MW01678078

Solomon's Decision

Coming soon from Judith B. Glad

Never the Twain

Published by

Treble Heart Books

SOLOMON'S DECISION

By

Judith B. Glad

Published December 2001
ISBN: 1-931742-20-0

Cover photo: Judith Glad

Treble Heart Books
1284 Overlook Dr.
Sierra Vista, AZ 85635-5512
http://www.trebleheartbooks.com

DEDICATION

For Richard R. Halse.

I'll slog through wetlands with you anytime, Dick.

And for Neil, of course.

ACKNOWLEDGEMENT

My thanks to Karole E. Scott, Chief of Public Affairs, and Sgt. K.L. Kistner, Flight Engineer, 939th Air Rescue Wing, Air Force Reserve, for information about rescue helicopters and methods of lifting people out of dense forests. My brother, Charles E. Bogard, helicopter pilot extraordinary, also contributed with many tales of his adventures in the air.

CHAPTER ONE

She was an emotional basket case when she walked into the conference hall. Perhaps that was why he affected her so strongly.

Kathryn didn't know what she'd do if the insemination didn't take this time. She'd been so certain she was pregnant following the first one that when her period came she felt like a failure. Having to be at the Wetlands Conference at approximately the same time as her next fertility period had had her chewing nails until her temperature began to climb and she knew she'd be able to do both.

Coming here directly from the clinic wasn't the most intelligent thing she'd ever done. Nor had her doctor approved. He was a firm believer in rest and relaxation. "I can't imagine any self-respecting embryo wanting to imbed itself in a tense uterus," he'd said. "Go home. Put your feet up, and pamper yourself for a day or two."

Instead she'd caught the next shuttle flight to Seattle.

The auditorium was almost full. She saw her boss waving at her from a seat in the middle of a row about halfway back. Stifling her desire to be anywhere else but here, she wove her way through the crowd. At least she could sit down.

"Did I miss anything this morning?" she said, slipping past two jeans-clad young women and gratefully sinking onto the molded plastic chair he had saved for her.

"Not much." He handed her a plastic-covered name badge and a handful of literature. "Registration lasted until ten, then they introduced the VIPs and talked about the philosophy of wetlands preservation." He pushed his attaché case under her feet, grinning as he did so. Around the office it was an acknowledged fact that her feet didn't reach the ground. "Oh, yeah. We had a slide show, with pictures of wetlands."

"What else?" she said, smiling in spite of herself. There was absolutely no reason she should feel so fragile. It was as if a single cross word from any perfect stranger would make her dissolve into a puddle of tears.

The first and second speakers of the afternoon were undistinguished, although the information they shared was interesting. Kathryn didn't think, however, that she'd ever have much need to create urban wetlands, or to work with industrial complex designers to incorporate existing wetlands into site plans. She was really waiting to hear about "The Responsibility of Local Regulatory Agencies in Wetlands Preservation." Sooner or later she would have to deal with a wetland threatened with destruction. When she did, she wanted to be prepared.

"I've heard this next fellow is a pretty dramatic speaker," her boss murmured as the audience rustled programs and whispered before the third speaker was introduced.

Kathryn started to reply, to say she'd heard that before, a long time ago, but the words caught in her throat.

The man who bounded onto the stage was beautiful! Even from forty feet away, she could see the lively sparkle in his eyes, could feel the energy he radiated.

More than that, she sensed his pure virility. Her mouth grew dry, her heartbeat accelerated. A heavy warmth flared in her lower belly and her breasts were suddenly sensitive and tender.

"Omigawd!" she gasped, but the tiny sound was lost in applause. Kathryn was grateful for the sudden darkness, because she was certain her instant lust for the man on the stage was written all over her face.

Under other conditions she would have been thrilled to be finally putting a face to the name. Ever since Jesse had gone off to Boys' State when he was a Junior in High School, she'd heard stories of the young man for whom he'd felt immediate liking. Erik Solomon had charisma—a word she doubted Jesse had ever used before in his life. He was committed, was directed. His name would be a household word in a few years.

Jesse had never again met Erik, but they'd kept in touch. Kathryn had been impressed more than once by Erik's inspiring, impassioned letters to Jesse, his espousal of ideas and concepts that might bridge the gap between conservation of natural resources and the needs of a growing world population. Perhaps Erik's letters had even contributed to her choice of careers.

Waiting at the edge of the stage, Erik closed his eyes and pulled the tatters of his psyche into a tight sphere at the center of his being in the last moments before he was introduced. He was so tired! It was getting more and more difficult to generate the enthusiasm that put him in such demand as a speaker at these conferences.

After six weeks of them, back to back, he felt drained. He just didn't have that much of himself to give, anymore. Each conference, each encounter with questioning, demanding audiences took a little more away, until sometimes, back in his everywhere-the-same hotel room, he felt as if he was an empty shell of a man mouthing platitudes about a resource loss that didn't matter to nine-tenths of the people in the world.

"When you're up to your ass in alligators, it's hard to remember that your initial objective was to drain the swamp," had been a popular quip about overwork when he was in college. The attitude it reflected was all too prevalent, even today. To the general public, a swamp was for draining. It wasn't a member of a class of highly productive ecosystems that were vanishing at an alarming rate.

The rustling of the audience continued, taking on an impatient pitch. With one last deep breath, he opened his eyes and bounded onto the stage, ending in front of the lectern. Shoulders back, arms loose at his sides, chin high, he stood in a carefully dynamic stance, a leader, a prophet, a wise man.

Silence. So quiet the proverbial dropping pin would echo and re-echo from the hard, undraped walls. No one challenged his fitness to lead them wherever he chose.

He raised his chin a little higher and narrowed his eyes, so no one would see how he was searching the audience for those two or three faces to whom he would speak directly, convincingly.

Erik Solomon was well known as an intimate, charismatic speaker. He'd never told anyone how he faked it—with arrogance, drama, and by pretending he was talking with his best friends.

There. A middle-aged man with a friendly, open face, a good listener.

And there. That young, pony-tailed, bearded fellow in the brightly colored parka, one of the save-the-world crowd.

One more. His eyes roved over the crowd and were caught, held, by a face so endearing, so yearning, that he almost forgot where he was, what he was doing.

A quick, automatic chop of his left hand signaled darkness. After that the swiftly changing slides kept the audience enthralled while he calmed his breathing and forced his thoughts back to wetlands.

His presentation following the slides must have been competent, for the questions were the ones he always got. Finally he brought the session to a close with a promise to elaborate on many of the points of confusion in his workshop tomorrow. As he concluded, he allowed himself another quick glance toward the woman whose face had filled his mind throughout his talk, hoping his extreme physical—sexual—reaction to her had been a momentary aberration.

She was gone! Her wide, yearning eyes, her curly mass of dark hair, her daffodil blouse, were nowhere in sight. And he couldn't even search for her, for the brief recess following his talk brought many of the audience to the side of the stage, full of questions.

Would she be at the banquet tonight? And would it matter? He knew from experience that his attention would be demanded by half the people there, leaving him little time for any sort of socializing.

Erik saw her, as he'd hoped to, across the banquet room. Everyone else faded into insignificance as he watched her, noted the way her lips lingered on the rim of her wineglass, imagined them lingering thus against his mouth.

She was only average in looks, not spectacularly beautiful, not plain. Her mop of curly black hair framed a thin face with enormous eyes, a straight nose, and lips that seemed to quiver on the edge of a smile. She should have a dimple in each cheek, but he had yet to be close enough to discover it, or to see the color of her eyes. They were light, but whether golden brown or sky blue he could not tell.

Her clothes were ordinary too. A straight skirt, a frilly lavender blouse, replacing the crisp yellow one she'd worn that afternoon, when his attention had first been captured by something about her. There was a glint of gold at her ear, a sparkle of white fire on her finger. Her right ring finger, not her left.

His relief was unreasonable.

Erik realized he'd been staring, oblivious to the conversation circling around him, when he heard, "Hey, man, come to the party!" A stocky, swarthy man in suntans was motioning to him.

Erik stifled a groan. It wasn't as if he'd missed much. Those guys dragged him into their unending disagreement every time they got together. He tried to look interested, but found his attention wandering after hearing, yet again, "We did what we had to do for the demands of the time. If the Soil Conservation Service hadn't managed those salt marshes back in the Thirties, they'd have been entirely lost to development."

And, as he always did, the other countered with, "If you guys hadn't put in floodgates and weirs, we'd still have salt marshes, instead of pastures."

"Bull! Erik, tell him how they filled—"

"You guys are wasting your energy. What's done is done. I'm concerned with saving what we've got left, not assigning blame for what's already gone." He swallowed the last of his wine and set the glass on a table beside him. "I'll see you around."

He began to weave his way among people, many of whom caught at his sleeve or tried to stop him with a question. Before he could reach her, the call to dinner came, and he watched her take a table halfway back in the large room, beside the older man whom she'd been standing with. Her partner? Surely not. He had a good thirty years on her.

He'd catch her after dinner. They could go into the bar and have a liqueur, while they got acquainted.

Kathryn wilted seriously during dinner, until she didn't know if she'd make it back to the hotel. Perhaps she should just lay her head down on the table beside her plate and give in to the seductive desire to sleep. Someone would surely wake her when it was time to go.

She laid her fork across her half-full plate and forced her eyelids back where they belonged. Wide open. Willing her head to turn, she looked about the banquet room for a focus, something that she could concentrate on, anything to keep her attention well enough that she could maintain consciousness for just a little longer.

The sight of him woke her like a jolt of direct current. His profile was sharply defined by the pale gray draperies behind the head table. His short beard glinted golden in the overhead light. He seemed removed from the conversation all around him, distracted. His hand lifted a coffee cup to his mouth slowly, as if he were operating on automatic. Lift cup. Sip. Set cup down. Wait thirty seconds. Lift cup. *Ad infinitum.*

He was beautiful, never mind that the word was not conventionally applied to men. Erik Solomon was beautiful. Sun-streaked hair curled rakishly around his ears and tumbled across his high, tanned forehead. His eyes were dark, darker than Jesse's had been, and just as startling in so blond a man.

Sleepiness deserted her as she watched him, wondering what those lean fingers would feel like, drifting across her cheek. Would his beard be scratchy, or soft, erotic, against her bare breasts. Like Jesse's.

Oh, God! Jesse. What was she doing? How could she compare anyone with Jesse—her first, her only, love? Kathryn closed her eyes and called up Jesse's image. Without success. The blackness of her inner eyelids remained blank, empty.

Desperately Kathryn tried to recall the individual parts of him—light sandy hair, cut short except in late summer when the demands of the ranch kept him from the barbershop. He had brown eyes lit by a teasing spark, a wide, mobile mouth always on the verge of a grin, a pug nose like a kid's—incongruous on a man otherwise totally masculine. As she put the pieces together, they took shape in her mind, but the vision that resulted was not Jesse. The hair was longer, more golden, and the nose was aristocratic.

She opened her eyes to see her vision still seated at the head table, now staring straight at her.

She stared back, peripherally aware that the tables had been cleared, the after-dinner speaker introduced, the keynote speech delivered. At least an hour had passed since she first locked her gaze on Erik Solomon—had she actually stared at him the whole time, or had she, as she desperately needed to, slept?

Her boss's grin told her that she had. "Did you have a nice nap?"

Feeling the blush lighting her cheeks, Kathryn returned the grin. "Lovely, but not nearly long enough. I think I'll pass on the rest of the evening and head back to the hotel."

There was a general protest from the group around them.

"Jeez, Kathryn, it's only nine-thirty!"

"Don't be a drag!"

The others, all planners from small towns in Idaho, Oregon, and Washington, agreed. This would be their only chance to talk shop in the relaxed atmosphere of a quiet bar, since most were leaving as soon as the conference ended tomorrow.

Kathryn regretted her exhaustion, but she shook her head. "I'd be no fun, people. All I'd do is sleep in a quiet corner. I'll see you tomorrow. Okay?"

Amidst more argument, she picked up her raincoat and stuffed the program into her purse, checking to make sure of the name of her hotel. Given her state of fatigue, she was liable to do all sorts of dumb things.

The touch on her arm and the low, rumbly voice in her ear startled her.

"Leaving so soon?"

Tired or not, her body went on alert. It was the same inexplicable reaction she'd felt this afternoon, an intense awareness. Almost a yearning.

She jerked her arm away from Erik Solomon's light touch. "No! I mean, yes." *Wake up Kathryn!* "Yes. I'm leaving. I'm tired. It's late. I—"

"Me too," he said, his hand lightly cupping her elbow. "Let's see if I can find us a cab."

Before she knew it, he was bundling her into a cab. "Which hotel?" he asked.

She told him.

"Just down the street from mine." He relayed the information to the driver, leaned back as the cab accelerated into the heavy early evening traffic with a slight screech of tires.

Kathryn relaxed back into the seat, wishing she were already in her hotel room. She appreciated his taking care of her, but now she just wanted him to go away and let her alone. She was so terribly, terribly tired. She let her eyes close, her spine relax.

Erik couldn't decide whether he was insulted or complimented by the complete trust she showed by falling asleep. He knew he sometimes bored his dates, sometimes forgot that everyone didn't share his enthusiasm for wetlands preservation. But he couldn't remember ever having put a woman to sleep before. He slipped his arm around her, tipped her head to rest against his shoulder. It felt right—she fit.

He closed his own eyes, aware of being more than just tired. His mind refused to relax, kept worrying at problems facing him back in Washington, D.C., anticipating questions from tomorrow's seminar attendees, wondering why the woman's name seemed familiar.

Kathryn Pierson. He must have met someone by that name and it stuck in his mind. He knew he'd never met this particular woman before. He wouldn't have forgotten her.

At her hotel, he couldn't wake her. If he hadn't been feeling like some kind of ghoul for his body's reaction to her warm breath on his neck, he would have been more patient. "Damn it, lady, wake up," he growled. The driver waited, watching him in the rear view mirror. Finally Erik gave up and reached for his wallet. "Keep the change," he told the now-snickering cabby as he pulled her awkwardly out of the back seat.

He had to lean her limp body against the building while he dug in her purse. Not knowing her room number would have been a distinct disadvantage when he asked for her key. Her wallet was, of course, at the very bottom of the confusion of keys, notebooks, conference program, cosmetics, pens, a stamped but unmailed phone bill, disposable flashlight, and a fat Swiss Army knife. She started to slide to the sidewalk while he was unzipping her wallet, forcing him to pull her firmly into his embrace.

His body reacted predictably. Damn it! Ever since he'd seen her at the conference this afternoon, he'd been randy as a teenager at a girls' camp. He grimaced. It had been a long time since Erik Solomon had suffered instant lust. Too many dangers, both medical and emotional, prompted his scientist's mind to rule his all too human libido.

He was finally able to steady her drooping body and peer over her shoulder at the receipt tucked between two credit cards. As he did so, a photo in a plastic sleeve caught his eye. It looked like...God, it was! Jesse Zenger. That was why her name was so familiar.

Stuffing her wallet back into her purse, he swung her into his arms and climbed the seven stone steps to the small lobby. "Ms. Pierson was taken ill at the banquet," he told the suspicious desk clerk. "May I have her key?" But he had to produce identification—hers and his—before he got the key to room 512. Even then he felt the clerk's suspicion as he entered the elevator.

God! What if he hadn't lied? Was she ill? He'd never seen anyone sleep so soundly. Erik struggled to get them both inside her room and gently laid her on the double bed. Laying the back of his hand against her cheek, he was relieved to find it cool. He left her alone while he closed the door and switched on a lamp on the dresser.

Bonelessly she sprawled along the bed, in exactly the same position he'd put her. He should leave, but he didn't want to. What if there was something wrong with her that didn't cause a fever? "Kathryn!" He spoke harshly, demandingly. "Kathryn, wake up!"

"Hmmmm?"

"Wake up, Kathryn. You need to get into your nightgown, to brush your teeth." He could see her trying to force her eyelids open. When she finally did, he saw that her eyes were a deep, clear, vacant green.

"Jesse? Oh, Jesse, I had the most awful nightmare." She clutched his wrist and pulled. Pulled hard, so he either had to go to his knees beside the bed or pull her upright. He knelt.

"Hold me, Jesse. Please. I dreamed you were dead." The tears welling from her eyes streaked across cheeks so pale that they might have been carved from the purest ivory. The pain behind them wrenched at his heart, for he didn't want to tell her it wasn't a nightmare, but reality. Jesse was dead.

Without reservation Erik lay down beside her and pulled her into his arms. Her sobs continued for several minutes, as if they'd been contained for a long time. She clung to him, even when her breathing quieted and she slipped again into sleep.

For a long time he stared at the ceiling in the dimly lit room, wondering at the deep feeling of rightness he experienced, just from holding a sleeping stranger—yet she was no stranger, for Jesse's infrequent letters had been filled with stories of his wonderful, beautiful Katie.

Kathryn woke in Jesse's arms. The room was pitch black, with a strange smell and small, strange sounds. She had no idea of the time, or even how she had gotten here—wherever here was. All she knew was that her nightmare was over.

She nuzzled against Jesse's neck, smelling his clean, soapy odor, feeling the slight, soft prickle of his whiskers. His arm tightened around her. "Love me," she whispered, stroking her hand down his lean chest, across his tight abdomen, teasing him into readiness through the soft wool of his trousers. "Oh, sweetheart, love me, please." She needed reassurance. It had been so cold, so lonely in her dream.

He responded by tightening his hold on her, by seeking and finding her mouth. His kiss was gentle, yet insistent. She ran her fingers through his hair—he needed a haircut as he always did in the summertime—holding him close while he gave meticulous attention to her cheeks, her eyelids, her mouth.

She felt herself climbing perilously close to the edge, as if it had been forever since he'd kissed her. "Now," she urged, impatient, needing him inside her, filling her. She fumbled at the fly of his trousers, frantic to free him. "Please, Jesse."

And he pushed her away!

Roughly he grabbed her wrists, forced her to release him. Before she could react, he was off the bed, away from her.

A click and light flared. Kathryn blinked, seeing a hotel room that was at once foreign and strangely familiar. "Jesse," she cried, "what's wrong?" She reached toward him, where he stood by the dresser, his back to her. A tall man, with wide shoulders hunched, as if in pain. Then he turned.

"Jess...*you*!" The recent past came flooding back, with all its pain. Tears welled up and flowed, burning tracks down her cheeks.

"I'm not your Jesse, Kathryn, and I'm sorry."

His voice was deep, gentle, full of sympathy, the mellow, convincing baritone she'd listened to just...today? Yes, today.

He sat beside her on the bed, tipping her face up with one hand while he pulled tissues from the box on the bedside stand with the other. "Here," he said, holding one to her nose. "Blow."

She tried to smile. Taking the tissue, she wiped her eyes and, holding it to her nose, sniffed. "I'm mortified," she whispered, trying not to notice that he was still mildly aroused. As she looked everywhere but into his face, she saw that she was completely dressed, even to pantyhose. Well, almost completely.

His smile was crooked. "Lady, you really know how to wake a guy up."

Kathryn burned. Not just her face, which she knew was

glowing bright enough that the lamp was unnecessary, but her hands, from the remembered feel of him. "I'm sorry."

"So am I. If I'd thought you knew what you were doing, I'd have cooperated with enthusiasm." His finger touched her cheek.

And now the burning threatened to become a wildfire. The wanting had been born when she first saw him, had grown since then, until it was consuming her. Jesse was gone, gone forever. No one would ever again cherish her, defend her, love her as he had. And she was so desperately lonely, so incredibly empty. "Make love to me," she said, not looking at him. "Please, just for tonight?"

The silence stretched until she wanted to break it with a scream. "I wanted you the instant I saw you," he said, his voice hoarse. He didn't move from where he sat, as far away on the edge of the bed as he could get.

"I've never felt like that before," she admitted. "As if I'd perish if I didn't have you." She traced a meaningless pattern on the sheet. "I still feel that way," she whispered, knowing what she was doing was wrong, but needing him. Needing to be held, to be kissed, to be loved.

"I was going to leave after I tucked you in," he said. "But I couldn't. I knew nothing would—could happen, but I needed to hold you just a little while longer. I couldn't resist lying down beside you, for just a few minutes before I left."

His sheepish smile told her he really hadn't intended to fall asleep. She took a deep breath. "Will you?" She looked at him, her eyes asking the rest of the question that she hadn't courage to put into words a second time.

"Are you sure?"

Kathryn nodded. Just to be held once more, even for a few moments, and she'd be able to face the lonely years ahead.

He leaned forward, his fingers touching her face again. Heat spread from the point of contact, flooding her body. "I've never wanted anyone as I do you."

She touched a questing finger with her tongue. "Can you protect me?" she asked, with the one last vestige of common sense remaining to her.

"Yes," he said, his eyes holding hers. " But I don't usually."

She could see the effort he was having, to hold himself in check. "Neither do I," she agreed. Licking dry lips with a tongue devoid of moisture, she said, "but this time..."

CHAPTER TWO

Eight Years Later

"I never thought Jethro Zenger would sell out. His family's been there forever." Emaline Cohoon, County Treasurer and Garnet Falls' unofficial news bureau, pushed a stack of files aside and cocked her feet on the edge of her desk.

Kathryn set her coffee cup on the wide windowsill and scooted up beside it. "Neither did I, but Jesse once said both his brothers could hardly wait to get away. They swore they'd never willingly come back."

"I wonder if Jethro'll have trouble finding a buyer. With cattle prices what they are, I can't imagine how anyone could run the Z-Bar-Z Bar at a profit, not if they pay anywhere near what it's worth," Emaline said. It was a few minutes after five on a Friday night and the entire courthouse staff was still reeling under the news that one of the area's oldest ranches was for sale. No one could imagine Jethro Zenger in any other environment, or doing anything else but cattle ranching, particularly living in a condominium in Phoenix and chasing a little ball around a golf course.

"You know what really gets to me, Em? The Zenger kids have this wonderful heritage, have marvelous, loving parents who would welcome them home with open arms. Jethro likes to rant and rave about them forgetting their roots, but even before Jesse died, he was planning on making sure all his children were treated fairly." Kathryn sighed, half in envy. "Jesse told me once it nearly broke his folks' hearts when the other kids left for good."

"Jesse's death kinda took the starch out of him, didn't it?" Em's voice was gentle, as if she were at a funeral.

Kathryn sometimes wondered if people actually believed she still mourned Jesse, after almost eight years. "No more than losing any of his children would have. Jesse might have been the one who loved the ranch, but he and Jethro were on the outs with each other as often as not."

The door opened. Eddie Webster, Kathryn's young and very eager intern, stuck his head inside. "Hi, ladies. Goin' to the Wooden Nickel tonight?"

"Not me. I'm scheduled for a decadent evening letting my kids beat me at Monopoly," Kathryn said, hopping down. She stretched, working the stiffness from her shoulders. She'd spent the better part of the afternoon searching through old records for some early property ownership maps of Mica City.

"Me neither," Em said. "It's our anniversary and my sweetie's taking me out to dinner."

"See you Monday, then." Eddie started to close the door, then stuck his head back in. "Hey, Kathryn, didn't I hear there's a humongous wetland on the Zenger place? We could have some real excitement around here if whoever buys it petitions for a zoning change." Again he disappeared, slamming the door behind him.

"Excitement?" Em sounded puzzled.

Kathryn didn't answer. She was remembering a talk she'd heard, a long time ago—and trying to forget the speaker. "The Responsibility of Local Regulatory Agencies in Wetlands

Preservation." Sunset County had been relatively free of the environmentalist-developer conflicts that plagued much of the country recently. So much of it was National Forest, and there were no major lakes or rivers, no outstanding scenic areas within its boundaries. The occasional tourists who strayed off US 95 soon went back to its wide, well-designed curves, for Idaho's second smallest county had little to distract them for long.

Jesse had taken her up to Wounded Bear Meadow once. She remembered it being one of the most beautiful, most untouched places she'd ever seen.

"This is what my great-grandfather must have seen," Jesse had said, gesturing widely. "We've never run cattle here, never wanted to. It's sort of a family tradition that we keep this one place like it was in the beginning, just so we'll appreciate what we've got."

And now there was no one but Jethro left to do the appreciating. What a shame it would be if someone came along and drained or dammed the meadow. With a little luck—all bad—she could find herself smack dab in the middle of the kind of battle there'd been in the White Clouds, back in the Seventies.

Excitement? Kathryn hoped not. "Never mind, Em. Eddie likes to overdramatize everything." No sense in borrowing worry. The Z-Bar-Z would always be a cattle ranch. What else could it be? "Have a good weekend," she said as she followed Eddie from Em's office. "And don't celebrate too wildly tonight."

On the way home she did her best to banish once again the memory of the man who'd spoken so eloquently on what she might be facing if Wounded Bear Meadow ever came under her department's jurisdiction. It had been quite a while since Erik Solomon had invaded her thoughts and, as always, he did so with devastating effect.

He still owned a piece of her heart, even after eight years. And she never wanted to meet him face to face again.

* * *

"This one has the potential of getting nasty." Walter Thomlinson tossed a file folder on Erik's desk.

Turning from the window, where he was contemplating the wall on the other side of the airshaft and wondering how long it would be before he went insane from lack of fresh air and sunshine, Erik slipped his glasses back onto his nose. The first letter inside was a photocopy, and the stylized sunset, which on the original must have been in bright pastels, obscured some of its first paragraph.

Sunset County, Idaho. What was he supposed to remember about Sunset County, Idaho? He knew he'd heard of it before, but when? The memory eluded him.

He read. A local ranch had recently been put up for sale and a consortium of developers had indicated interest in purchasing it for a planned recreational community. The county planner knew there was a large wetland on the ranch and was asking for advice from a more knowledgeable planner in the state government. What should he—Erik glanced at the signature—what should she do first, to ensure that all the right actions were taken?

He was halfway through the next paragraph, which described the wetland, when the signature penetrated his consciousness.

"Kathryn Pierson, City/County Planner."

No! Coincidences like this just didn't occur!

Erik turned again to his view of the airshaft and stared into infinity. He hadn't thought of her in a long time. There had been a time when thoughts of Kathryn Pierson had intruded on his every activity, a time when he could hardly manage ten minutes without remembering her piquant expression, her sweetly curved mouth that always seemed to be promising laughter.

It would have been so easy to go back, to find her. But he hadn't. Once the urgency of his need for her faded into a memory of heaven touched but not grasped, he'd realized she was all wrong for him. Kathryn Pierson had been very young then. She would have wanted all the traditional trappings of marriage and babies, something he wouldn't—couldn't—give her.

Was her hair still a short, curly mop framing her pointed face? Were her eyes still as green as spring leaves, as deep as the sky just before dawn? His fingers curved, remembering how they'd filled with her breasts, and his body awoke, also remembering.

With a snort of self-disgust, Erik tossed the photocopy aside and read the letter from the state planning office in Boise. Wounded Bear Meadow—he loved it!—sounded like a perfect candidate for purchase by the National Wetlands Trust. Several of the people in the state office often alerted conservation organizations like NWT and The Nature Conservancy when likely property came on the market. Idaho might not always be able to commit public funds to preserving natural resources, but there were people who made certain that someone did it.

Erik had known the planner who'd forwarded the letter from Sunset County in graduate school. He trusted her judgment. When she said she seconded Kathryn's opinion that the wetland was worth a second look, he took her seriously, even as he snorted at her handwritten postscript.

"I'm hoping Erik will investigate this one. It's high time he got out into the field. The last time I talked to him, he was crosser than the old bear the meadow was named for."

He was tempted. Not because of Kathryn, but because he was getting stale. The Trust's senior associates spent their time testifying as expert witnesses, lobbying for wetlands protection, and pursuing funding for future purchases, not doing on-site evaluations. He picked up his phone.

"When do I leave?" he said, when Walter answered.

* * *

Kathryn looked up as her door opened.

"He's here!" Eddie said, sounding awed.

"Who's ...Oh! The man from National Wetlands Trust." She laid her pen down as she sighed. Her colleague in Boise had warned her that NWT would probably send a young and idealistic staff member to do the initial evaluation. That probably meant he'd be in her hair all summer, despite NWT's assurance that he'd cause very little disruption. Kathryn didn't believe that. All consultants, by definition, got in your way. Those doing the baseline work for the reopening of the Styx Valley Mine were already causing her more trouble than enough, and they'd barely begun. "Well, you might as well bring him in."

But Eddie only pulled the door closed behind him. "They must really think the meadow is important, Kathryn. Wait'll you see who they sent!" His whisper was loudly theatrical and, she was sure, carried throughout the old courthouse.

At times like this, she knew she was getting old. Either that or Eddie was very young. "What's so special about him?" She wanted to chuckle. Her intern was standing with his back to the door, as if he were barricading it against ravaging hordes.

"He spoke to my environmental planning class last year. I've never forgotten how he stressed the importance of wetlands and how the local planner is their first line of defense." Eddie looked as if he were ready to die in the trenches. "He said wetlands are an invaluable global resource and if the human race lets them be destroyed, it'll be signing its own death warrant." His tone was definitely awed.

Kathryn had heard someone say those same words, once.

Impatiently she checked her watch. "I guess you'd better bring him in, Eddie. The Chairman won't be here for another fifteen minutes and we can't let a VIP cool his heels in the corridor that long."

"Can I stay? Please?"

Oh, God. Eddie was suffering a king-sized case of hero worship. She wouldn't get any work out of him for days. On the other hand, why couldn't he entertain his hero and let her get a little more done on her budget plan? "Take him across the street," she said, digging out a five dollar bill, "and feed him a piece of Lester's pie. Just have him back here in twenty minutes."

Twenty-five minutes later, Kathryn was wishing she'd invited the VIP into her office. At least she would have had him here on time, in the courtroom where the County Commissioners met. Then the door opened and she was glad she hadn't.

She simply stood dumb while Eddie introduced Dr. Erik Solomon to the commissioners. When it was her turn to greet him, he interrupted Eddie by saying, "Ms. Pierson and I are old friends, aren't we, Kathryn?"

Eddie's mouth dropped open, but his surprise was nothing compared to hers. She did manage to smile as she shook Erik's hand. What she wanted to do was run screaming. Even after so long, his touch still softened her backbone, leaving her quiveringly ready to do anything he asked of her.

"Old friends?" she managed to say. "Yes, I guess you could say that. How are you, Dr. Solomon?"

This man had taught her that she was still alive, that she hadn't died with Jesse. Although the healing had taken a long time, her brief and shocking encounter with him had been the strong medicine she needed to start the process. He'd given her memories to last through the rest of her life, as well as a terminal case of embarrassment.

Yes, she guessed they were "old friends."

She paid little attention to the content of his meeting with the commissioners, except to notice that Charlie Bittenbusch wasn't buying whatever Erik Solomon was selling. The others were reserving judgment, as they should. Even she wasn't convinced that Wounded Bear Meadow would be better managed by NWT, although she understood and agreed with wetlands protection in general.

Five years of college hadn't overcome her ingrained belief that a man's land was his to do with as he chose. That was one reason she'd stayed in Sunset County, refusing offers for better-paying jobs. She'd grown up here, and she felt she understood better than an outsider the philosophy and character of people who lived and worked in the high country. It took a special kind of human being, one who didn't take kindly to rules and regulations. Being a planner here was a challenge, because zoning was a foreign concept to most of the residents.

It would be up to Erik to convince the commissioners that Wounded Bear Meadow should be preserved. The concept of land stewardship for preservation of natural resources wasn't new, but it hadn't been seen before in Sunset County. There were several Nature Conservancy preserves in Idaho, and one NWT wetland. According to many planners, such environmental preserves were in some ways better than having the state or federal government set land aside. Wounded Bear Meadow could be the first national Wetlands Trust property south of the Salmon River.

If Erik managed to make the deal. Jethro Zenger was willing to preserve the meadow, but he'd already said he wasn't going to give it away. He'd never put up with a lot of red tape.

She shifted restlessly in her chair. Erik was telling Commission Chairman Harry Lindholm that he was planning on spending several weeks in Sunset County, making sure Wounded Bear Meadow was actually worth consideration by NWT. There was no doubt in her mind that his investigations would require her help and cooperation. Would she be able to carry it off with élan, or would he reduce her to a quivering mass of desire with only a touch and a single word?

She'd like to believe the former. She feared the latter.

Erik watched her across the courtroom. If her body language was to be believed, she was uncomfortable as hell. Good, because he wasn't any too relaxed himself.

It had been more difficult than he'd imagined, and he didn't understand why. He'd met former lovers before and the worst that had happened was a momentary twinge of embarrassment.

Now that the meeting was about wound up, he hoped to catch her. They had to talk. He wasn't going to spend weeks—perhaps even months—here in Garnet Falls, tiptoeing around her just because she was self-conscious about having slept with him.

He rose with the others, stretching his arms behind him to work out some of the stiffness of a long air flight, a drive almost as long, and an interminable meeting. An unobtrusive glance at his watch told him it was after five.

"Well, Dr. Solomon, you just go on up there and take yourself a look. You'll see it ain't nothing but a big ol' swamp. Me, I don't see why anybody'd want to do anything but drain it."

My God! He'd just spent two hours explaining to them why wetlands were so important, how they functioned and how few of them were left. Had this fellow been asleep?

"Charlie, you just stop your pushin', now." Harry Lindholm nudged Charlie Bitten...Bitten-something.

Erik had a hunch he knew where his biggest headaches were going to originate. Charlie seemed to fancy himself an entrepreneur, and was all in favor of any kind of development that would, as he'd repeated several times, "Put Sunset County on the map." From what he said, that meant sidetracking rich tourists on their way elsewhere and luring summer home owners to the area.

"Have you found lodgings yet, Dr. Solomon?" Short, weathered, and gravely-voiced, Amelia Warren, the only woman commissioner, slipped between Charlie and Harry.

He smiled. He had to, for Amelia was, for all her incongruous appearance, an old fashioned lady. "No, ma'am, I haven't. I checked into the hotel, but I don't imagine I'll stay there very long." The Conestoga House—he'd done a double take when he saw the sign—was full of poorly done antique reproductions, glowed with red plush, and had the thinnest walls he'd ever tried not to eavesdrop through.

"Come see me tomorrow, then. I've got a mobile home out by the creek..." She pronounced it *crick*. "...and there's no need for it to sit there empty."

"Thank you." Erik was determined not to accept her offer. Renting from one of the commissioners would not be politic. "I'll be in touch." He turned as the young planning intern sought his attention.

God, but he was tired. Flying west was always harder on his body than going east, and this trip had been particularly tiring. He'd missed connections at Denver and his Red Eye flight had turned into an early bird. Add to that an inability to sleep because his mind had insisted on replaying scenes from a long ago morning in Seattle—one of the more incredible experiences of his life.

Harry finally called the meeting to a close about quarter to six. "You know where to reach me," he told Erik. "Just give me a call when you're ready to go out and see Jethro."

"I'll want to take a quick look at the meadow first," Erik said, "to see if it's worth discussing with Mr. Zenger." He stepped aside to let the local people leave before him. He was in no hurry, for Kathryn had disappeared into an office across the hall.

He stood alone just outside the double front doors until a slight figure slipped from a door at ground level and started away from the courthouse. "Kathryn, wait!" Erik went down the steps two at a time.

She stopped in the middle of the sidewalk, but didn't turn to look at him. The brim of her rain hat, shadowing her eyes and nose, made it difficult for him to read her expression.

"We need to talk."

"Why?" Her face gave nothing away, neither her thoughts nor a second of her time.

"Well, about, uh..." He faltered. "About us."

"Erik, there is no 'us.' There never was." Her mobile lips twisted in a grimace. "There was only a one night stand." The grimace became a thoughtful smile. "A memorable one, I'll admit."

"That's what I want to talk about, Kathryn. I've never forgotten you." Well, that was the truth, because no other woman had ever stayed in his memory the way she had.

"Oh?"

"Well, you know what I mean." He felt as clumsy and inept as a sixteen year old boy on his first date—with the Prom Queen.

"I don't see what good talking about what happened so long ago will do. I'd rather begin again today and go on from here."

"But that's what I mean," he said, growing increasingly uncomfortable. Why wouldn't she look him in the eye? "We can't let an old relationship interfere with our working together. I could be here for quite a while and you're the county planner, and well, we've got to be professional."

With the lowering sun at her back, her eyes were in shadow. "I think that's a good idea, Erik. By all means, let us behave professionally." She turned and began walking north.

"Hey, wait!" He caught up with her. "Can I buy you dinner?"

She kept walking, perhaps even sped up a bit.

He'd had enough. Grabbing her arm, he pulled her to a stop. "Kathryn, all I want to do is visit with you for a while, not seduce you."

Standing before him, head bent and body tense, she muttered something, but he only heard, "...already did that."

"Okay, now let's try it one more time. I'd like to take you out to dinner, Kathryn. Are you free?" Looking along Main Street he wondered where he'd take her if she accepted. Garnet Falls wasn't exactly a gourmet diner's paradise.

"I have to go home." She silenced his automatic response with a gesture. "I've got a previous commitment. Perhaps another time."

He heard the reluctance in her voice, but he wasn't going to let it stop him. He was a firm believer in facing up to whatever made him uncomfortable. Kathryn made him damned uncomfortable. Feeling like a masochist, he said, "Sounds good. I'll look forward to it."

"Fine. Now, I really do have to get home." She began walking.

Erik fell into step beside her, enjoying the chance to stretch his legs after all the sitting he'd done yesterday and today. "I'll walk you there." Given the bucolic atmosphere of Garnet Falls, his rental car would be perfectly safe sitting in front of the courthouse all evening. All night, for that fact.

They crossed a side street and were in front of the Conestoga House. Once again he vowed to find other lodging. Next was the Baptist Church, an old stone structure lovingly preserved. Across another side street, the Methodist Church was newer brick, but just as well cared-for. They turned east then, and were immediately out of downtown. He liked this town. It was just the right size.

"When did you leave the Fish and Wildlife Service?" Kathryn's question broke an increasingly comfortable silence. "Isn't that where you were working, when we...when you came to the Seattle conference?"

She was looking straight ahead, head high and shoulders swaying with her brisk walk. Her hands were in the pockets of her pale gray raincoat. The curve of her cheek, faintly highlighted by the rosy sunset, was exquisite. Erik experienced a strong resurgence of the compelling desire he'd felt at his first sight of her.

"I've been with the National Wetlands Trust for three years. Actually, I'm an associate, rather than an employee. I also do some consulting."

"So you're a consultant?" She sounded—what? Disgusted? No, more like scornful.

"You don't like consultants?" He wasn't surprised. He

commonly ran into local officials who'd had a few bad experiences with consultants who came in and demanded instant cooperation. They gave the whole profession a bad name.

She shrugged. "We're here," she said, turning into a narrow, cracked sidewalk under an ornate iron arch.

Erik wondered what color the roses were. His grandmother had had a rose arbor like that, before she died and the old place was sold to a developer. He hoped they were pink. Pink and fragrant, filling the warm summer night with their provocative scent. With luck, he'd still be here to see them bloom.

He waited while she unlocked the front door. The top half of it held an oval window, etched with a floral wreath. He wondered why she bothered locking it. Any self-respecting burglar would be inside in less time than it took her to turn the key.

She slipped inside and turned. "Thank you for walking me home, Erik. I'll see you Monday."

Before he could find his tongue, the door closed in his face. He heard the dead bolt slide into place with finality.

CHAPTER THREE

"And there's this great-big gold statue of a lady with wings but no arms, right there in the middle of the round floor under the dome!"

Kathryn listened with half an ear while she scrambled eggs. The twins were still excited over their school field trip last week, bubbling over with the sights they'd seen in Boise. "Um-hmmm," she responded to Ginger's next question, before she realized she hadn't even heard it.

"Oh, wow! Can we really? And can Jace and Denny and Abby go too?" Kyle bounced in his chair.

Oh, lord, what *had* she promised? Hurriedly she scraped the eggs into a bowl and took the toast from the oven where it had been keeping warm. "Well, perhaps. Let's talk about it, okay?" With luck they'd tell her what she'd agreed to do.

Both children reached for food. They always woke up ravenous, excited, anticipating the wonders in store for them in another bright new day. She'd often wondered about their father, who must have been a day person. Perhaps she should have specified slow starting among the other characteristics she wanted in a sperm donor. She swallowed more coffee. Two or three cups usually were required before she and the twins were moving at the same speed. Especially on Mondays, after a weekend at the ranch.

"Steven said his dad has lots of extra inner tubes we can borrow," Ginger said, between bites. "He said there's one really big rapid where lotsa people got drownded."

"And we can take a cooler inside an innertube, too, so we can have a picnic on an island."

"Steven says sometimes there's so many people on the river that it's like a great big swimming pool."

"But it's always fun, 'cause of the little waterfalls and the chan...channels around the islands."

"All you have to do is call Steven's mom and she'll let us sleep in her family room again."

"Hold it! Wait just a minute! We can't just go to Boise and stay at a perfect stranger's house." She had agreed—actually, mindlessly agreed—to taking the twins to Boise some summer weekend to go tubing on the river. Although she'd done it herself once, with Jesse, she didn't think it was an activity she wanted to undertake with two adventurous children. Not to mention descending on this Steven's mother like a horde of locusts.

"Steven's mom said she likes having company. And besides, he's my friend," Ginger said, with the heartrending expression that never failed to melt Kathryn's resolve.

"We'll see," she told them, taking refuge in every parent's evasion. "It'll be quite a while before the river's low enough to tube in, and we'll talk about it then."

Kyle's lower lip went out. "You'll forget," he accused.

"No she won't, 'cause we won't let her," Ginger promised. Her grin was pure devilment.

Kathryn knew she was in for constant reminders, until her good intentions were worn away like rock under a waterfall. She glanced at the clock. "Finish your milk, Ginger. Kyle, did you remember to feed King Alfred?"

Eventually they were on their way to school and she was alone, left with the usual puddles of milk on the table, fragments of breakfast on the floor, and a house still echoing with their childish laughter. Was ever a woman so blessed, she wondered, as she quickly tidied the kitchen.

The decision to have Kyle and Ginger had not been arrived at easily. Kathryn knew she would cause more than raised eyebrows in Garnet Falls when she produced a baby out of wedlock, particularly so soon after Jesse's death. But she had been so desperately *lost*. The Zengers had contributed to her decision, too, with their outspoken regrets that she and Jesse had been too good, too careful.

"I never thought I'd be wishin' one of my boys was careless with his seed," Jethro had said, one of those Sunday afternoons when she had gone to the Z-Bar-Z because she'd gone there with Jesse since they were in high school and had nowhere else to go. "But if he had, and you was pregnant, nothin' would make me happier."

"That way we'd have something of him left," his wife agreed. "And so would you."

She shared their regret. Jesse had been a part of her life since the awful day she arrived in Garnet Falls, newly orphaned and unsure of her welcome in the big house where her father had grown up. Her grandparents hadn't been easy with children, but they'd given Kathryn a home, and as much love as they were capable of. But they'd never been demonstrative.

Jesse gave her hugs. Jesse always gave her hugs, from the time she was eight and he was eleven until she was sixteen and he showed her that there was more, much more than hugs, to loving a man.

How desperate they'd all been to salvage something from the disaster of losing their son and her lover. She and Jesse had stopped practicing birth control as soon as she returned to Garnet Falls after her graduation from Boise State. They wanted babies. Lots of babies. But he had died, alone and bleeding in the mud, just a week before their wedding. When her period came, a few days later, it had nearly destroyed her.

In retrospect, her decision to be inseminated had been for all the wrong reasons. It was a good thing there hadn't been any kind of psychological evaluation to determine her suitability as a parent. She would have failed spectacularly. Four months after Jesse's death, she was in Portland for her first attempt. She'd specified a sperm donor with Jesse's physical characteristics: sandy hair, brown eyes, long and lanky. On her second try, she'd caught.

Jesse's mother hadn't approved. But Jethro had, saying, "It ain't like having Jesse's own blood children, Katie, but the babies do make me feel almost like a grandpa." He remembered them on birthdays and at Christmas. His approval made it possible for her to be an unwed mother—by choice—in a small town where the sexual revolution was merely a topic on the evening news.

Now Jethro was selling out and moving to Arizona. "The winters are just too much for these old bones, Katie. If Jesse had lived...well, never mind. But I'm tired of fightin' the beef market and the weather and the government. I've worked hard all my life and I want to do a little playin' before my time comes."

She couldn't blame him. But oh, lord, she would miss him! He was as dear to her as her own father would have been.

The telephone's ring brought her back to her kitchen. Harry Lindholm's request made her wish she could cancel Monday and go back to bed.

Erik looked down onto Main Street as he sipped his instant coffee. The studio apartment above the Wooden Nickel was a far cry from his condo in Vienna, Virginia. According to Lester Wood, who owned the building, the only time noise could be a problem was on Friday and Saturday nights. "If you're like most young bucks," he had said when he was showing Erik the place, "you'll be out whoopin' it up with the rest of 'em, so it won't make no never mind."

Erik had refused the free use of Amelia Warren's mobile home, for taking favors from a County Commissioner would have been a conflict of interest, not to mention putting him all too close to her interested view. But he hadn't been able to resist this apartment, particularly when his own search for semi-permanent lodging had proved futile. Amelia had sent him to Lester, and the furnished apartment had been cleaned and made livable on Saturday.

Home! For the next few weeks, at least. When he wasn't off on another of his active projects. He'd certainly have to get back to the Gulf Coast no later than next Tuesday to check on the progress of the coastal wetland. The Trust was attempting to restore.

Damn, but it had been inconvenient, arriving on a Thursday, in order to meet with all the commissioners. Friday had been wasted, too soon to make arrangements for a helicopter to fly them in to the site. The only good thing about the delay was finding this apartment. He'd spent Saturday exploring as much of Hells Canyon as he could reach by road, Sunday moving in and getting settled. And now, finally, he was going to see the supposedly incomparable wetland that had brought him almost three thousand miles.

He was willing to bet it was a mess. A century of cattle and sheep grazing had left little of the West in its pre-settlement condition.

He rinsed the cup under the tap and set it to drain. It was a good thing he was compulsively neat, for a single thing out of place in this tiny apartment would make it look unkempt. Time to go.

Harry Lindholm wasn't at the airport—a grassy landing strip

with a single unattended hanger. Neither was the helicopter, which was flying down from New Meadows. Perhaps he should have insisted on chartering the helicopter himself, since NWT funds were paying for it. But Harry had said using the flying service in New Meadows would be much cheaper than chartering out of Boise, so Erik had let him go ahead and make the arrangements.

Erik leaned against the fender of his rental car, enjoying the quiet, the solitude. Except for a distant mechanical murmur from the sawmill on the other side of town, he could hear nothing but birdcalls, the whisper of wind in the cottonwoods along Garnet Creek, and his own thoughts.

Moments like this were becoming more and more precious to him, the longer he stayed in D.C., and more and more necessary. Perhaps it was time he did what he always said he'd do when he got tired of life in the fast lane—settle down.

There were worse places to settle down than Sunset County, Idaho.

The distant thwump-thwump of a helicopter reminded him that he was only here to do a job. When he settled down, it would be someplace where the hand of man had touched the land but lightly. He wanted no reminders of civilization in the view from his front porch—if he ever had one.

Tires on gravel signaled the arrival of Harry Lindholm, Chairman of the County Commissioners, John Deere and Ford dealer, and his guide for today. He heard a door slam and, without turning, he said, "We couldn't ask for a nicer day, Harry."

"Harry could." There was laughter in the husky, feminine voice.

He spun around. Kathryn was pulling a daypack out of the back of a dark blue minivan. Her black curls held glints of red in the morning sun and her pert little bottom filled a pair of jeans quite nicely.

"What are you doing here? Where's Harry?"

"Harry and his hunting dog had a disagreement over which way they'd walk this morning," Kathryn said, walking toward him. "Ace won, but in the process he pulled Harry off the porch and broke his leg." She smiled. "So I'm your guide."

Excitement flared in him. All weekend he'd done everything he could to avoid thinking of her, for his thoughts always ended in the same place.

He wanted her, with an ache that was enormous, overwhelming, all-consuming. Erik swallowed. "That's great," he said, wondering if she heard the tremble in his voice. How the hell was he going to spend a day in her company and keep his hands off her?

The helicopter landed, preventing any further conversation. While he loaded the duffel containing his field gear, Kathryn returned to the minivan for a roll of maps and a pair of rubber boots.

Soon they were airborne. Erik sat alone in the rear seat, not touching Kathryn. It was difficult enough to ignore the vulnerable line of her neck when he shifted his gaze past her from one window to the other. He watched the world revolve under them as the pilot turned the aircraft and soared over the high ridge that rose just west of Garnet Falls. This wasn't the green and lush land he was used to, but it had a bleak beauty of its own.

Sagebrush gave way to scattered timber as they climbed higher. Soon ponderosa pine and Douglas-fir grew tall and straight on steep mountainsides, forming an open forest where deer and elk abounded, where grouse and squirrel, bear and bobcat lived in uneasy proximity. Erik knew that if he were on the ground he would see signs of human disturbance, but from up here, the forest looked as it must have for ten thousand years.

They swooped over another ridge, into a valley where a dirt road pointed to clean white buildings on a knoll. The bottomland was green, spotted with red cows and their gamboling calves. He caught the glint of a meandering stream as they turned to follow the road.

"...cousin Jon...Double J...borrow a horse...." The noise from the rotor, carried inside through the open window, stole Kathryn's words.

"I can't hear you," he shouted as she looked back, obviously expecting an answer.

"Never mind," she said, but he read the words on her lips rather than hearing them. Her smile twisted his heart; it was so incredibly sweet.

They were in the air for almost an hour. After the ranch with the white buildings—the Double J, he assumed—they went over another ridge, followed another stream up a narrow canyon, and then hovered above a hillside where the stream entered the canyon. Kathryn pointed and Erik looked as the helicopter slowly rotated counter-clockwise so that the view was directly outside his window.

He looked. He rubbed his eyes and looked again. "Oh. My. God!"

There weren't any places like this left on Earth. Somehow they'd crossed a dimensional barrier and come out in another time, on another planet.

"Wounded Bear Meadow." Kathryn's words came clearly to him, despite the rotor noise and the wind.

Erik knew that nine hundred acres was close to one-and-a-half square miles. He knew that Wounded Bear Meadow was primarily a palustrine wetland comprising several types: forested, shrub/scrub, emergent, and submergent. He'd seen from the map that Wounded Bear Creek meandered through the valley containing the meadow, here dammed by beaver, there running free over its rocky bed. And he'd read in Kathryn's letter that the meadow had never been plowed.

Nothing he'd heard or read or known had prepared him for what he was seeing.

A touch on his shoulder broke his enchantment. With raised eyebrows, Kathryn gestured at the ground. He read her lips: "Do you want to land?"

Erik nodded vigorously.

As they descended, he wondered if the fizzing excitement in his blood was because of Kathryn's light touch, or because he was going home, to a place he'd never been.

She was slipping into her daypack when he slid from the helicopter's door. "The pilot has got another job that'll take him about three hours. I brought lunch, so if it's all right with you, we'll look around until we get hungry."

"Sounds good to me," he agreed. He couldn't wait to explore Wounded Bear Meadow, to see if it proved as pristine as it appeared.

"I still don't believe there can be a place like this in cattle country," Erik said as they stuffed the remains of lunch back into her daypack. "In a few minutes, I'm going to wake up and start living today all over again."

"Jethro's gotten a lot of ribbing about it. This is some of the finest bottomland pasture on the Z-Bar-Z and he's always kept it fenced off. He always says that what was good enough for his grandpappy is good enough for him." Kathryn zipped the pack and slid her arms through the straps. "Actually I think it was his great grandfather who first decided it was too beautiful a place to spoil. Back in the 1870s, if I remember rightly." For a moment she felt a twinge of regret that there would never be another Zenger to preserve Wounded Bear Meadow because it was the 'prettiest place this side of heaven.'

She stood, waiting for him to finish inserting fresh film into his camera. "Now you see why I called for help. I just couldn't let it become part of a planned community, with jogging paths all around the edge and boardwalks out to the beaver dams."

"That's better than being drained. Twenty years ago, that would have been the first thing they did, right before they paved the whole place." Erik closed his camera and advanced the film. "There. Now, what are our chances of getting to that copse of trees out there? I'd like to look it over."

Kathryn looked dubiously at the stand of evergreen trees on a low island surrounded by the many-branched stream and several beaver ponds. "I'm game, I guess. When I was up here before, we didn't really explore too much." Instead she and Jesse had picnicked on the wooded slope overlooking the meadow, then made long, delicious love under a pine tree.

She half-expected an old, familiar pain to catch at her heart with sharp talons. Instead all she felt was a gentle melancholy, a sorrow that Jesse's vitality, his deep capacity for love, was no more a part of her life. She missed him still, but she no longer felt half a person for his absence.

"The worst thing that can happen is that we'll get caught in the mud and have to wait for Bill to hoist us out," Erik said, heading out onto the hummocky area between them and the nearest beaver pond.

She could see the ground give under his feet, and knew he would sink were it not for the thick mat of roots that lay just under the surface of the wet soil. "No, the worst thing is that we'll fall into a beaver pond and get captured and stored for next winter," she countered, willing to join in his joking.

"Even worse than that would be to find a pool of slow mud and gradually sink out of sight." He turned around to grimace at her. "Ugh! Can you imagine feeling the mud climbing higher and higher on your body, slick and slimy and completely remorseless?"

"And pretty soon it reaches your mouth, and you can't say scary things any more." She caught up with him and gave him a gentle shove, barely causing him to break stride. "What in the world is slow mud?"

"It's like quicksand, only mud, and very, very slow. Haven't you ever stepped in a mud hole and started to sink?" He gestured. "Your feet get stuck, and the only way to get loose is to take off your boots. But there's no place to grab hold of for leverage, so you just keep sinking. It takes a lot longer, but it's just as deadly as quicksand."

"I don't believe you."

"You should. I'm the wetlands expert. Besides, it happened to me."

"How did you get out?"

"I didn't. I sank out of sight." The twitch of his mouth and the twinkle in his eye belied his serious tone.

The going got rougher. Little ponds appeared on the surface and the grasses—and sedges, according to Erik—became more sparse. Several times Kathryn felt the mud grab her boot and try to hold it. Once it released her with a wet, sucking sound.

Erik smiled and said, "See, I told you."

It was all she could do to keep up with him. His long legs seemed tireless, his feet never seemed to miss landing on solid roots instead of hungry mud. They crossed the first branch of the creek by wading a free flowing stretch between beaver dams. The water wasn't quite deep enough to overtop her boots, but she felt some slop inside, wetting her tucked-in jeans. Her boots, knee high and easily slipped on and off, were really too large around the top. She could have bought women's boots, but they were a couple of inches shorter, and she had wanted all the protection she could get when she helped irrigate two summers ago while her cousin Jon was laid up with his smashed foot.

Erik stopped often, taking photographs or just looking around. His comments were mostly technical ones, more talking to himself than to her, she guessed. Kathryn didn't have much breath left for speech, so she didn't try. It was humbling to find that her daily walks to and from work—half a mile each way—had inadequately prepared her for this kind of walking. She strode along briskly in town and here she was traveling at a slow stroll, but it was work! She had to watch where her feet landed, had to test the uneven and often yielding surface before setting her weight on each foot. It was getting more and more difficult to breathe through her nose, when her lungs demanded oxygen in large gulps. Erik made it all look so easy and she'd be darned if she'd pant along behind.

Eventually they reached the copse. It was a lovely place, shady, with leathery-leaved low shrubs and tall grass under the dark green branches. Kathryn sank gratefully onto a fallen log while Erik loaded still another roll of film into his camera. Watching his long, nimble fingers handle the camera as if it were an extension of themselves, she recalled how knowing they had been another time.

She pushed the thought back, 'way back. She was going to have to work with him for weeks, perhaps months. If she allowed him to affect her the way he had in Seattle—the way he had ever since he came to Garnet Falls—she wouldn't be able to do anything effectively.

That brief, unforgettable episode had been a temporary aberration from her usual practical, sensible behavior. It had been part and parcel of the insanity she'd sunk into after Jesse's death. That was all. She'd never do something that...that stupid again.

"...mud on my face?" Erik said, breaking into her thoughts, alerting her to the fact that she'd been staring at him.

"Oh...oh, no. No, I was just...just thinking about...about something."

She had to stop thinking of what might have been and concentrate on what was. After one night of insanity—she never would have been so wanton if she hadn't been out of her mind from stress and exhaustion—she'd come back to Garnet Falls and gone on with her life. And it had been a good life, filled with family and friends, with love and satisfaction.

Only the nights were empty.

And now the cause of that emptiness was here, confusing her, making her remember feelings best left forgotten, needs best left unfulfilled.

Then he was before her, looming, his eyes catching and holding hers.

"Were you remembering, Kathryn?" He ran one finger across her cheek, in a gesture that reduced her to a pool of melted will. "This?"

Before she could do more than gasp, his lips were touching hers softly, teasingly. "Or this?" he breathed, as he kissed his way all around her mouth. "I've never forgotten either," he said, taking her earlobe between his teeth, gently tugging.

"No!" She pushed him away and nearly tipped herself backwards with the same convulsive motion. "No, damn you!" She grabbed her daypack and headed back they way they'd entered the copse, but his hand caught her upper arm and brought her to a sudden halt.

"No? I saw the way you were staring at me. Hungry, Kathryn. You're as hungry for me as I am for you."

"I'm not!"

"Liar."

She didn't move as his arms came around her, pulling her back against his chest. Her buttocks were nestled against his pelvis and she could feel the stirrings of his awakening desire. Kathryn couldn't speak, could hardly breathe.

"Are you lying to yourself, too? Or just to me?"

His hands flattened across her midriff, his thumbs touched the sides of her breasts lightly, fleetingly. Again the breath caught in her chest. The sleeping hunger in her belly stretched, yawned. Before it could awake, ravening, demanding fulfillment, she jerked herself free and spun around.

"Listen to me, Erik Solomon, and listen good! There's not going to be a repeat performance, do you hear me? Sleeping with you was the dumbest thing I ever did, and I don't intend to make the same mistake twice."

"Was it a mistake?" He hadn't moved, but was looking at her in the strangest way. Almost as if his feelings were hurt.

"Oh, yes," she said, knowing she had to conquer this awful hunger for Erik Solomon. She had to!

"Then let's talk about it," he snarled, pushing her back onto the log and sitting beside her. "You wouldn't talk to me the other night, and you weren't at work Friday. Where were you? Hiding?"

She had been, but he didn't need to know that. "I was out at the ranch. My cousin's ranch, the Double J." She'd pointed it out to him on the way up here. "And why should I talk to you? We slept together eight years ago. You went your way and I went mine. That's all there was to it." She shrugged, aware that her voice trembled and hoping he'd interpret the quaver as anger, not regret.

"And now we're back together again," he said, his voice soft and full of promise. Taking her hand, he turned it palm up and traced across it with one finger. His light touch sent arrows of heat up her arm and through her whole body. "Can you tell me, honestly, that you don't feel anything for me?"

She snatched her hand free, clenching her fist around the memory of his touch. "No," she admitted. "No, I can't." Closing her eyes, she called up the decision she'd agonized over this past weekend. "But we're not going to do anything about it. Not unless you can tell me we'll be together longer than a few weeks."

He stared out across the meadow, and she heard her answer in his silence.

CHAPTER FOUR

Damn her!

Erik pivoted on a heel and aimed the camera out across the meadow. He'd already gotten all the photos he needed, but at least the viewfinder gave him somewhere to look. His fingers were tight on the camera, as he wanted them to be on her lovely white throat.

He *knew* she wanted him. He'd seen the desire lurking in her eyes at the courthouse, when he'd caught her watching as he explained the National Wetlands Trust to the commissioners. He'd felt her hunger for him that evening, as they spoke of trivialities on the way to her house. And he'd read it in her face a few minutes ago.

Hell, he still wanted her. He felt the same inexplicable pull he'd felt the first time he'd seen her. The strong feeling of inevitability he felt then was even stronger now. As if their lives were fated to be tangled together.

And it scared him. He should not allow himself to get involved with her again, no matter how his body lusted mindlessly for her.

A dark shape swooped across his peripheral vision, not quite so much seen as sensed. He turned to look and saw wide wings just disappearing into an untidy mass of sticks atop a dead tree. Letting the camera swing from its strap, he raised his binoculars. Nothing.

He held the binocs on the mass—a nest? Patiently he waited, until finally he was rewarded by motion. A head. No, two. Three? He couldn't be sure. But it was a nest, and there were young in it.

"Kathryn," he called, softly, even though he knew a human voice wouldn't disturb the birds at this distance. "Look."

There was no answer. Erik lowered the binocs and turned around. She was nowhere in sight. He shrugged, and returned to watching the nest. After a long interval of bobbing heads and undefinable motions barely visible over the irregular rim of the nest, the parent bird flew.

"Osprey," he identified, not surprised. The large raptor, once called a fish hawk because of its hunting and feeding habits, was a common habitant of wetlands, although it was not nearly so often seen as it had been a century ago.

A second adult bird landed on the nest, before the first was out of sight. It held something in its talons, possibly a fish. Again he saw the bobbing heads. Dinnertime for the kids.

Reluctantly he lowered the binoculars. He could stand here all day and watch the osprey, but he had work to do. He pulled his field notebook from his hip pocket and made notes of the approximate location of the nest and the fact that it seemed to contain three healthy chicks. The first thing he'd do, once NWT assumed title to Wounded Bear Meadow, was have large-scale aerial photos flown. Then he'd put his summer interns to work mapping all nests and perches, as well as the beaver dams and game trails. Satisfied he'd seen all there was to see from here, he returned his camera and binoculars to his knapsack.

"Kathryn." This time he called loudly, hoping she hadn't wandered off. She was little more familiar with the meadow than he was, and he didn't want to have to search for her. He still wanted to see if he could cross the main stem of the creek. It had looked like there was some higher ground over there, near the nest tree.

"I'm here," she said, coming from behind a screen of elderberry bushes. "I had to...ah, I went—"

He grinned. "No problem. Are you ready to go?"

"Anytime." Her voice was still tinged with frost. Well, hell! She'd been living in another dimension if she really expected him to hang around Garnet Falls, Idaho, any longer than he had to.

The next task was to convince his body that sexual frustration was good for it.

He pointed out the route he wanted to follow. "Can you manage that?" She was tired, he could tell, and had been having trouble keeping up, just before lunch. He often forgot how difficult many people found the going in a typical wetland.

"You lead, I'll follow," she said, her chin set stubbornly.

By the time they reached the creek, Erik wasn't sure it was worth their while to go any farther. The ground was barely supporting their weight. He'd gone in almost to the top of his boots more than once. Thankfully the mud wasn't the heavy, clayey kind—the slow mud he'd kidded Kathryn about. So far.

There was a log wedged across the creek, the remnants of its root ball rammed into the near bank by a spring flood. Water poured under it, barely wetting it. Years of pounding by spring floods and scorching by summer suns had eaten away the bark and left a shiny, silvery surface, probably slippery under the thick rubber soles of his boots. "You'd better stay here," he told Kathryn, testing the footing. The trunk was only about a foot in diameter. He was used to walking logs like this—or even narrower. She probably wasn't.

"I can make it," she said, and he heard the unspoken challenge: *Anywhere you can walk, I can follow.*

"At least wait until I get to the other side."

She looked mulish.

"Look, Kathryn, if I fall in, I want you ready to pull me out, not standing on the log, ready to fall yourself. Okay."

"Okay." She glared.

His first few steps were easy. Along about the middle, he hit a patch of rotted wood that crumbled under his feet, but he was ready and managed to get past with no trouble. "Watch your step here," he called back. "It gets a little dicey."

On the other side, he waited as Kathryn inched her way across. "Don't watch me," she said, windmilling her arms and carefully putting one foot in front of the other. "I'll fall if you do."

He obeyed, knowing exactly what she meant. Balancing on a log was bad enough, but having someone watch while you exhibited your innate clumsiness was another thing entirely. He waited until she was on solid ground, then struck off across the patch of sedge between the creek and the next tree.

Ten steps and he was in up to his right hip. The other leg was only buried to the knee. Immediately he flopped forward and grabbed handsful of the tough-rooted sedges. Working his left leg free was easy, but the right one seemed solidly mired. He rolled onto his back and began working his leg back and forth, using all his strength to lift it out of the sucking mud.

Water seeped around him, wetting his butt. With a curse, he wriggled out of the knapsack, not wanting its contents to be ruined. As he was doing so, he heard a squeal, then another one.

"Kathryn!" With renewed effort, he struggled to release his right leg.

"I'm all right." Her voice faded as she went on speaking, until it was only a faint sound without comprehensible words.

He continued to struggle, but felt no give to the mud. Whenever he tried to use his left foot or his hands to gain leverage, they too began to sink. The only way he was going to get out was to lift the right leg while he was lying flat on his back. Even sitting made him sink.

Finally he gritted his teeth and reached for the knife sheathed at his belt. He'd heard of trapped beaver biting off their legs to escape, but this was ridiculous. He plunged his hand into the mud beside his leg, holding the knife blade up, parallel to his wrist. The mud resisted, but little more than thick soup or heavy pancake batter would have. Eventually he found the knotted ties of his boot and slid the sharp blade along them. He felt the prick of the blade against his arch and carefully withdrew his arm, laying the knife at the limit of his reach. He didn't want to lose it. His grandfather had carried that knife in World War II.

"Erik! Where are you?"

"Stop!" He put command into his voice. "Don't take another step." She was somewhere between him and the creek.

"What on earth?"

He took a deep breath, then gave a mighty pull. His foot slipped free of his boot and slid through the clinging mud. Once it was at the surface, he rolled to his belly and carefully crept backwards, imitating an inchworm. A few feet and he felt the ground grow firm.

Pulling his knapsack to safety, Erik just lay there, breathing deeply and wondering how the hell he was going to get back to the pickup point with one bare foot.

He looked down. One bare and bleeding foot. The knife had done more than prick his arch.

"Is that slow mud?" He opened his eyes. She was standing over him, dripping.

She looked like the proverbial drowned rat. Erik wondered how she'd managed to fall in after she'd crossed safely. All he could think of to say was, "Did the maps get wet, too?"

Kathryn sank to the ground, more miserable than she had ever been in her entire life. It wasn't exactly cold, but clouds had drifted in, concealing the sun. A fitful breeze stole her warmth as it evaporated the water dripping from her clothing.

"I could have drowned," she said, as she wrapped her arms around her quickly chilling body, "and you're worrying about maps?"

Erik rolled over and raised himself to a crouch. He was covered in mud to his waist and seemed to be missing a boot. She couldn't be sure, for the mud was so thick and so black that it made his legs appear knobby and misshapen. "So could I," he said, his voice shaking. "I was stuck in the mud—slow mud." He gestured at a patch of crushed and mud-smeared weeds about ten feet away. His hands became as muddy as his legs when he began scraping his legs and feet clean.

Yes, he *was* missing a boot. "What happened?"

He explained, and she was instantly contrite. "You weren't kidding—I thought you were pulling my leg." His tall tale of slow mud had sounded so farfetched she hadn't really believed him.

"I was. You looked so gullible." Pulling his knapsack to him, he began rooting inside. "I made it up—slow mud, I mean. But I just discovered it's for real." He pulled his binoculars and camera out and examined them, "Ah, good. They didn't get wet. How about the maps?"

Kathryn muttered to herself as she shed her own knapsack. While she hadn't really been in any danger when the bank had crumbled under her feet—the creek hadn't been over three feet deep—she'd have appreciated a little concern. But she apparently wasn't anywhere nearly as vital to Erik Solomon as his precious maps were.

She pulled them out, knowing as soon as she touched the roll that they had gotten as wet as the rest of her. The paper disintegrated under her touch and blue drips ran from it. The maps she'd brought had been diazo copies—blueprints—of enlarged topographic maps. While new copies would be easy enough to obtain, these had been annotated by Erik at each of their stops, including in the copse where they'd eaten lunch.

Unrolling them was impossible. The paper stuck to itself and tore when she tried to separate it. Erik, watching, cursed under his breath. She recognized the cadence, if not the syllables.

"I'm sorry," she said, wondering if he really would hold her responsible.

"Don't sweat it," he said. He took the roll from her. "I'll take 'em back to my room and see if I can get them dry before they mildew. I should have insisted you stay on the other side."

Kathryn admitted, just to herself, that she'd have crossed the creek, come hell or high water—well, no matter how strongly he'd insisted she not follow him, anyway. She watched as he stood and took a couple of testing steps back the way she'd come. She noticed he only put his weight on tussocks of the harsh, grass-like stuff that grew everywhere on this side of the creek.

"What's the matter?"

"I'm checking to see if it's stable. I don't want to fall in again."

"I didn't have any trouble. It didn't even feel wet."

"You lead then. Any route's better than the one I took." He stood aside and let her lead him back to the creek.

Kathryn didn't even bother trying the log. She had always had a problem keeping her balance on things like logs and railroad tracks. She would rather get wet by choice than make a fool of herself falling off again. Get wetter, that was. She waded through the creek, splashing great sheets of the icy water on either side of her. Perhaps if she moved energetically, she'd be warmer. Right now she felt like a refugee from an ice cream factory.

She was warmer by the time they reached the spot where the helicopter was to pick them up, but at the cost of every bit of stamina she had. Erik had walked in a straight line between the scene of their wetting and the landing area and let nothing stop him. He didn't slow down once, despite the rough walking, the numerous creeklets they had to jump, or the nettle patch they traversed, bare hands held high to protect them. He didn't even limp or otherwise favor his bare foot. Right then, she hated him.

The sky was completely overcast and the wind had quickened. Erik slipped out of his knapsack and began picking up branches and twigs.

"What are you doing?" The words came out almost unintelligible. Her teeth were chattering and shudders shook her frame.

"Help me," he commanded. "We've got to get warm. No telling how soon the helicopter will get here."

She picked up a few twigs, but her hands seemed incapable of grasping. Most of them slipped through icy cold, nerveless fingers. She finally sat on a rotting log, too cold and too defeated to keep trying.

"Get up!" Erik was on his knees, blowing on a pile of tinder in the midst of a pitifully small collection of wood. "Keep moving."

"I-I-I c-c-c-can't-t-t-t." The shudders wracked her with greater force and her teeth clacked together until they hurt.

Wisps of smoke rose from the wood. Erik kept blowing, until at last he was rewarded with a few tongues of flame. When it seemed as if the fire would maintain itself, he came to her and pulled her roughly to her feet.

His arms went around her and his hands moved hard and fast up and down her back. The friction and the pressure seemed to help, but her body still shivered uncontrollably. Finally he pulled her to her knees and held her, back to his chest, close to the fire. Its warmth soothed her icy cheeks, but barely penetrated her sodden sweatshirt and clammy blue jeans. Kathryn was beyond caring. She grabbed the bottom of the sweatshirt and pulled—or tried to—it over her head. "Help m-m-me," she whimpered when its wet folds wrapped around her head and shoulders.

Erik did, and Kathryn found that her shirt was just as cold, just as clammy. She tried to unbutton it, but her fingers refused to manipulate the tiny buttons. Again Erik helped her, until, with relief, she felt the wind, warm by comparison, on her bare skin. "My jeans," she gasped, warmer now the shirts no longer robbed her upper body of precious heat, but still shivering and fighting an urge to just quit, wrap her arms around herself, and give in to the cold.

Erik wrapped his wool shirt around her, scratchy against her bare shoulders and through the lace of her bra. Then he attacked her boots.

Even her socks were wet. No wonder she'd squished when she walked. With relief she rolled from side to side as Erik peeled her tight jeans down, thinking how much warmer the grass in the clearing felt than she did. Perhaps she could just lie here and...

"Turn your back on the fire," Erik said. Kathryn was amazed to see that the twigs and branches were being consumed by leaping flames. "You'll be able to sit closer."

She obeyed and immediately felt wonderful warmth on her back. Gradually the shivers lessened, until they occurred as occasional spasms rather than constantly shaking her body. She pulled her legs up and clasped them, resting her chin on her knees. Eyes closed, she tried to relax as her body slowly regained the heat it had lost.

"Turn around now," Erik said, some long time later. Kathryn opened her eyes. He was standing before her, clad in nothing but very scanty, very red briefs.

A new warmth began in her lower belly and flowed through her. She knew that body, knew its pulse points and its erogenous zones. She had buried her face in the springy pelt on his chest and nipped at the dark, almost concealed nipples. She had dipped her tongue into the deep indentation of his navel, tasting his musky, male scent.

Some of her feelings must have showed in her eyes, for he kneeled before her, one hand reaching out to touch her cheek. "Kathryn?" His voice was husky, little more than a whisper.

She found no words. All she could do was look at him, still wanting him and still certain that they had made a mistake.

Her certainty could no more resist her body's need than a drifting feather could resist the wind. She fought to keep from leaning into his touch, resisted the urge to find his fingertips with her lips. She told her eyes to close, rather than drowning in his fiery gaze.

When his breath blew hot on her mouth, she silently screamed at her lips to close, her jaw to set. And when his lips brushed hers, with a touch as delicate as a spider's silk, she was still telling herself not to welcome him back into her life.

"Kathryn." Her name was almost a prayer on his lips.

Pull back, her mind screamed. *Don't let him!*

Just this once, her body argued. *Just this one time more, for the memory.*

His lips found hers and were hot, oh! so hot. Demanding. Pleading. Promising.

His arms were strong around her. Protective. Cherishing. Kathryn had forgotten how good being held in a lover's embrace could feel. No one had held her since Jesse. No, since Erik.

"Ah, Kathryn. You smell so good, taste so good." His tongue toyed with her lips, begging entrance.

She welcomed him, telling herself that she would allow only this pale imitation of what they both wanted. Soon she would stop him, tell him they'd gone far enough. Soon.

Her heart pounded in her ears, growing louder as Erik explored her mouth, as his hands stroked along her spine and framed her waist, shaped her buttocks, relearned the lines of her thighs.

Louder and louder, until Erik ended the kiss with a soft curse. "It's the helicopter," he said, framing her face with hands that almost seemed to tremble. "It'll be here any minute. Get dressed."

Quickly he rose to his feet and reached for their clothing, draped on branches and shrubs all around them. For a moment Kathryn sat, stupidly staring, still hearing the pounding of her heart.

"Kathryn! Get dressed. Hurry!" Her jeans, still almost dripping, hit her in the face.

The shock was enough to bring her back to reality. The helicopter. Of course. She forced her feet into the clinging denim, shivering again as it robbed her legs of their little warmth. Her shirt was somewhat drier, but still damp enough that the wind made it feel even colder and clammier.

"Keep my shirt," Erik said, taking the sodden sweatshirt from her. He twisted it until trickles of water ran out.

"And what'll you wear?" She'd give anything for the warmth of the wool, but having him cover his broad chest and wide shoulders was more important. Now that she was shocked back into common sense, she didn't want anything to distract her from her resolution. "I'm fine," she insisted. "Once we get into the helicopter, I'll be warm as toast."

He didn't argue, and was decently covered and kicking dirt over their fire when the 'copter finally set down in the meadow.

By Friday Kathryn had herself convinced her lack of judgment had been due to incipient hypothermia. Erik had played least in sight all week, and she'd heard, from various subscribers to the Garnet Falls grapevine, that he was holed up in his apartment, making long distance calls and pacing the floor.

At the Grade School Spring Program on Wednesday, Sandy Oliverio mentioned that he had a fancy little computer and printer set up and papers scattered everywhere. "He told me not to touch anything," Sandy complained. "How does he expect me to clean the room when I can't ever dust or make the bed? It even had papers piled on it."

Since he hadn't come in to her office, or called her at work or at home, Kathryn figured he was as embarrassed as she at what had almost happened Monday. She hoped so, because she didn't want to have to keep pushing him away all the time he was in town. Sooner or later, she was afraid, she'd forget to push.

"Do you ever do anything but work?" Erik's voice at her door called Kathryn away from her computer screen Friday afternoon about three. For an instant, before she resolutely told it to behave, her heart leaped in excitement.

She kept her smile impersonal. "All the time. My children and I spend every weekend playing."

"*Your* children?" His eyes flicked to her left hand, still poised over the keyboard.

"My children. I have twins, Kyle and Virginia. They're in first grade." As always, when she spoke of the children, she let more than a little joy creep into her voice. They might not be Jesse's biological children, but they were the son and daughter of his heart.

They were all she had left of him.

His mouth was grim. "What about their father?"

"He's dead. A long time ago." Strange how it didn't hurt any more to say that.

"I see." He stepped into her office and set a file folder on her desk. "Here's a memo to your commissioners stating my preliminary conclusions. It looks like Wounded Bear Meadow is a candidate for purchase by NWT, but I want some more information before I make a definite recommendation to the Board. I'll send a final report and our decisions as soon as they're compiled."

The shift from friendly bantering to business caught Kathryn by surprise, but she ignored it. She preferred the business. It didn't threaten her equanimity or test her resolve.

"I'm sure the commissioners will be pleased you're finished so quickly." She fiddled with her pens, straightened the papers in the folder beside the computer. "Will you be back, then?"

"Hard to say. I'm not usually involved in the in-depth studies."

His tone said, *Thank God*. She suspected he was far too important to waste his time on checking out insignificant little marshes out in the wilderness.

She couldn't understand why she felt so...so let down. She'd known all along he'd be leaving as soon as he did what he'd come to do. That was why she'd held him at a safe emotional distance. Or tried to.

"I hope you'll cooperate with whoever we send to continue the studies as fully as you have with me."

Frowning at the lined-up pens, she pushed a memo pad beside them. "Of course. Anything I can do to help..." *Well, not quite anything. I won't fall in love with your replacement.*

Where had *that* come from? She hadn't, she *wouldn't* fall in love with Erik Solomon, or anyone else. Her life was fine just the way it was. She was glad he was going away. Glad!

"Assuming you don't change your mind and your Board accepts your recommendation, what would be the next step?" She wasn't really trying to postpone his departure. She just wanted to know what to expect.

"Getting funding for the purchase. Usually we have more time than Mr. Zenger gave us and can plan ahead. This time we'll have to get pledges for the entire amount over and above our annual acquisitions budget."

Kathryn sensed rather than saw him checking his watch.

"Look, I've got to go. Take care of yourself, okay?"

Finally she allowed herself to look up. She wanted one last mental image, one last memory of him. "I will," she managed to say, just above a whisper. "You too." Her throat closed and no more words could escape past the threatening sobs.

He reached, then pulled his hand back before his fingers could touch her cheek. The lines in his cheeks deepened.

He spun on his heel and was gone.

"Goodbye," she said to the empty space he left behind. "Goodbye, Erik."

* * *

"I'm not surprised," Emaline said. "I've always thought those conservation organizations were a lot of hot air." The County Treasurer wasn't much of an environmentalist. Not only did her husband work at the sawmill, but their oldest son was a logger.

"I expect they have to rely on contributions for their funding," Kathryn said, noncommittally. She was disappointed, and knew Jethro would be too. Last time she'd taken the children out to the Z-Bar-Z, he had told her how much he'd liked that young fella from the National Wetlands Trust. Would he wait, or would he sell Wounded Bear Meadow along with the rest of the ranch? She was almost afraid to ask him.

"I think it's a damned shame," Eddie said, setting his Pepsi on Kathryn's desk. "It seems like there's always money to build fancy houses and buy big new cars, but nobody's willing to spare a few dollars to save the nation's resources."

"Oh, come on, Eddie, don't make me vomit." Emaline cupped a hand over her mouth. "One little swamp isn't anywhere near 'the nation's resources.'"

"If everybody thought that, pretty soon we wouldn't have any wetlands or forests or anything left," the young planning intern's voice rose and his ears grew red. "Erik said—"

"Stop it, both of you. I've got a headache." Kathryn found she tightened up inside every time Eddie went into his "Erik says" routine.

That was the problem with being young and idealistic. Your heroes were perfect.

Then you got older and more worldly wise, and discovered your heroes were nothing more than ordinary human beings.

She had to admit she was as upset as Eddie was that NWT wasn't able to fund the purchase of Wounded Bear Meadow right now. Erik's letter had arrived yesterday by courier and as soon as the commissioners were all notified, they'd converged on the courthouse. Soon its contents were common knowledge, as was the news that Erik Solomon would be returning to attempt to put together some sort of alternative deal with Jethro.

That was, she realized, when her headache began.

Eventually she managed to push both Emaline and Eddie from her office so she could get some work done. Not much though, for it seemed like everyone in the Courthouse dropped by to comment on Erik's report.

"I've been up there," one of the fellows from County Roads said, as he leaned against her doorframe about two, "and I don't see what makes it so special. Not even a road in."

The mayor's secretary stopped by shortly after. "My husband's going to be really disappointed. He loves to camp up there come elk season. I'll bet whoever buys the place from Jethro won't be so hospitable."

"I doubt NWT would welcome hunters either," Kathryn said. "Erik said they operate their preserves like wildlife refuges." My God! She was doing the "Erik says" thing too.

There was another letter from Erik waiting when she got home. It was totally impersonal, entirely concerned with the meadow. "...understand you've been his friend for a long time. I was hoping you could convince Mr. Zenger to postpone a decision on Wounded Bear Meadow for a reasonable time—perhaps until September—so we can explore some other avenues of funding."

He hadn't even signed his letter. She knew his indecipherable scrawl from a short note requesting some information while he'd been in town. This neat, almost childlike signature was almost certainly his secretary.

"How come you're so set on me keeping the meadow with the rest of the ranch?" Jethro Zenger leaned back in his easy chair and fiddled with his pipe. He hadn't lit it for nigh on to twenty years, but it made a good gadget to hide behind when you were tryin' to think what to say.

"Well, Jethro, it seems to me that anybody wanting the ranch would want all of it." Charlie Bittenbusch smiled, showing every single one of his teeth.

Jethro wondered if the teeth were false. They were just too perfect. He never had trusted a man with straight, white teeth like Charlie's. "Anybody wantin' my ranch is gonna take what I'm willin' to sell." He wished Charlie would make his pitch and get it over with.

"Don't be too sure of that. I know some fellows who want it all." With slimy pride, Charlie leaned back in his chair and beamed some more. "They particularly want the meadow."

"Ranchers?" Jethro knew the chances of Charlie knowing any honest-to-God ranchers was pretty slim.

"Well, as a matter of fact, they aren't." He fidgeted. "You know that Sunriver place over in Oregon?"

"Yeah?" Jethro laid the pipe aside. He didn't need the distraction.

"Well, these fellows are looking to do something like that. A planned community, sort of, for people who want a summer home with all the amenities."

"What kind of amenities?"

"Well, a village with gift shops and clothing stores, maybe a bakery and one of them fancy espresso bars. You know. Kinda like McCall, only smaller and upscale."

"Upscale! Shoot fire, Charlie, what kinda word's that?"

"It means fancy, Jethro. Expensive. My cli...uh, my friends want to appeal to people with more than average money to spend." He rose to his feet and began pacing. Shortly he had outlined his plans to Jethro, plans that would, he claimed, bring a lot of outside money into Sunset County. Considering the state of the cattle and timber businesses, that wasn't all bad, Jethro had to admit.

"And what would happen to my meadow?"

"Well, they'd probably make it the center of their development," Charlie said, not meeting Jethro's eyes. "There was some talk of putting in boardwalks and maybe damming one arm of the creek, so they could have a small marina." He paused and seemed to take alarm at Jethro's frown. "For rowboats and canoes. No motor boats," he said, backing off and making peaceful motions with his fat hands.

Jethro pushed himself out of his chair. "Now you listen to me, Charlie Bittenbusch. Ain't nobody gonna turn my ranch into an amusement park." He shook his fist as Charlie backed away. "We Zengers have held this land for more than a hundred years and we've used it in the way the Lord intended."

Charlie was backing toward the door as Jethro advanced. "Not an amusement park," he protested. " A planned community, with houses and condominiums."

"And streets and sidewalks and tennis courts," Jethro continued as he followed Charlie out onto the porch. "Well, it may come to that for the rest of the land," he admitted, "but the only way they're gonna put a dam in Wounded Bear Meadow is over my dead body, Charlie." He stood on his porch as Charlie scurried toward his big, fancy Cadillac. "And I plan on bein' around a good while yet."

Watching the plume of dust rise behind Charlie's car, Jethro hoped he wasn't lying. It wasn't that he *had* to sell the Z-Bar-Z, but if he and the wife was to ever get to Mexico and Hawaii, like she'd always wanted to do, he had to get rid of the ranch.

And he was tired. Dang tired. Man and boy he'd worked this land, and now it was time to rest.

If only Jesse had lived, he'd have someone to pass the Zenger heritage on to, but he was buried up there on the hill, alongside his great-great grandpa, who'd first claimed this land back in 1874.

And the others didn't care. Of his four children, only Jesse had the love of the land that could make ranching in this high and lonely land worthwhile. If he were to ask his other children's advice, they'd tell him to take what he could get for the ranch and stop being a sentimental old man.

Dang it all! He'd just have to convince his wife that Solomon fella had a good chance of comin' up with the money by September.

CHAPTER FIVE

"He's back!" The excited voice was nearly unrecognizable, but after a few seconds Kathryn recognized Sandy's shriller-than-usual soprano. Her best friend never remembered to identify herself, but always jumped right into the middle of what she wanted to say.

"Who?" She missed a few words as she switched the receiver to her other ear.

Her query was lost in Sandy's breathless monologue. "When he left, he said somebody else'd be coming in a week or so, and they'd call me to get the place ready and probably they'd want me to clean and change the beds, like I do for Amelia and Lester. Only I don't know where they're going, now that it's rented."

"Whoa, Sandy," Kathryn soothed. "You always talk faster than I can listen. Back up and start again. Who's back?"

"Erik Solomon, that's who, and I thought you liked him. I do, and I've already got a man, but that doesn't mean I can't appreciate a hunk when I see one. He's the first really eligible man to come to town in years and if you aren't interested in him, you need your head examined. I mean, the way you live all alone and devote your time to the Wednesday Club and the PTA and all, well, I just think—"

"Sandy."

"...it's time you started dating again but there aren't any likely candi—"

"Sandy!"

"—dates in Garnet Falls and you won't even go to McCall for any of the dances and—"

Kathryn practically shouted, "Sandy, that's enough!" She couldn't help smiling, because Sandy was determined to get her married off. The silence on the line lengthened. After a suitable wait to make sure she had Sandy's attention, she said, "I am not interested in dating. I am not interested in getting married. I am particularly not interested in Erik Solomon."

"I don't believe you."

"Believe me, Sandy. I'm fine the way I am. I've got the twins and I don't need any complications in my life."

"Yeah, but—"

"But nothing. Let's talk about something else. Are you still planning to bring the girls out to the ranch Sunday?" Sandy's daughters were the same ages as her cousin's two boys, and were tomboys enough that Jace and Dennis considered them suitable playmates.

"I may have to work Sunday afternoon."

"Didn't you work last Sunday?" Kathryn knew Sandy only waited tables in the Conestoga House when one of the regular waitresses was absent. She secretly thought three jobs—hotel maid, cocktail waitress, and part-time waitress—were too many for her friend, but resolutely kept her mouth shut. Sandy and her husband were saving for a house of their own.

"Why don't I take the girls out Saturday morning when I go? Then you can come out Sunday evening." She wouldn't mind company on the twenty mile drive out to the Double J.

Shortly it was settled and Kathryn hung up. Thank heaven, she thought to herself, she'd been able to distract Sandy.

When were her friends going to give up and accept that she wanted to spend the rest of her life single? Probably about as soon as she convinced herself.

Erik wasn't here to make a decision on Wounded Bear Meadow this time, but to resolve a question about his future. The studio apartment above the Wooden Nickel gave him a place to set up his computer, have a second phone line installed for his modem, and work just as well as he could in Washington, D.C.

It wasn't the first time he'd left the nation's capital to set up shop in more congenial surroundings. Since about half of his work was consulting, it really didn't matter where he hung his hat. His clients could contact him in Idaho as easily as in D.C., and he'd be a lot happier here than in the impersonal rooms of his seldom-used condo.

With summer approaching, he needed no other excuse to seek the clean, dry air of Idaho's mountains. Last year he'd had to be available as an expert witness until Congress adjourned. He'd sworn then he'd never spend another summer in the nation's capitol.

So he'd told Walt it was his turn to have some fun. Never mind his astronomical charge rate. He'd work for technician's wages, just to get out of the city and into the high country. Or did the NWT director think he'd forgotten how to run a transect and interpret soil cores?

And while he was here, he'd work through his feelings for Kathryn.

Kathryn, whose eyes had told him to come back, even as her voice told him goodbye. Kathryn, who was the only woman he'd ever known who could make him wonder if going through life alone, as he'd long since chosen to do, might be a dismal and lonely process.

Since absence hadn't lessened his hunger for her, it was time to try proximity. He'd never known a woman who wore well, not when he was with her every day.

Once Kathryn's glamour was dimmed, he'd go on with his life.

Yeah. A summer with Kathryn would be a sure cure for the way his body surged with desire whenever he was anywhere in her vicinity.

It had always worked before.

He finished stowing his belongings and looked around. A far cry from elegant, the large room with a kitchen tucked into one corner and a small bathroom walled off in another, was nonetheless comfortable. The varnished knotty pine walls were warmly welcoming and the brightly floral slipcovers on the two chairs added color. What he found the most remarkable was the king-sized waterbed that dominated the north end of the room, under a large skylight set into the sloping roof. The place looked more like a love nest than an occasionally rented "spare room" available to guests of local residents.

He picked up the phone and dialed. Now that he was settled, it was time to begin his campaign to get Kathryn Pierson out of his system once and for all.

Surely she would have answered after fifteen rings. He cradled the phone and looked around the apartment, no longer so welcoming and warm. In fact, it felt positively cramped. Music and laughter filtered faintly from the tavern below, inviting him to socialize, instead of hiding up here in his cave.

Not enamored of his own company tonight, Erik followed the sound of music down to the Wooden Nickel. Capturing a corner table, he ordered a beer and a sandwich. One of the fellows at the bar seemed familiar, so Erik gave him a casual wave which was, after a slight hesitation, returned. When the waiter came back with his roast beef on sourdough—he hoped they gave doggie bags—Erik introduced himself and mentioned he was the upstairs tenant. The men at the next table overheard, as he'd intended them to, and he was soon in the midst of a conversation about the Seattle Mariners' chances at the pennant.

By ten that night, he was one of the guys.

"Not too many single women in Garnet Falls," Sheriff Wally Blanchett said, in response to his query about feminine companionship. "Leastways none past twenty-five or so. I had to go up the road, to New Meadows, to find my lady."

"There's Katie Pierson," Steve Lindholm said. "She's not so old. And she's pretty."

Alf Wallace snorted. "Pretty is as pretty does."

"What d'ya mean by that, Alf?" Steve half rose from his chair. "Katie's a real nice girl."

"I didn't say she wasn't," Alf said. He was older than the others, and his face bore the imprint of years of viewing everything in the worst possible light. "But she ain't always been, has she?" He waved the waiter over and ordered another round without asking if anyone was ready. "How'd she get them kids if she's pure as the driven snow?"

Erik's ears pricked up.

"I wondered about that myself," Wally admitted. "She and the Zenger boy never did get married, did they?"

"He was killed a couple of weeks before the wedding," Steve said. "Tractor rolled on him."

Alf snorted. "But those kids ain't his. Not unless that was the longest pregnancy on record."

"What do you mean?" The words burst out of Erik despite his resolution to keep quiet and listen.

"Figure it yourself. Jesse died in July. The twins was born more'n a year later." Alf sat back, a smarmy grin on his fat face. "I figure she got herself knocked up on one of those "business trips" she's always takin'. Funny business, if ya ask me."

"Aw, come on, Alf, Katie's not like that," Steve protested.

"She sure seems like a lady to me." Wally leaned forward across the table, holding Alf's eyes with his own. Erik bet himself the sheriff had been a holy terror in the Marines. "I don't like to hear you talk about her like that."

Erik's fists were knotted on his lap. It was either that or paste Alf's bulbous red nose all over his face. No matter who her children's father was, no one had a right to speak of her in so derogatory a manner.

"Alf, I've told you before to keep your big mouth shut." The deep, gravely voice came from behind Erik. He'd heard it before. Lester, the tavern's taciturn owner, seldom came out from behind the bar, rarely spoke to his customers.

"Well, this here fella was askin' about Katie Pierson, and I had to tell him, didn't I?"

"Yeah, you had to tell him the stories your dirty little mind dreamed up." Lester pulled a chair from the next table. "Alf here knows the truth but he don't believe it," he said. "But Katie's one of the finest women ever lived in Garnet Falls and I won't let anybody badmouth her. Not in my tavern."

"Do *you* know who fathered her twins?" Steve asked, looking almost ashamed of his curiosity.

"No, and it's none of my business, either, is it?"

Everyone but Alf nodded. Lester returned to his seat behind the bar.

"One time when I was home on leave," Wally said, "my pa said something about her going up to Portland and getting herself artificially inseminated. He was real disapproving, Pa was."

The other men began discussing the possibility, while Erik mulled the question over in his head. He liked it better than the alternative. The Kathryn he knew wouldn't be so careless as to get herself pregnant by accident. She'd been so particular that he protect her.

"Well, I still say she had to get them twins some way," Alf said as he stood, "and I don't believe no doctor done it to her. She had herself a one night stand up there in Portland or somewheres, you mark my word."

Erik felt his face flush and was grateful for the dark corner in which they sat. Kathryn had had at least one affair, up in Seattle, not all that far from Portland. Had she had others?

"Alf, you either find somewheres else to sit, or you and me's goin' out to the parking lot and have us a little dialogue," Wally said. "Got that?"

"Need any help?" Steve grinned, but Alf was getting to his feet, mumbling as he did so.

"Sour old fart," Wally said when Alf had stomped to the door. "He's one of them fellas can't say nothin' nice about nobody."

Steve agreed. So did Erik, but contented himself with a nod. "Tell me more about Kath...ah, Ms. Pierson," he said, after the waiter had brought them another round. He was beginning to feel pleasantly mellow. One beer was usually his limit, and here he was sipping on his third.

Wally shrugged. "I don't know much to tell. Just what Ma wrote me when she was still alive. Katie was about eight or nine when she came to Garnet Falls to live with her grandparents. Her parents had been killed in an auto accident and the old folks were her only kin willin' to take her."

"She was a cute little kid," Steve put in. "Lived next door to my cousins, so I saw her a lot. Then she started followin' Jesse everywhere, so I saw even more of her. She thought he was right up there with Superman and Santa Claus."

"She got some kind of scholarship to college, didn't she?" Wally asked.

"Two or three, I think. She was top of her class at graduation."

"So what happened with her fiancé? You said he was killed? Just before the wedding?" He never had heard how Jesse had died. The note from his sister had been brief and tear-stained.

"It was really awful." Steve shuddered. "Jesse was usin' an old Massey Harris tractor to pull a load of fenceposts up to one of the high pastures, 'way back of the main house. There was a culvert—a big old wooden thing goin' back a long time. They figured the back tractor wheel hit it just wrong and caved it in. Jesse was thrown and the tractor wheel caught in the barb wire fence and sorta wrapped it around him."

Erik really didn't want to know any more, yet he had to. "The tractor kept moving?"

"Nope. Just the wheels." Steve looked sick.

So did Wally.

"The doctor said Jesse bled to death. It didn't take long, 'cause the big artery—the feme...fero...anyhow, the big one in his groin was torn clear open."

"The femoral artery," Erik said, although he didn't know why it mattered.

"Yeah, that one. The doc said he was probably unconscious in minutes, dead soon after. And even if somebody had been there, they probably wasn't anything they coulda' done."

"I don't imagine so," Erik agreed. God! That must have been devastating for Kathryn, to lose Jesse in such a horrible way. "What a tragedy."

"Yeah, Katie was pretty laid out," Steve agreed.

"I was home on leave right afterward," Wally said. "She lost a lot of weight, went around looking lost and half dead herself for a long time."

Steve emptied his glass and set it down. "Her boss back then probably kept her from goin' off the deep end. He kept her so busy she didn't hardly have time to think. My ma was his secretary, and she said he found all sorts of conferences and meetings and classes for her to go to. When the county wouldn't pay her way, he paid from his own pocket."

"What about her grandparents? Were they supportive?"

"They were both gone by then, I think." Steve thought a moment. "No, just her grandpa. Old Man Pierson died when she was in high school, and her grandmother went into the rest home about the time Katie graduated college. She was pretty sick all that summer."

"Didn't she pass away about the same time Jesse did?" Wally asked.

"No, it was closer to Christmas." He looked at his glass. "Do I want another? Nah. I've got to open the station in the morning. Dad'll kill me if I come in with a hangover."

"I'm gonna have some coffee." Wally pantomimed pouring into a cup and soon Lester was headed their way with a steaming carafe.

Erik realized the world was looking a little blurred. "Me too," he said. "Black and strong." Caffeine might keep him awake tonight, but it was better than passing out before he could even climb the stairs to his apartment.

Well into their coffee, Steve reopened the conversation. "Look, Erik, don't get the wrong idea about Katie Pierson, okay? She's a real nice lady, and nobody around here cares much who the father of her kids was. However she got them, she did it for a good reason and we don't worry about it."

"They're nice kids," Wally added, "and she's done right well with 'em. That's all that matters."

"It is indeed," Erik agreed. He went to bed full of food for thought.

"You're sure we did the right thing, 'Melia?"

Amelia Warren, widow, horse breeder, County Commissioner, and enthusiastically fallen woman, stretched voluptuously. It had taken her three weeks to get Lester to come to her house instead of meeting her in the apartment above the Wooden Nickel, as he did for the past six years. Somehow the change had done them both good. Lester made love to her with unusual vigor, and she'd been just enough titillated by seeing his broad, dark body against the white crocheted bedspread of her feminine bed that she was more, well, turned on—she thought that was the current term—than she had been in years.

She dropped a kiss on Lester's shoulder, too lazy, too sated, to stretch any farther. "I hope so, honey. If we hadn't let him rent the apartment, he might've gone up to New Meadows, and we didn't want that."

"We didn't?" Lester pulled her against his shoulder and held her there. "How's come?"

"Oh, honey, I told you earlier, but I guess you were just too busy to listen."

One big, ham-sized hand cupped her head and strong fingers sifted through her hair. "Had me better things to do," Lester rumbled.

Amelia shivered as his fingers, callused and hard, stroked the tender skin behind her ear. The worst part about growing older, she thought, was that Lester was no longer as randy has he'd been when they were both twenty.

For perhaps the jillionth time, she wondered what her life would have been like if she had stayed in Garnet Falls and married Lester, instead of going down to Idaho State and finding someone else. Less fulfilling, certainly, but more exciting. Lester warned her—oh, back when they were just kids—that with his chances of passing on Cystic Fibrosis, he wouldn't give her children. Today medical science could give the answers they hadn't dared take a gamble on, but it was too late, had been for a long time.

"I don't want Katie to end up like me," she said, hearing the tiniest hint of regret in her voice. She couldn't say, even now, that she'd made the wrong choices in her life. The twenty-eight years of marriage had been all right, just not exciting and passionate. She'd had the children, and a lot of money.

Would those same years have been any better with Lester? She didn't know, and it really didn't matter, except that now, as she saw the big six-oh staring her in the face, she was aware of how much she had missed when she was young. Every woman needed to be loved. It kept the skin clear, the juices flowing. "Kathryn needs more than a father for those twins, Lester. She needs a husband for herself. It's such a waste, her bein' alone at her age."

Lester's voice was slow and deep, as if he were on the edge of sleep. "She's got family—Jon and Janine, and their young 'uns—" he mumbled, "and those little hellions of hers." His voice dwindled with the last few words, and she felt his breathing deepen and become the regular, long inhalations of early sleep.

Was there a man alive, she wondered, who could stay awake after sex? She'd heard her share of beauty parlor and bridge table talk, and one of the most common complaints of even the best satisfied wives was that their men never cuddled them enough afterward.

Idly she wondered how Erik Solomon was in bed? Did he stay with his women after loving them, sharing the afterglow, or did he, in Candy Lindholm's inelegant and earthy words, "start to snore before he'd rolled clear off?"

She smiled into the room's dimness. Not that she'd ever know, because even if Amelia's plans came to fruition, Katie Pierson was not one to kiss and tell.

Too bad. She really would like to know if the sensual promise she read in Erik's rich brown eyes was for real, or just a product of a dirty old woman's imagination.

Kathryn turned the heat down under the potatoes and went to the door, hoping someone interesting had come to call. The twins had been out at the ranch for two weeks now and she still wasn't used to the peace and quiet of an empty house in the evenings. She was so lonely she could cry.

She had so far resisted calling them this evening, but knew that if something didn't distract her, she would before their bedtime. It wasn't that she doubted their well being—Janine and Jon treated them like their own children. Ginger and Kyle were so much more content out there with their cousins than at Wanda's Childcare, which was all right to go to after school, but not for all summer. The real problem was her own loneliness, pure and simple.

She opened the door.

"Good evening, Kathryn. Is supper ready?" Amelia Warren slipped past her and into the living room, immediately making herself at home.

"Hello, Amelia. No, supper is not ready. I've already eaten."

Amelia sniffed. "What's that I smell cooking?"

"Potatoes." Kathryn had to chuckle at Amelia's anticipatory expression. "They're for the committee potluck tomorrow night."

"That's all right then," Amelia said, leaning back comfortably into the sofa. "I'll eat some tomorrow. I'm not really hungry tonight, anyhow."

Shaking her head in amusement, Kathryn started for the kitchen. "The tea will be hot in a few minutes," she called back over her shoulder. "And I've got snickerdoodles this week."

"No chocolate chips?" came a forlorn wail after her.

That Amelia! She was a caution. Rich and feisty, she had a finger in nearly every Sunset County pie. Besides being a County Commissioner, she sponsored several of the soccer teams in the county's league, organized outings for the elderly—she didn't consider herself one of them, being only fifty-nine—and wrote frequent, impassioned letters to the *Idaho Statesman* whenever one of her causes needed support. This summer she was championing the preservation of Wounded Bear Meadow, trying to shame the state into purchasing it for a wildlife refuge if NWT didn't come up with funding. Kathryn hoped she'd be half the woman Amelia was when she reached fifty-nine. Even at thirty-one, she wished she had that much energy.

She wouldn't mind having Amelia's love life as well. Everyone in Garnet Falls knew—but no one ever mentioned—that Amelia and Lester Wood met every week in the apartment above the Wooden Nickel for an afternoon of lovemaking. Since both were widowed and free of familial responsibilities, it was generally accepted that whatever made them happy was fine with their friends and neighbors.

"Have you heard from the novelty company?" Amelia asked when Kathryn returned to the living room carrying a tray with two cups of peppermint tea and a plate of cookies.

"No, but I didn't really expect to yet. It's only been a week since I ordered the prizes." As co-chair, with Amelia, of the Wednesday Club's annual fund-raiser, her job was to follow the older woman's orders and keep all the loose ends tied up.

"They should have acknowledged our order by now," Amelia fretted. "What if they never got it?"

"Amelia, we still have more than three weeks before the carnival. But if it makes you fell better, I'll call them tomorrow."

"Please do." Amelia took another handful of cookies, making Kathryn envy her metabolism. Only slightly over five feet tall, Amelia was as slim as a girl and never seemed to worry about her weight. She ate like a logger—Kathryn had personally seen her put away eight pancakes, three eggs, and a huge slice of ham at the Legion breakfast last April. Life was definitely not fair, not when Kathryn had to subsist on yogurt and vegetables for lunch just to be able to eat normally at supper.

"So. Are you and Erik Solomon seeing much of each other?" Amelia said after the plate was cleared of cookies.

Aha! thought Kathryn, now we come to the point of this visit. "Should we be?" she said, with as much innocence in her voice as she could put there.

"Well, I just thought, since you're about the only single people in town your age, it just seemed like, you know, you could get together and do things." Amelia didn't meet Kathryn's eyes.

"Do things? What did you have in mind?" She knew good and well what Amelia was envisioning, but she wanted her to say it, straight out.

"Well, bowl, maybe. Have picnics. Go up to McCall and have dinner. Maybe see a movie."

"But I do those things with my children. Why should I be interested in substituting Erik Solomon?"

"Oh, pshaw, Katie! Don't play dumb with me!"

"Play dumb? What on earth do you mean, Amelia?" She was biting back laughter at the transparency of Amelia's thoughts.

"You know good and well what I mean! It's high time—it's way past time, in fact—that you started living like the young and pretty woman you are. You've played like a widow woman long enough, Katie, and it's time you came back to life."

Kathryn sobered, wondering if the whole town still saw her in the role of grieving widow, a role they'd willingly allowed her at Jesse's death, even though she'd never been wed. "I'm alive, Amelia. Really I am. And I'm happy, too. How could I not be, with Ginger and Kyle."

"Children are no substitute for a man in the house, Kathryn!" Amelia snapped. "You can't cuddle up to a child in the night."

At Kathryn's raised eyebrows, she backed down. "Well, maybe that isn't quite what I meant to say. You need love, Kathryn, and don't tell me you get it from those two. They're little hellions, just like all that age, and they can keep you busy and wear you out, but they can't bring you to life like a man can."

"And if I don't want to be brought to life that way?" Kathryn couldn't help asking.

"Then you're a damn fool, girl. Wasting yourself like you are, you'll end up a lonely old woman someday."

"I'll still have my children."

"Sure you will, just like I have mine. One's in San Diego, one's in Columbus, and I'm not sure from one day to the next where the youngest is, the way her cruise ship wanders all over the globe." She leaned forward and patted Kathryn's hands where they lay on her lap. "Children don't complete a woman, Katie. They fulfill her. But a woman's only half a person without a man to love her."

"Then why haven't you married again?" Kathryn had always wondered why Amelia and Lester maintained their not-so-clandestine affair instead of marrying.

"I'd marry him in a minute, if he'd have me," Amelia said. She bit her lip and blinked rapidly for a moment. "But some men get an idea into their heads and there's no convincing them otherwise." Looking every day her age for a moment, Amelia, with visible effort, renewed her smile. "Besides, we're talking here about you, not me. I'm practically over the hill, and you're still a spring chicken. Why, if I were twenty years younger, I'd go after that gorgeous man myself, but since I'm not, well, I guess it's up to you."

Kathryn smiled. "He is awfully good looking, isn't he?"

"That he is, Katie. And nice as he is handsome." Amelia picked up the fanny pack she used as a purse. "I've got to be goin'. You'll be sure and check up on that order, now won't you?"

Kathryn promised, and escorted her visitor to the door. She was pretty sure Amelia wasn't at all worried about the order for carnival prizes. She'd just been doing a little matchmaking, in her own steamroller way.

Closing the door, Kathryn leaned against it, feeling the cool glass of the window on her forehead. Who would be next? It seemed like the whole town was determined to pair her off with Erik.

* * *

"Good morning."

Kathryn didn't have to look up from her desk to know who was standing in the doorway of her office. She knew that voice as well as she knew her own.

"Good morning, Erik. What can I do for you?"

He was leaning against the doorframe, looking impossibly handsome in a pale yellow cotton sweater over a madras shirt, light tan chinos, and tasseled loafers. No one in Sunset County ever dressed like that, except for the annual Christmas play at the grade school, maybe, or the high school graduation ceremonies.

"How do I get a list of all the civic organizations in the county?"

"A list of civic organizations? What for?"

"I thought I'd put together a luncheon program, telling why preserving Wounded Bear Meadow would be good for the area. I kind of got the impression that most people around here don't think too much of the idea."

"I see," she said, wondering if he would believe her. "I can tell you. There's the Wednesday Club, the American Legion, the Odd Fellows, and the Sunset County Boosters." Smiling, she pressed her forefinger against her lips. "I don't think any of them have luncheon meetings."

"What about the ones that do?" He strolled into her office and sat in the old oak chair she kept for her occasional visitors—mostly Emaline and Eddie.

"You don't understand, Erik. There aren't any civic organizations that hold luncheon meetings. Not in Sunset County."

"Okay, then, how about evening programs?"

"The Legion and the Odd Fellows meet at night. Talk to Lester. He belongs to both." She wanted to laugh at his incredulous expression.

"And the others? What were they? The Sunset Boosters and the Wednesday Club? What's that?"

"The Boosters are our local version of a Chamber of Commerce. And the Wednesday Club is a women's club that—"

"Oh, never mind then," he interrupted. "They wouldn't be interested."

If that wasn't just like a man! She would have expected a comment like his from a man raised in Sunset County, but not from Erik. Surely he wasn't a chauvinist.

"The Wednesday Club," she said, putting a touch of frost in her tone, "is the most active, largest civic organization in the county. It raises thousands of dollars a year for children's and senior citizens' benefits, helps support both Garnet Falls City Park and Pine Hills County Park, contributes to the junior soccer league, the county library, and the immediate care clinic, and awards two college scholarships a year to deserving county students. We are *not* a social club."

"'We?" Does that mean you're a member?"

"Almost every woman in Sunset County belongs, although some aren't active. Besides being a lot of fun, it's sort of a civic duty." She had joined the Wednesday Club when she was sixteen, along with her two best friends. How grown-up they'd felt, and how important, when they were chosen to work on the carnival committee for that year's Fourth of July Social.

And now she was co-chair of the whole Social. She was still proud!

"I didn't mean to belittle it," Erik said, holding his hands up in a gesture of peace. "It's just that I haven't had very good luck getting women's social clubs involved in environmental protection."

She sniffed. "If you tried to tell them you were out to save the world, I'm not surprised. We had a speaker from some environmental cause or other in to talk to us a couple of years ago. He made saving the environment sound noble and important, but he didn't show us how it would affect us directly."

"I'd planned to talk about how rapidly we're losing wetlands everywhere, and how valuable they are as wildlife habitat."

"And women in Sunset County are supposed to care about that? Give me a break, Erik. Most of these women are related or married to loggers and ranchers. They've seen how endangered species have cost jobs in Oregon, how the environmental movement threatens the federal grazing lands they depend on to make a living." Kathryn leaned back in her chair and nibbled on the tip of her forefinger. "What you need is something to make them realize what a unique resource Wounded Bear Meadow is. And how keeping it unspoiled will make their lives better."

"Usually it's the birds and bunnies people relate to," he said. With one leg laid across the other and the old chair tilted slightly back, he looked perfectly at home in her office.

"Country people?"

He shrugged. "I generally talk to civic groups and professional organizations. I've not been closely involved in drumming up local support for one of our preserves before."

She wondered why he was doing it this time, but didn't feel it was her place to ask. "If you're looking for money, I don't think you'll find much here. There's not a lot of industry in Sunset County beyond timber and cattle, and neither one is making anyone rich these days."

"I was thinking more in terms of local people putting pressure on county and state government to preserve the meadow."

She chuckled. "I hate to tell you this, Erik, but 'local government' in Sunset County is the County Commissioners. Garnet Falls is the only incorporated city in the county, and all we have is a part-time mayor and a city clerk. Not even a police force. Wally Blanchett, the county sheriff, takes care of town, too."

He was silent for a time. Finally he unwound himself from the chair. "Local support is important, even if all the funding comes from outside an area. I still think I ought to speak to as many of the residents of Sunset County as I can."

"Just be as convincing as you were in Seattle," she said, remembering how charismatic a speaker he was, "and you'll have them willing to follow you anywhere."

As soon as the words were out of her mouth, she wished she could swallow them. Erik's brows raised and his lips quirked into a half smile.

"Oh?" He stared at her for the longest time, until Kathryn was sure her face was as bright as a ripe, red apple. His voice changed, took on a smoky, seductive quality. "And how about you, Kathryn? Would you follow me anywhere, too?"

She shook her head vigorously and looked down at her desk. "Go away, Erik. I've got work to do."

After a little while, he went. But it was a long while before she remembered what she'd been doing when he came in.

CHAPTER SIX

At noon a week after his return, Erik was waiting for her at the bottom of the courthouse steps. Kathryn commanded her foolish heart to cease its excited flutter. Hadn't she decided that he was hazardous to her emotional health?

"Are you going home for lunch?" He fell into step beside her.

"No, I'm meeting Amelia at the Bon Ton." She hoped she sounded purposeful and hurried. Surely he'd think her fast walk was the cause of her breathlessness.

"I'd like to see you, Kathryn. Sometime when you're not too busy." The echo of her words sounded in his.

Had she remembered to bring the folder of committee work plans? She stopped in the middle of the sidewalk and flipped though the stack of files she was carrying. Yes, there it was, but where was the...? Oh. There. She became aware that he was looming over her, waiting for a response. "That'll be sometime in July," she said. "After the Social." Wondering why she'd ever volunteered to co-chair the darn thing, she pulled the screen door of the Bon Ton Cafe open. "Why don't you give me a call then." She slipped inside, leaving him standing on the sidewalk.

There! She'd handled that situation. Short of telling him to take a hike, she didn't think she could have been any more clear about not wanting to spend time with him.

If only she could convince herself.

"Afternoon, Katie." Lester's gravely basso came out of the dark hallway separating the Bon Ton from the Wooden Nickel as she slipped into the back booth. "Amelia'll be there in a shake. You want some coffee?"

"Iced tea, I think, Lester. D'you suppose summer's here to stay?" The sun hit her office around eleven this time of year, turning it into an oven despite the valiant efforts of a window air conditioner.

The young waitress set a lemon-trimmed mug before her just as Amelia came through the passage from the bar.

"I seem to have fallen behind on my bookkeeping," she said, setting a fat, untidy file folder on the table between them. "I thought perhaps you could check over these few invoices, since your children aren't home and all." She pushed the folder across the table, almost knocking Kathryn's iced tea over in the process. "Just initial them, once you're sure they're correct, and drop them by the treasurer's on your way home."

"A few invoices!" From the looks of the folder, none of the expenses they'd incurred since starting to work on this year's Social had been paid. "Amelia, in case you haven't noticed, I *do* have a job. One that the County Commissioners," with a pointed look across the table at one of said commissioners, "expect me to devote eight hours a day to."

"I know that, hon, but I just thought you could do these during your lunch hour or something."

It was time to take a stand. "Amelia, I will not donate my every waking minute to the Social. Since you don't have time to do what you volunteered to do, I suggest you find someone who will." She would let herself be taken advantage of to a point, but Amelia had long since passed that point.

"As a matter of fact, I'd had the same idea myself. I know you're overworked, and I thought I should find you an assistant. When I mentioned it last night at the Wooden Nickel, several people volunteered."

Kathryn could just imagine who they were. She knew most of the habitués of the town's most popular tavern, and she didn't think any of them would make much of an assistant for her. "Uh, Amelia," she began, "I don't think—"

"He should be here any minute," the older woman said, looking at her watch. "I told him we'd be lunching together and he said he'd join us for dessert, so we could get our business out of the way first."

Kathryn groaned. In the first place, their "business" had consisted of Amelia issuing directives, making excuses for tasks not completed, or complaining about committee members who weren't doing their jobs to her liking. In the second place, Kathryn needed an assistant like she needed a flat tire on her car.

"Afternoon, ladies," a deep, familiar voice said, just behind her. "Am I on time?"

"You are, Erik," Amelia said, "and welcome, too. Katie was just saying how much she appreciated your volunteering to help her for the next few weeks."

Kathryn felt her mouth drop open, and knew she was gaping like a fish out of water. Before she could say anything, Erik had slid into the booth beside her, trapping her between himself and the wall.

"My pleasure," he said, smiling at her. "I'm yours to command, so just tell me what you want from me."

Oh, God! If only his eyes didn't hold such promises. If only his voice didn't send shivers up her spine and raise the hairs at her nape. If only she could want just his help on the Social, instead of all of him. She wondered just how long her fine resolutions would stay intact—she was through lying to herself. She wanted Erik with a deep and abiding hunger. And she wanted him forever.

"Well, if you two young people will excuse me, I have some errands to run. After all, I can't let Kathryn do all the work for the Social, now can I?" Amelia picked up the check and slipped from her side of the booth. She waggled her fingers at them as she walked away. Again Kathryn was speechless.

"Well, Kathryn?" Erik said after watching Amelia leave with a broad grin on his face.

She turned to look at him. He seemed to be waiting for something. "Well what?"

"What would you like me to do for you?" His grin showed he understood every implication of his words.

"I...ah...I haven't got time to tell you now," she stammered. "I've got to get back to work."

"This evening, them." He shook his head. "No, that won't work. I'm speaking to the Odd Fellows. And tomorrow I'm catching a plane out of Boise at ten." He rubbed his nape. "How about Monday?"

Kathryn shook her head. "I'm busy. Make it Tuesday."

"Then it'll have to be right after work. Unless you can take the afternoon off?"

Feeling backed against the wall, Kathryn bit her lip. He couldn't come to her house. She wasn't ready to be alone again with him. "No. No, I can't do that." She heard the thready whisper of her voice and cleared her throat. "Tuesday afternoon, then. In my office. I'll have Lester send sandwiches over, and we can eat supper while we get organized."

"Fine." Standing, he tossed some bills on the table, a far larger tip than a local would have left. Kathryn bet he was an extremely popular customer. "I'll walk you back."

"You don't need to do that." She picked up her purse as she slid out of the booth. It nearly slipped through her fingers and she gripped it tighter. "It's only across the highway. I'll be perfectly safe."

His hand on her back burned through the light cotton of her blouse. "I know that. I'll walk you back because I want to be with you, Kathryn, not because I'm worried about your safety."

"'Afternoon, Katie," Lester said as she sped past his seat behind the cash register. "Erik."

"Lester," Erik acknowledged, but he didn't hesitate. "Kathryn, will you slow down!"

She walked even faster once she was on the sidewalk. Only the pickup coming down the road kept her from dashing across the street to the courthouse.

By the time she was at the corner, she was nearly trotting, but she had to wait for a log truck to pass and Erik caught up with her.

"What the hell?" He grabbed her wrist as she started to cross. "Are you running away from me?"

"I'm trying to," she said, pulling as hard as she could, but his grip was unbreakable.

He didn't resist as she pulled him across the street, but he didn't release her either. By the time they reached the courthouse steps, she felt like she was dragging a dead weight, because he was making no effort to catch up with her.

"Way to go, Katie," came a call from the open door of the cigar store. Two old men, regular occupants of the courthouse benches, watched with bright, interested eyes.

She realized she appeared to be dragging Erik behind her, against his will. Jerking her arm once more, she finally was able to repossess her hand. "You...you stinker!" she muttered, seeing his smile and reading his amusement at the situation. "You did that on purpose, didn't you?"

"Did what on purpose? Me?" His smile would have done one of Botticelli's cherubs justice.

She glared at him. "Made a fool of me." Furious, but more at herself for falling into his trap than at him, she ran up the fifteen steps to the courthouse door.

Safely in her office, she sank into her chair and breathed deeply. She was all but breathless, her legs were weak, and her heart was pounding.

Darn that Amelia, anyway. If she hadn't intended to do her share of the chair's duties, why'd she volunteer, anyhow? Candy Lindholm had been willing, but Amelia had talked her out of taking on the responsibility for the second year in a row.

Candy might have a mouth on her, but she always did what she said she'd do. And she was kind of fun, besides.

How could Amelia have let the bills slide like that? She'd better just check them over, to see if there were any really late ones.

Oh, no! In her panicked attempt to escape from Erik, she must have left them on the table in the cafe. With a sigh, more of frustration than of disgust, she reached for the phone. Surely one thing, just one little thing, could go right today.

A few minutes later, she said, "You're sure he took it, Lester? It didn't fall onto the floor, or something?" Not even one thing.

"Nope. I saw him carry it out myself, Katie." His voice rumbled in her ear. "'Melia told me he's going to be your assistant, so why don't you just not worry about them bills until Tuesday?"

Had he heard everything they'd said? She wouldn't be surprised. When she was small, it was a gospel truth that Lester Wood heard anything anyone said, anywhere in Sunset County. And he did it all from behind the cash register in the hallway between the Wooden Nickel and the Bon Ton Cafe, where he sat for eighteen hours a day, except when he and Amelia snuck off on one of their supposedly secret assignations.

"I think I will. Thanks, Lester." She hung up. If Erik was determined to be her assistant, let him worry about those bills.

Or not. She was going to finish her Friday afternoon tasks and take off for the weekend. Between five o'clock today and Monday at eight, she wasn't going to give a single thought to the Fourth of July Social, the problems she was having with the consultants for the Styx Valley Mining Company, or those special reports Charlie Bittenbusch insisted he needed "to help make an informed decision on Wounded Bear Meadow."

As if there was anything to decide. The National Wetlands Trust would either find the funds to purchase it or they would not. Either way, Charlie would have little to do with the final outcome.

The old gate protested as Kathryn squeezed through its meager opening Tuesday evening. She usually walked around the block instead of using the alley, but as late as she was running tonight, any shortcut was worthwhile. Thank heavens Erik had called to tell her he couldn't make their after-work meeting. She'd gotten a call from Boise at four and had to work overtime to put together the information the state highway people wanted first thing in the morning.

The club really ought to get a work party together and clean up this back garden. It would be years, if ever, before the library needed to expand again and they couldn't just let it go to weeds in the meantime. When the Wednesday Club voted to establish a County Library in the building they'd owned since the early 1900s, they hadn't included a budget for grounds-keeping, nor had subsequent Boards of Directors. As a result, the small lawn in the front of the building was usually at the mercy of not-too-enthusiastic volunteers and the back yard was entirely ignored. Perhaps she ought to make that part of her platform, if she decided to run for president next year.

She slipped through the kitchen door, hearing a cacophony of women's voices from the assembly room. Good. The meeting hadn't started yet. It wouldn't do for the co-chair to be late. As soon as she stepped into sight, she was the center of a noisy crowd.

"Katie, have you got that list of donations to the auction? I can't seem to find my copy."

"I need another five volunteers to work the ice cream booth, Katie."

"Amelia called me. She'll be a little late."

"Wally says we're going to have to pay wages for extra security this year, Kathryn. He's not going to ask his men to volunteer their time like they always have."

"Did we store the leftover carnival prizes at your place last year, Katie?"

She could answer that. "No, Sandy, they're in Emaline's basement. I'll have her drop them off here tomorrow." She shouldered her way through the mass of demanding workers, waving her hands and smiling. Finally she was at the podium—where Amelia ought to be.

"Okay, people, let's get started. I'll try to deal with your problems later, after we've gone through current business, okay?"

Heads nodded, but there were a few frowns, as well. Most of the milling crowd gradually sank into seats. Those still standing—mostly men—slowly drifted toward the back of the room where they leaned as if it were their duty to hold the walls up.

Most of the committee chairs had things well in hand. Those who didn't offered no surprises. She'd worked with them all before.

"Charlie, I heard your people working as I left to come over here. How are the booths coming along?" She didn't like Charlie Bittenbusch, but she had to give him credit for doing everything he could to make the Social a success. He saw it as one way to bring in tourist dollars, something he was almost rabid about.

"Just fine, Katie. Me and Erik, we'll have 'em all built well before Friday."

An older woman waved to catch her attention and Kathryn groaned mentally. There were always a few who always had to complain about something and she was the worst. "And when the driver unloaded the cartons, he refused—absolutely refused, and in such a nasty way—to carry them down into my basement. And you all know how careful I have to be about my back. I called that nice Erik and he came over and took it all downstairs for me."

Kathryn didn't know why she couldn't have had Erik bring the paper products here, to the clubrooms, but he could always do it later. If she gave him enough little tasks like that, perhaps he'd stay out of her hair. "Great. Okay, Candy, I know you're on top of everything for the parade. Can you deal with Wally about security patrols? He's being difficult again."

"You bet your butt, honey. I'll twist his arm a little, and if that don't do it, I'll sic Erik on him."

Kathryn felt her mouth drop open for a moment. Erik seemed to be everyone's answer to problems this year. He'd been officially her assistant only a few days, but it sounded like he'd been doing his job.

She felt like she should resent his interference, but she couldn't. She needed all the help she could get.

Kathryn had finished with the committee reports and was starting to deal with specific problems before Amelia arrived.

Amelia and Erik. They came through the back door, both laughing fit to be tied. All semblance of order ended as everyone turned to share the joke.

"We've got the most wonderful news, everyone!" Amelia announced. She was hanging on Erik's arm like a smitten adolescent. A twinge of irritation tightened Kathryn's fingers on the edge of the podium. Why couldn't Amelia act her age? "Tell 'em Erik!"

"It's your surprise, Amelia," Erik said. His voice still had the capacity to send tingles down Kathryn's spine.

Her hands clasped under her chin and her small body practically quivering in excitement, Amelia took a deep breath. "Well!" she said, "you'll never guess!" A cascade of giggles broke free as she beamed at Erik. "We're going to have a celebrity at our little Social."

A chorus of "Who? Who? Who?" made it sound like a herd of owls was loose in the hall.

"Erik was telling me," again the roguish glance at her companion, "about this fellow he went to school with who sometimes sings with the Grand Ol' Opry. He called him and he said he thought it was a great idea and he offered to pay his airfare but he said no, he'd do it for nothing as long as the profits went to saving the Meadow, and he'll be here Friday, sometime. Isn't that wonderful!" She looked around, waiting for applause.

"Amelia," Erik said into the expectant silence, "maybe you'd better tell them his name." His grin was almost as wide as Amelia's.

"Oh. Of course. Trace Pickett. That's who. He's coming here! With his band!" Amelia clapped her hands together like a happy child, but the sound was lost in the sudden outburst of exclamations.

Even Kathryn, who paid as little attention as possible to Country Western music, knew who Trace Pickett was. His renditions of folk and traditional cowboy songs were haunting and memorable; his spectacular good looks made him popular with girls who otherwise would have been swooning over MTV stars.

Oh my. Getting Trace Pickett as the star attraction of their little Social was going to complicate everything immensely. Kathryn remembered the year Jesse's brother, who'd built himself a fair reputation as a saloon guitarist, had come home for the Social. Attendance had nearly tripled.

She'd better speak to the food committee about ordering more paper products. And to the butcher about more meat for the barbecue. What if they ran out of ice cream...?

Kathryn sank into the chair beside the podium, her mind working a mile a minute. With a little over a week until the Social, she wasn't sure she had time to do all the additional tasks she would have to do. The appearance of a famous singer would turn their small town Social into a major event, and the Wednesday Club wasn't really equipped to handle anything like that.

She almost wondered if Erik had done this to plague her.

Erik found he wanted to go to her and smooth the worry lines from her forehead. She'd looked harried this morning when he'd passed her office, but nothing like she looked now. According to her intern, the two consultants with her made nuisances of themselves, wanting old records pulled from dead storage, asking questions no one had answers to, and apparently unable to understand that the County's work couldn't come to a complete halt just so their demands could be satisfied.

Eddie had nothing good to say about consultants, and Erik wondered if he'd ever made that kind of impression on local officials. He hoped not.

"Yessir, this oughta put Sunset County on the map," Charlie Bittenbusch said, rubbing his hands together in satisfaction. "We need to get it in the paper first thing tomorrow. I'll call the *Statesman*, maybe the Salt Lake paper. Spokane, Portland."

Erik tuned him out, although he knew he should remind Charlie that Amelia was handling publicity. Maybe it would keep Charlie out of Kathryn's hair.

"Can I help?" He leaned over the table Kathryn had her papers spread out upon.

Her sigh was heartfelt. "Can you ever! Have you any idea of what you've done?" She laid the pen beside the stack of file folders. "Erik, we rarely get more than five hundred people from outside Sunset County at the Social. Do you have any idea what a draw Trace Pickett's going to be?"

"I hadn't thought about that aspect," he admitted. "How many do you usually plan for?"

"Two thousand, tops." She leaned back and closed her eyes. "We'll probably get twice that many people to see Pickett's show. I've got to make sure we can handle them."

"We'll handle them. I'll help." He began stacking all the spread-out papers together. "But not now. It's too noisy in here and everyone's too excited."

As if to confirm his words, Candy and several of her buddies broke free of the crowd around Amelia. "Katie, we're going to have to get Wally involved in this. We're gonna have one hell of a parking problem. I figure we'll get five, six thousand people here for the show."

"And we don't have anywhere near enough plates and cups to feed that many. What'll we do?" Sandy wailed.

"I figure we can charge fifteen bucks a ticket," Charlie said, from behind Erik. "Besides the carnival profits and the food." His lips moved as he toted up profits.

It was time to calm things down. He whistled a loud, shrill sound that cut through the voices. "Kathryn and Amelia will want to meet with all of you again tomorrow night, after they've had a chance to assess the impacts of having Trace as a star attraction. Can you all be there?"

"Well, I guess I can drive back in," one woman said, sounding reluctant. Erik didn't blame her, since she lived nearly thirty graveled and twisting miles from town.

"I'll need a baby-sitter," another said.

"Bring 'em over. My girl can keep 'em," someone else responded.

"You all come to the Conestoga House for supper," Charlie said.

"On me," Charlie added, into the dead silence that followed his words. "Well, it's the least I can do, if we're gonna have everything ready by next week," he said, sounding apologetic.

Erik gathered, from the *sotto voce* comments as the crowd was departing, that Charlie's invitation was a first for Garnet Falls.

"...wouldn't buy his own mother's supper if he didn't think he'd get something back," was the kindest comment.

Erik and Amelia went home with Kathryn. She hadn't invited them, but they came anyhow. Before she knew it, Erik was in the kitchen, making coffee, and Amelia was on the phone.

"Well, you just get yourself over here to Katie's right now,

Wally, and I don't care if you are in your slippers. You don't need your fancy trooper boots to drive three blocks."

Kathryn went in to the kitchen, thinking Erik might need her help finding things. But he didn't. Four mugs and spoons were on her fancy red lacquer tray. He was washing her china sugar and cream set—the one she didn't use from one year to the next.

"Got any cookies?" he asked.

Since the twins weren't here, she hadn't been baking. But she'd picked up some Oreos the other day and there should be enough left for four people. She poured the remainder of the package on a plate, set it beside the mugs.

The coffee maker spoke its "I'm brewed" set of gurgles. As she reached for it, Erik's hand caught hers.

"Wait," he said. "We need to talk, and now's a good time." He jerked his chin toward the kitchen door, through which they could hear the murmur of Amelia's voice. She was still on the telephone.

"Talk? What about?" They would probably be talking most of the night, just making sure they had all the bases covered. Candy's five or six thousand people was certainly an exaggeration, but they had better be prepared for twice their usual attendance.

"About what I've done. You're going to be really angry, and I want you to yell at me in private. Okay?"

"I wouldn't yell at you," she said, pulling her arm free of his clasp. Why was it that every time he touched her, some sort of bone-dissolving force flowed from him to her, making her want to melt against him? "You've done something wonderful for the Social and everyone in Sunset County will benefit from it."

"Trace's condition was that all profit from his concert would go to preservation of Wounded Bear Meadow," he reminded her.

"Oh, I understood that. But we usually make several thousand from the carnival. Oh, lord, that's something else I have to do. Get more prizes." She reached for the pad and pen beside the phone.

"Kathryn, before you do anything, there's something you really need to know." Putting his hands on her shoulders, he guided her to the table and pushed her into a chair. Perching on the table, one leg swinging, he stared at her. His expression seemed troubled.

"Oh?" She wasn't sure she wanted to hear.

"Last year Trace did a concert for the Trust in North Dakota. Same kind of deal—there was a wetland we wanted to purchase and he donated the proceeds."

"That's very nice of him, but I don't see—"

He placed his fingers across her lips. It was all she could do to keep from kissing them.

"Kathryn, that concert was more than a hundred miles from the nearest moderate sized city. There was no bus service into town, no train, not even a landing strip." He waved his hand in the general direction of the Garnet Falls airport. "How many people do you suppose came to the concert?"

How should she know? Taking the first figure that popped into her mind and doubling it, she said, "Four thousand?"

His expression was amused. "Try again."

"Darn it, Erik! How should I know? I've never been to a concert like that in my life. For all I know, we won't have any more people than we did last year." And last year had set an attendance record.

"There were nine thousand four hundred thirty-two paid admissions, Kathryn."

She stared. "You're kidding me," she finally said, after assimilating the meaning of his words.

"Nope." His grin spread. "We managed to buy the wetland and put some extra into our permanent acquisition fund."

"We won't have that many here," she said, "will we?" What would little Garnet Falls, Idaho, do with an influx of nearly ten thousand people? Where would they all park?

"We'll probably have more. That's why Amelia called Wally, and why she's talking to the State Police right now."

The doorbell pealed. Erik's hand stopped her from jumping to her feet. "Just remember, Kathryn. I'm here to help you. And I've been involved with an event like this before, so don't be afraid to ask for my help."

What she'd like to do was dump the whole problem in his lap. Ten thousand people! How much food would ten thousand people eat? Could the women of Sunset County make enough ice cream to feed them all? And if they could, was there enough home freezer space in Garnet Falls to store it? In the county?

Maybe it was time to take her vacation. She could go to Hawaii until the fifth of July, maybe. Mexico, hot as it would be, sounded more tempting than staying here for the next ten days.

The doorbell pealed again and she heard Amelia call, "Keep your pants on, Wally. We're comin'!"

Wally proved the easiest of her problems to solve. Where the Wednesday Club would never have paid public officials for doing their regular job of policing the park and school fields, both Kathryn and Amelia recognized that the expected crowd would far exceed the capability of Garnet Falls' five-person sheriff's force to patrol. Wally agreed to cooperate with the State Police on traffic control and to contract for the necessary personnel from a private security firm in Boise, as long as the Wednesday Club guaranteed their fee.

But the time Amelia and Erik left, about eleven-thirty, Kathryn actually believed everything was going to work.

Erik hoped she was dressed. He didn't need any more frustrations this morning. Of course, wanting to mash someone's nose across his face was a far cry from fighting his body's mindless response to a woman who made it plainer every day that she wasn't the slightest bit interested in being more than a friend.

His finger was about to press the doorbell again when the door opened. Even through the screen, he could smell warm, just bathed woman, redolent with the lingering scents of shampoo, soap, and toothpaste. His whole body clenched. Damn! She was still in her bathrobe.

"Erik! What on earth?"

He jerked the screen door open and forced his way inside as she backed away from him. "Kiss me!"

"What?"

Taking one more step forward, he clasped her around the waist. "Kiss me, I said. Now!"

Before she could do more than think about arguing, he possessed her mouth, slipping his tongue into its minty depths. She was soft and yielding, her breasts flattening against his chest, her bottom round and lush, filling his hands.

Her relaxation was gradual, and Erik gloried in every bit of it. First her arms slid up and around his neck, pulling him even tighter against her. Then her tongue came to meet and play with his. Finally, her feet left the ground as her legs, one at a time, wrapped around his. She moaned as he lifted her higher, until only the thickness of his jeans and her light robe kept them apart. She was hot against his arousal, hot and ready.

He lost himself in her, finding renewal and an end to anger in her mouth, her sweet response. He wanted more. He wanted all of her.

Some small vestige of sanity remained, and he ended the kiss, loosened his clasp on her buttocks. She clung to him with a little whimper of protest, but her legs dropped to the floor and took her weight. He stroked her back until her breathing calmed, letting his own slow, his heartbeat return to normal at the same time.

"I can't believe I did that," she said, her face buried in the angle of his shoulder. Her whole body had gradually stiffened, but he prevented it when she tried to remove herself from his embrace.

"I can't either," he acknowledged, "but I'm not sorry I did. At least something's gone right this morning." He released her, but kept one arm around her waist so she wouldn't run away. "Have you got any milk? That stuff they call coffee at the Conestoga House is enough to dissolve carbon steel."

He followed her into the kitchen and nodded his thanks when she poured him a glass of milk. "Don't let me delay you," he said, as she looked indecisively at the toaster. Two slices of dark bread sat waiting in its slots. "I thought I'd walk you to work and catch you up on the latest developments. I didn't mean to interrupt your morning routine."

"I usually dress while the coffee's perking," she said, sounding uncertain, shy. "But it got done while we...while I was answering. Would you like some toast?" Her chin came up with her question, as if she had decided to ignore the kiss.

As if she could. Her desire had been as strong as his, and he had a hunch she was as uncomfortable with that little fact as he was.

"Go," he commanded. "Get yourself dressed. I'll make myself at home."

She hesitated, but she went.

Erik didn't really want toast, not with his mouth still feeling sticky from the overly sweet, doughy cinnamon roll he'd eaten at the Conestoga House. But an egg, some protein to overwhelm the effects of all that sugary icing, would taste just right. He delved into the refrigerator.

When Kathryn returned, wearing a full-skirted dress the colors of summer flowers, he had poached eggs and toast waiting for her. He'd even placed a daisy in a water glass, to center the table.

She stopped when she saw the table. "Oh, Erik, how thoughtful!" Her smile brightened his day considerably. It was too bad he was going to have to tell her the bad news.

"All right," she said, pouring them both more coffee, "what are these latest developments you came to tell me?" She looked so happy this morning, so fresh and eager for the day's surprises.

"Charlie Bittenbusch got me out of bed at five-thirty. He wanted a breakfast meeting about the Social."

She frowned. "I wonder why he didn't call Amelia, or me."

Erik gritted his teeth. "He's planning on seeing you at the Commissioners' meeting this morning."

"What? What Commissioners' meeting? There isn't one sched— Oh, I see. He's calling one, isn't he?"

"Can he do that?"

"If he can get a majority to agree, he can. But I don't understand. Why?"

"Oh, he's got a grand agenda, Charlie has," Erik said, his anger growing again. He'd met some self-serving bastards in his time, but Charlie Bittenbusch was about tops. He glanced at the clock. Quarter to eight. "I'll fill you in while we walk downtown. Just so you won't get too many nasty surprises all at once."

As they walked, he told her about Charlie's plans to capitalize on Trace's visit to Garnet Falls. The singer would be the Grand Marshall of the parade, instead of Erik—not that Erik cared, because he'd only reluctantly accepted the honor in the first place. There would be a formal reception at the Conestoga House on Thursday night—Erik had made the mistake of telling Charlie when the band would arrive—and Charlie thought he might be able to get the Governor to attend. He'd only grudgingly given in on leaving Trace's schedule open Friday because Erik said his famous friend already had plans.

"He's got something else up his sleeve, I think, but I don't know what it is." Their swinging arms brushed, and Erik caught Kathryn's hand in his. It felt as if it belonged there.

"With Charlie, there's just no telling. Whatever he proposed—and he'll say it's for the county's benefit—you can be sure Charlie's going to make a profit on it."

Had she squeezed his hand? Erik couldn't be sure, but he responded, just in case. "That sounds like a conflict of interest." They were nearing the corner of Oregon Street and Sunset Highway, entering what passed for downtown Garnet Falls. He wondered if she would make him release her hand now.

They were in front of the Baptist Church before she wriggled her fingers free. “Kathryn, I didn’t mean to come on to you quite so...so forcefully this morning. I was frustrated and mad, listening to Charlie’s ideas about how Trace is going to put Sunset County on the map. He doesn’t seem to understand that the concert is all in benefit of the Trust.”

“I’m the one who should apologize,” she said. “I practically climbed all over you.”

He sensed her moving away, both physically and emotionally. “We’ve got to talk about all this, Kathryn. We can’t keep working together and tiptoeing around how we feel about each other.” Catching her hand again, he pulled her to a stop, just before the stone bench at the end of the Courthouse steps. “I don’t understand it, but I can’t get within ten feet of you and not want you.” He touched her cheek, marveling at its soft texture, its warmth.

“I don’t think talking about it is gong to do any good, Erik. We’ll just have to show a little maturity, instead of groping each other like a couple of randy adolescents.” She stepped back, almost bumping the bench. “I really can’t get involved with you. Not now. Especially not now.” She spun around and practically ran up the Courthouse steps.

That was all right. He’d see her in an hour, unless he missed his guess about Charlie’s ability to convince two other commissioners to approve the meeting.

The trouble was, he wasn’t sure he wanted to be at that meeting. He had this awful, gut-deep feeling that everything was about to go to hell in a hand-basket.

CHAPTER SEVEN

"Charlie, stop wastin' our time," Amelia snapped. "If you've got something to say, say it. We've got better things to do this morning than sit around listenin' to you."

Several heads in the audience nodded. The room was almost as full as for a regular Commission meeting.

"Well, now, I'm a little concerned about those crowds," Charlie said, as if Amelia hadn't interrupted, "and their effect on our little community. We'll have parking problems, sanitation problems."

Kathryn reached into her skirt pocket for the list she'd been adding to all morning. Portable toilets. Why hadn't she thought of them? The park facilities simply weren't built to handle a crowd of the magnitude Erik predicted, even if the high school restrooms were all opened as well.

Charlie was droning on. "Not to mention the amount of food needed to feed that multitude." He lifted his arms as if intending to provide loaves and fishes for all.

Kathryn wanted to vomit.

"What are you getting at, Charlie?" Bob Wolfe, who had

obviously had come to the meeting right out of his corral, drawled, "Isn't that the Wednesday Club's problem? It's their Social."

"Yes, Charlie, what makes you think we can't handle all these problems?" Amelia said, her voice deceptively sweet. "We've been putting on the Social for almost a hundred years, and we've never had anything we couldn't handle yet."

"Not even the flood, back in '48," someone in the back called. Kathryn thought she recognized Lester's voice despite the background noise.

"How about the year they had to close the highway because of the big fire? We just put everything on ice and held the Social the next day," a woman called.

"Fed all the firefighters, too," Emaline Cohoon boasted. "Least we could do, after they kept the fire from comin' into town."

Kathryn remembered that year. The range fire had all but surrounded Garnet Falls. Her grandparents, and most of the other residents, had been on the verge of evacuation when word came that the raging flames had been contained. That had been one of the memorable Socials, for it had also been a feast of thanksgiving.

Harry tapped his gavel. "That's enough, folks. Let's let Charlie have his say."

"Well, now, all I wanted to do was take some of the burden off you ladies," Charlie said, his tone appeasing. "As the elected officials of Sunset County, I felt we ought to consider offering the County's resources to help you out."

"Exactly what resources are you thinking about?"

Kathryn craned her neck to see who had sounded so skeptical, but there were too many tall people between her and him.

"These fine folks don't have a stage, or much seating out there at the City Park," Charlie said, "so I thought we'd make the rodeo arena at the Fairgrounds available. Of course, we'd have to charge a moderate rent, but I don't see why it couldn't be added onto the concert tickets. And I'd be proud to open the old ore facility to parking, for a small use fee. Now, if you ladies need more storage for your ice cream," he nodded at Amelia and Kathryn, in turn, "we've got a big, walk-in freezer at the Conestoga House. And you're welcome to use the kitchen, too, of course."

"How much do you think we should charge for the use of the grandstand, Charlie?" Amelia sounded almost friendly. Kathryn couldn't believe she was going along with Charlie. The Wednesday Club provided more social and civic support to Sunset County than any other organization. If the county couldn't donate the fairgrounds for something as beneficial as a Trace Pickett concert, she was going to vote for some new Commissioners, come election day.

"Oh now, let me figure." Charlie stroked his chin. "I'd guess about two dollars a ticket would be about right."

"Ahuh." Harry nodded. "And parking on your property?"

"Well, I just couldn't afford to hire me one of those street sweepers and mend the fence for less than about five dollars a car." He said it as if he were doing the county a favor.

"For God's sake!" Bob Wolfe stared at Charlie in amazement.

"I suppose you'd charge for the storage space in your freezers?" Amelia said, still mildly.

Charlie shook his head, looking as innocent as the day he was born. "Oh, I don't think so. After all, it's for a good cause."

"Let me get something straight, Charlie," Harry said. "What exactly would be the reason the county would need to charge for use of the Fairgrounds?"

"Upkeep, Harry. All those people, they'd be real hard on the facility. And improvements. Why, if this is a success, we could look at doin' it again. Get us a famous performer in here every summer. The ladies could go on with the ice cream part of the Social, but we'd want to contract with a real carnival—rides and all—and probably some more experienced caterers. After all, we can't expect our good ladies to feed ten thousand people every summer, can we?"

Kathryn sat open mouthed, not really believing what she'd been hearing. She was conscious of a growing buzz of conversation all around her. Before she could tune in, the gavel silenced everyone again.

"Mr. Chairman, may I speak?" Erik was standing in the front row, looking totally at ease.

Harry waved permission.

"Thank you. I spoke to Commissioner Bittenbusch earlier and so I had an idea of what he planned to propose. So I called Trace Pickett and asked for an elaboration of the terms under which he will appear at the Social."

The silence was complete. "Trace will not perform if the tickets are priced higher than ten dollars each, and he will not perform in a facility for which the sponsoring agency—the Wednesday Club, in this case—is charged a fee. He prefers to perform in a park or other open area." Kathryn would swear he'd winked at her. "Furthermore, he will not give interviews locally, but will allow an interview to be aired on Boise television as part of the promotion for the concert."

"Well, I guess that settles the question of the fairgrounds," Harry said. "And I don't think the question of how much help the Wednesday Club needs is the Commission's business." He lifted the gavel.

"Just a minute, Harry," Bob said. "I'd like to suggest one condition. If, within a year, NWT fails to raise the rest of the funds to purchase Wounded Bear Meadow, the county receives twenty percent of the take from the concert, to be used for upgrading the clinic."

Amelia waved her hand. "I'll second that motion."

"Is that gonna cause a problem, Erik?"

Erik shook his head. "It's not going to happen," he said confidently.

"Okay then. All in favor?" Harry silently counted his way around the table. "Four in favor. You opposed, Charlie?"

Frowning, Charlie shook his head. "What about next year?"

"Let's get through this year's Social first," Harry said. "Any other business?"

No one spoke.

"Okay. We're adjourned. Let's get back to work." Harry pushed back from the table and picked up his crutches. "Katie, I'd like to talk to you." He gestured her ahead of him and followed her to her office.

Once the door was closed, he said, "I'm going to exceed my authority, girl. But you'll thank me for it."

"I will?"

"You sure will. I want you to take from now until after the Social off."

"Harry, I can't." She really couldn't. Just last week she'd learned that the roof on her house wasn't good for another winter. "I can't afford to take unpaid leave, and the twins and I—"

"Yes, you can. I'm gonna put you on my own payroll. Call it my contribution to the Social." He reached out and rumpled her hair, just as he'd often done when she tagged along with Steve and Jesse. "You know Amelia can't do it alone. There's a whale of a lot of work to do between now and then, Katie, and I don't want you wearin' yourself out."

"Thanks, Harry. I'll do it." Kathryn enveloped him in a big hug. "You're a pretty nice man, you know that?"

"And you're a nice little lady." He dropped his crutches to squeeze back. "Let me know if there's anything else you need. I always have a man or two I can spare in a pinch."

Kathryn spent the rest of the day briefing Eddie and her secretary on what had to be done while she was off work. Fortunately, except for dealing with the consultants investigating the Styx Mountain mine property, there was nothing they couldn't cope with or postpone until her return. And the consultants could be put off too. She'd spent enough of her time at their beck and call lately.

* * *

It was a good thing Harry told her to take time off, because otherwise she'd have found precious little time for sleep. Ever since Erik's announcement that Trace Pickett would perform at the Fourth of July Social in Garnet Falls, she'd done nothing but talk, talk, talk. She talked to committee chairs, to suppliers, to people whose help they desperately needed, to local merchants—most of whom were concerned that their stocks were too low to supply the thousands of tourists who would arrive next Saturday—while at the same time being certain that all those outsiders would create chaos in their sleepy little town.

The best and worst part of the past few days had been working closely with Erik. She didn't know what she would have done without him, despite Amelia's sudden competence and willingness to do her share. He'd thought of a million things she would never have dreamed of, kept her calm in the face of uncooperative suppliers. He made her laugh when the whole world seemed determined to frustrate her.

The novelty supplier had called the day the shipment was due to arrive, with the unpleasant new that they would be closed the week of the Fourth and would be unable to put together a shipment of the size the Women's Club needed. "Someone's just going to have to go get them," she'd said calmly, wanting to scream instead.

"I'll take care of it," Erik said.

She knew he would.

When a usually dependable club member called to say she wouldn't be able to freeze the four gallons of ice cream she'd volunteered to do, Erik picked the phone out of Kathryn's hand before she could explode. She didn't know how he'd done it, but he'd managed to talk the woman into making the ice cream anyway, before she went off on an unplanned visit to her sister in Seattle.

But the best of all had been the way he'd handled Charlie.

"Charlie, I've got a great deal for you," Erik said, leaning back in the plush booth and turning on his charm to full power. "The Social Committee will guarantee cleanup of your ore facility before and after the Fourth, if you'll agree to waive any charge for parking."

Kathryn hadn't been down to the old ore facility since she was a kid, not until that morning, when she and Erik had slipped through the break in the fence and walked around. Other than the abandoned tipple, looming near the equally abandoned railroad tracks, it was a vast, empty space, level and covered with an inches-deep layer of crushed copper ore. Litter had blown against the chain link fence and empty beer and pop cans lay here and there across its emptiness. It would make an ideal parking lot. She had no idea of how to judge capacity, but it looked bigger than any supermarket lot she'd seen anywhere.

"I don't rightly see how I can do that. It just ain't good business," Charlie opined, finally.

Erik sat relaxed, but she felt his contained energy. It was as if he had enough to sweep the whole world along in his wake, leading them to new places and new experiences. Showing them levels of experience they'd never had before. Did he affect everyone this way, or was she the only one?

"You know," he said, as if it didn't matter either way to him, "up at the Kingdome in Seattle, people might be willing to pay five dollars to park. I don't think they'd like it too well here in Garnet Falls."

After thought, Charlie said, "I could go as low as two and a half. But that's my best offer. I've got a right to make a decent profit from the use of my land." He had that mulish expression on his face that meant he was finished talking. Kathryn had seen it enough times when he'd stonewalled commission decisions.

"Oh, come on, Charlie. You're not making any profit on the lot as it sits." Erik sat back while the waitress refilled his cup. Charlie waited, too. Kathryn just watched.

Erik sipped.

Charlie fidgeted.

Finally, setting his cup down, Erik leaned forward. "We've talked to the school district and they'll lease us their busses next week."

"What are you gonna do with them?"

"We sort of thought we'd route people up to Backwater Creek to park, then bus them down here for the concert." It was the first she'd heard of such a far-fetched plan. Backwater Creek, an abandoned mining town, didn't have an acre of level ground anywhere around. Erik's hand squeezed hers under the table and Kathryn bit back her astonishment.

"But that's ten miles!" Charlie looked as astonished as she felt.

"Well, yes, we know that. But we figure people would rather park free up there and be bussed down than pay five dollars to park at the ore facility."

Charlie hemmed and hawed. "I was just trying to recover my expenses of cleaning up the place."

"Of course you were," Erik agreed. "But if the Committee sees that it's returned to its pre-Social state, you won't have to worry about that." He smiled, and Kathryn wondered if even Charlie could resist.

He couldn't. After a suitable wait, so as not to seem too easy, Charlie said. "Oh, hell. You win. Use it for nothin'." He stood and looked down at Erik, his expression sour. "But there'd better not be so much as one beer can in there come July fifth, or I'm gonna have me some words with the Commission about a license fee for the Social next year."

"Make that the sixth. You don't want the volunteers out there in the dark, trying to clean up, do you?"

Charlie snorted, but his nod was all the agreement Erik seemed to need. As soon as he was out of earshot, Kathryn turned to Erik. "How could you tell all those lies? The Committee didn't—"

He put one finger against her lips and again Kathryn had the insane urge to kiss it, or maybe nibble it. "Later," he said, in a voice so full of promise she almost melted, right there in a red plush booth.

Later, Kathryn challenged him about his lies again.

"Lies? I'd prefer to say I anticipated the Committee's actions." He smiled at her this time, and she was ready to follow him anywhere—as usual.

"What do you mean?"

"If the Committee had acted on the problem, wouldn't they have refused to allow Charlie to extort five dollars a car for parking."

"Well, yes. We've never had anyone charge for parking at the Social before." They'd never needed to. The Fairgrounds had accommodated all the cars in the past.

"Well, then, I merely took a shortcut. Nobody on the Committee has time to meet about something so minor as parking, and I saved them the inconvenience."

She had to look twice to make sure there weren't canary feathers all around his mouth. "And the school busses?"

"That was legitimate. I had breakfast with the principal of the high school. He mentioned that the school district would be amenable to renting their busses, if we needed them."

Kathryn gave up. The bottom line was that he'd outwitted Charlie in a matter of money. Not many people in Sunset County managed to do that.

The last weekend before the Social went too fast. She went out to the ranch and helped Janine make six batches of ice cream. "Only one more week," she promised Abby and Ginger as she tucked them into their beds Sunday night. "And yes, you can eat all the ice cream you can hold." Abby had been disappointed when Janine had refused to let her have thirds this evening. Kathryn was certain that her niece could eat a whole quart of home made ice cream if allowed to. Ginger was almost as bad.

"Mama, can we come to town the night before?" Ginger's drowsy voice had a lonely sound to it.

Kathryn was immediately overcome with guilt. "No, honey," she said, smoothing the child's black hair from her forehead. "I'll be as busy as a one-armed paper hanger all day."

Ginger and Abby both giggled.

Kathryn wished she found it so funny. She was almost dreading the coming week. Even with Erik and Amelia, even with committees who did everything they were supposed to, on time and correctly the first time, it was going to be sheer hell. She just knew it was.

She kissed both girls again, with a special, nose-rubbing, raspberry-blowing smooch for her daughter. How she missed having the twins with her, but it wouldn't be fair to make them stay in town and spend their days at Wanda's Childcare, when they could be here on the ranch with their cousins.

Kyle was waiting on the trundle bed in the boys' room. "Mama, are you gonna get married?"

Quickly she knelt by his side. "Of course not, honey. Where on earth did you get that idea?" She slipped an arm under his head and pulled him to her, noticing that Jace and Denny were propped on their elbows and listening.

"I heard Aunt J'nine sayin' you oughta marry that wet guy." He looked worried. "Is he wet *all* the time, like a fish?"

She chuckled. "No, honey. He's just a man." So was Superman.

"Well, then, I think you should marry him. He could go to soccer with me."

In a town where everyone was related to everyone else, often Kyle was the only child on his soccer team who didn't have a masculine voice cheering him. Jon simply couldn't get into town at the early hour the peanut teams played and there wasn't anyone else she felt comfortable asking. Perhaps she should work to conquer her discomfort. Steve Lindholm would probably be willing to come to an occasional game, if she asked him.

But did she want to leave herself open to the obvious conclusion on Steve's part? She'd known him as long as she'd lived in Garnet Falls, and she'd never found him anything but a nice man. Sort of like vanilla pudding, when chocolate mousse was the industry standard.

"He's not going to be in Garnet Falls very long, Kyle, but I'll bet he'd come to a game, if you'd like that." Erik wouldn't misunderstand her invitation. If anything, he'd turn her down. Her children were the last thing about her he was interested in.

More's the pity, a tiny voice said in the back of her mind. He'd never asked about her children, had seemed uncomfortable whenever she mentioned them.

"Okay, but if you're not gonna marry him, it wouldn't be the same." Kyle snuggled down into his covers, his eyes closing. "G'night, mom," he said.

She leaned over and kissed him. "Good night, honey. Sweet dreams."

Marry Erik Solomon? What a wonderful, impossible idea.

"Do you like children?" Kathryn asked the question in the middle of a comfortable silence as she and Erik finished their sandwiches Monday noon.

Ever since she'd arrived in town, about nine, they'd been going over the revised plans and schedule for the Social, hoping they'd forgotten nothing. Amelia was due back from Cambridge soon, hopefully with a commitment from the Sheriff's Posse for a food booth like the one they were famous for at the Washington County Fair. Over the weekend, she'd contacted the Obon Festival Committee in Ontario and gotten their enthusiastic agreement to set up a Japanese food booth. Both the high school principal and the football coach had agreed to help out at the dunking booth and a contingent of women from New Meadows was coming down to help out at the carnival and the ice cream pavilion.

"I don't know anything about them," Erik said, after a moment's thought. "They're hard to talk to, though. I do know that."

"Why do you say that? I've always found children much easier to talk to than adults. They take everything so literally." Sometimes too much so, but she wasn't going to admit that.

"That's exactly what I mean." He pushed his plate away and leaned back in his chair. "I have this buddy back in New Jersey. Five kids. The oldest one's maybe twelve or so. The night I was there, they were helping him fix dinner—he and his wife trade off on household chores and it was his week to cook. He told one of the middles to put out the rabbit food while he dished up the pot roast." His mouth twitched. "When we sat down to dinner, there was a little dish beside each plate, full of rabbit pellets."

Kathryn fought to control her laughter. "Oh, my!" she gasped.

"The worst part of it was," Erik said, his own voice sounding suspiciously like he was trying not to laugh either, "was that for a minute I thought we'd have them with Thousand Island dressing. Wils didn't want to hurt the kid's feelings."

"It does take practice," she admitted. "And I still get caught sometimes, even though I'm really careful how I say things to mine."

"I guess some kids are okay," he said, sounding contemplative, "but I don't see how anyone could want as many as Wils has. Five! How do you suppose he keeps them all straight?"

"Each child is unique," she said, thinking of how different her own were. "And wonderful."

"You've got a boy and a girl, right?"

Kathryn began to gather the dirty dishes. This was the first time she'd invited him to eat at her house instead of at the Bon Ton. It hadn't been so bad. He'd been a perfect gentleman. "Uh-huh. Kyle and Ginger."

"How are you going to manage the boy as he gets older? I mean, how can you possibly understand?"

Before he could finish his question, Amelia was at the back door, calling out her arrival. Darn! She still didn't know whether he liked children.

That night, while she was courting sleep, she wondered about his question. Of course she would understand Kyle as he grew up. As much as any parent could understand a child.

Tuesday the paper products didn't come. Erik went to Ontario to pick them up.

Wednesday was the phone call from Trace Pickett. His converted bus had broken down in Wyoming. Could Erik locate housing and transportation for the band if they flew into Boise? Erik could, and Kathryn thanked her lucky stars that she had an assistant who got things done first, then worried about her approval.

On Thursday Sheriff Blanchett came into her temporary office at Lindholm Motors. "Mornin', Katie."

"Good morning, Wally." She wondered what his arrival meant. Wally was a good sheriff, but he could be the gloomiest, most pessimistic person she'd ever met. "What can I do for you today?"

"Money." He lowered himself into the folding chair across from her desk. "For the rent-a-cops." His tone made it clear he wasn't too happy about his request. "They want a retainer before they'll sign the contract."

"Oh lord!" Kathryn sighed. "How much?"

The sheriff looked as if he'd swallowed a lemon. Or something stronger and more bitter. "Fifteen hundred."

She gasped. "Dollars?"

Wally nodded.

"But that's more than we have in the treasury."

"Figured as much. What d'you want me to tell 'em?"

What indeed? They had to have extra security, if no other reason than for traffic management. Wally and his five deputies, even with the help of the volunteer Mounted Sheriff's Posse, simply couldn't do it all. Not with the volume of people and cars they were expecting.

"Will they take a check?" She had a little more than eighteen hundred in her savings. The Wednesday Club could pay her back next week.

"Certified. And somebody'll have to deliver it. They want it before the bank closes tomorrow."

Kathryn closed her eyes and took a deep breath. Why hadn't this happened Tuesday, when Erik was in Ontario? Another sixty miles wouldn't have mattered. Well, she could take the check up to New Meadows right away, so it could catch the FedEx delivery tomorrow.

There were times when living in a small town, back of beyond, was definitely a pain in the...the posterior.

Friday dawned clear and hot. Kathryn almost looked forward to the day since they'd gone home last night with every problem solved and every loose end tied into a tidy little knot.

Erik was down at the park, where she would be as soon as she processed the last few bills and dropped them off, so the club treasurer could write the checks during her lunch hour. Amelia would join them as soon as she came in with her pickup full of beef contributed by ranchers throughout the county. Their usual sources of beef for the barbecue had been inadequate, but Mike Peters had called around and gotten pledges for enough to feed twice ten thousand.

She hoped.

At nine that night, she was beginning to believe it was all going to come together. No one had let her down. All the supplies were here. The volunteers from New Meadows, Ontario, and

Cambridge had their booths set up and were ready to go. Even the ice cream had all been made and was filling every freezer in town, including those at the Bon Ton, the Conestoga Hotel, and Coleman's General Store.

She was exhausted.

It was too early for bed and she was too keyed up anyway.

Kathryn found one lone bottle of wine cooler in the back of her cupboard, a leftover from a party she'd had last Halloween. Filling a glass with ice, she poured the deep pink, fizzy liquid over it. She was going to sit out on the back porch and listen to the crickets until she felt like she could sleep.

Her front screen rattled. "Help!" a pitiable voice called. Or at least it sounded as if it were trying to be pitiable. Erik would probably sound warm and sexy after a month of sleep deprivation, starvation, and dehydration.

She carried her glass with her. He was leaning against her house, one hand holding a six pack of beer, the other propping him up. "How's your hospitality?" he said, as she peered through the screen.

"Not very warm," she said. She'd had about all she could take of people this week, and tomorrow would be infinitely worse. Tonight she just wanted to be left in peace and quiet.

"Shucks. I though maybe I could play on your sympathy." He turned to go, his shoulders slumping slightly. He sounded as tired as she was.

"Erik," she called, just as he started down the front steps. "Come in." She unhooked the screen and held it open. After his Herculean efforts on behalf of the Social this past ten days, she hadn't the heart to turn him away. "Sympathy I can spare, as long as I get some back." She led him through her house and out the back door. "Make yourself at home. Do you need a glass?"

"I'll take it straight," he said, twisting off a cap. "Ahhh!" Half the bottle was gone before he lowered it. "I needed that."

Kathryn settled in the chaise lounge, next to the one he'd taken, conscious as she did so that all she wore was her short summer nightgown. Her gown was sleeveless white cotton with lace trimming. At least it wasn't sheer.

They sat in silence for several minutes. Comfortable silence, as far as she was concerned. With Erik, Kathryn never felt the need to entertain, as she usually did on her rare dates. It felt good not to have to talk.

"Can you spare a room?" Erik asked.

CHAPTER EIGHT

As the silence lengthened, Erik gave an inward sigh. Perhaps he'd misunderstood, this past week. Kathryn had seemed comfortable with him. Tonight she did not.

He finished his beer. Trace and his wife were using his apartment, the band occupied spare rooms all over town, and the Conestoga House was bursting its seams. Amelia had said he could come out to her place, sleep on the sofa. Her single guestroom was occupied by an in-law or something. It seemed like every house in Garnet Falls contained at least one relative from somewhere, all here to see the legendary Trace Pickett perform.

He sighed again, involuntarily and aloud. Time to go. Picking up the six-pack, he stood. It wasn't so much that he dreaded the sofa at Amelia's, but that he wanted Kathryn to trust him.

"I'll have to change the sheets," she said.

He sat down again, aware that he'd been holding himself tightly and had suddenly relaxed. "No. Don't do that. I'll be fine."

"Erik, I don't think you know what you might find in a six-year-old's bed. I'll change the sheets." She went indoors.

Erik let his head fall back against the wall behind him. When he'd decided to come here instead of going to Amelia's place, he'd told himself it was because he was too tired to drive the seven roundabout miles to get there. Now he had to admit it was because he simply wanted to be with her.

He wanted to be with her in every sense. This week had taught him how much he wanted her in his life. No longer based on a memory of one delicious night, his need for her went far beyond the merely physical.

Then he remembered whose bed he'd be sleeping in tonight. Her son's.

Kids. She had two, he reminded himself. That was two more than any of the women in his life had ever had, for he'd always shied away from dating women with children. He didn't know how to relate kids, wasn't comfortable talking to them. Never had been, even when he'd been a kid himself. Except for Gail. She'd been far more than a sister; she'd been his best friend.

Kathryn's kids were certainly a complication to anything beyond mild friendship. But then maybe that's all Kathryn wanted from him, anyway. Erik admitted he was confused as hell. Sometimes he'd swear she wanted him as much as he did her. Then again, she seemed to be wholly self-contained and without any sort of sexual needs at all. Especially for him.

Well, he wouldn't worry about it tonight. Once his head hit that pillow, he'd be dead to the world. Planning a hometown festival proved more work than all the project management he'd done, even when he'd integrated several firms' personnel into a functioning, environmental assessment team.

He didn't miss the consulting business. The last six years had been enough to teach him that it wasn't his particular can of worms. Of course, an occasional project, where he could work with other dedicated wetlands preservation professionals, kept his skills honed and his contacts current.

Walt had called him just last week about a wetland in Minnesota. It was time for him to be moving on. He'd been in

Idaho more than a month now, and that was longer than he'd stayed anywh...

"Erik. Erik?" At a touch on his arm he swam out of the doze into which he'd fallen. "Your bed's ready."

Shaking his head, he looked around at unfamiliar surroundings.

"Erik?" The hand on his arm was warm, somehow comforting. "Wake up and go to bed." The voice was amused.

Another shake of his head and reality resumed. God! He hadn't been this out of it for a long time. "Thanks," he said. "Sorry I zonked like that."

Kathryn's smile seemed to light up the darkness. "Let me show you the way," she said, leading him into the house.

The kitchen was dark, but a light in the hall made a bright path. She had put a robe over her nightgown, he noticed. Even silhouetted as she was, he could no longer see the shape of her body as he had when she'd come to the front door, outlined by the same hall light.

He followed her up the stairs and along another hall. She indicated the bathroom. "I'll leave the night light on for you. Your towels are on the bar at the end of the tub."

"Thanks," he said, just as she opened a door and stood aside. The room was a typical boy's, or at least it looked like his had when he was a boy. Sports posters, a bird's nest sharing one shelf with thin books with bright spines, a soccer ball on another, and in the corner a cage that looked as if it might hold a rat or a gerbil. The important part was that there was a bed. Two beds, but it was the nearer one, sheets turned back invitingly, that mattered to him. "Thanks, Kathryn."

"I could take King Alfred," she said, gesturing at the cage, "if you think he'll bother you."

"No need. I've slept with critters all my life," he assured her. He started unbuttoning his shirt. "I really appreciate this," he said, wishing she'd go so he could collapse onto the bed.

"I...well, goodnight," she said. "Sleep well." She stepped out the door, pulling it closed behind her. Then she opened it again, just as he was pulling his shirt off. "Ah...what time?" She licked her lips, and despite his exhaustion, he felt a shaft of fire spear in his belly. "What time do you want to get up?"

"I don't care," he said. "But early." He could feel her gaze, almost physical on his bared chest.

Again her tongue flicked out. "Six?"

"Fine." Damn! He was too tired for this.

"I'll set the...the clock." Suddenly she was out the door and slamming it behind her.

Leaving Erik thoroughly awake.

Insomnia was probably much easier to endure, Kathryn thought, back in the days when clocks ticked and their hands went silently and invisibly around. The bright red digits of her clock reproached her as she pounded her pillow yet again, wondering where all the rocks came from. Eleven-thirty, and she hadn't slept a wink.

She didn't even feel tired. The blood was zinging though her veins and her mind was going a mile a minute. She'd thought about every possible thing that might go wrong tomorrow and had come up with half a dozen ways to prevent or solve each and every one of them. The sleepiness that had almost overtaken her just before Erik's arrival was lost, driven away with the awareness of his presence, just across the hall.

Had Emaline remembered to arrange for the sawhorses? Just this afternoon they'd realized they needed something to block the service road that went behind the athletic field at the high school. Sawhorses would have more authority than just a rope.

Was Erik asleep?

She wondered what time Jon and Janine would get to town. This afternoon when Janine had brought in the ice cream, she'd said Jon wanted to come in early so they could go home early.

He'd given the hands the day off and had to get back to milk their one cow and check the siphons on the hayfield they would be irrigating.

Was Erik comfortable? Kyle's narrow bed was probably too short and too narrow for him.

Where had she put the key to the high school? She was supposed to go over and open the north corridor in the morning. Was it in her purse, or still on her desk, where she last remembered seeing it?

A floorboard creaked. Another. Erik?

She pummeled her pillow again, determined to beat it into comfortable submission. The bathroom door rattled shut. Water ran. The shower? At this time of night?

Her mind on hold, Kathryn listened until the water stopped. Small sounds told her he was brushing his teeth, flushing the toilet. Then the distinctive rattle of the door again. She really should get it fixed. That rattle could bring her out of a sound sleep.

Waiting for the floor to creak again, she wondered what he was doing. The only boards in the house that gave notice of being walked on were between Kyle's bedroom and the bathroom. Their silence meant he hadn't gone back to bed.

Where was he?

She rolled out and went to her door. Carefully she turned the knob, not wanting him to know she was, well, spying on him. Inching it open, she tried to see into the dim hallway. The small night light in the bathroom only lit the hall so you could see not to run into the wall. But her eyes were used to the dark, and so she saw him.

Erik was waiting for her, standing across the hall from her bedroom door. She didn't have to ask what he was waiting for. She knew, for she'd been waiting too.

"Kathryn," he said, his voice low and just a little hoarse, "I tried." He shrugged. "Even a cold shower didn't help."

"I've always thought they were vastly overrated," she said, stepping back so he could come into her room.

He stopped at the foot of her bed. In the dark, she could only see his eyes as a glimmer.

"Wait," she said. Quickly she pulled the shades and lit the small crystal lamp on her dresser. It gave just enough light to make the room warm and mysterious, with shadows occupying the corners.

"I don't have anything to protect you," he said, standing a scant foot from her. He hadn't yet touched her, nor she him.

"I don't either," she said, wondering why she didn't. If only she'd acknowledged the inevitability of this happening as soon as he'd come to town.

"I guess we'll have to contrive, then, won't we?" He reached out a finger and touched her cheek, traced a line to her mouth, and down her throat to the demure neckline of her nightgown.

Her last hesitation vanished. "I guess we will." She took a fateful step forward and found herself caught and held. The solidity of his chest, the thrust of his erection, and the stroking of his eager hands were all familiar. Her body had remembered, even when she denied this need.

Ah, how lonely she'd been, with no one to caress her, no one to hold her and keep the nightmares at bay. As his hands slid over her skin, cupping her breasts, teasing the nipples, shaping and molding her to fit against him, she knew that she was made for twoness, not a solitary life.

A brief flare of anger burned within her. Life was so damned unfair! First taking Jesse away, then sending her this man who would never stay. Then the flame turned to a fire of another sort, as his fingers brushed across her belly and whispered across her lower curls.

Her legs grew weak, until she was clinging to him lest she dissolve into a puddle of desire at his feet. He seemed to sense her bonelessness, for he lifted her and laid her gently across her bed, tossing the tangled linens to the foot.

He returned to her breasts, worshipping them. Every touch of his mouth hurt, a delicious pain shooting thorough her. As he suckled her, she arched against him, willing offering more...all. Anticipation built within her, as heat suffused her body and threatened to consume her. Each flick of his tongue against her hypersensitive nipples enhanced the blaze, until she wanted to scream at him to stop...don't...stop...don't...don't stop!

His fingers left a blistering trail wherever they went. Between her breasts, down the line of her midriff to her navel, and then to her thighs. She knew she was writhing, moaning, in need as he slipped his hands under her, as his mouth left her breasts. The night air was cold on her wet skin, tightening her nipples even more, until they were yet another in a galaxy of aching hungers.

"Erik! Oh, please!" Was that her voice? That hoarse entreaty? That guttural demand?

"Tell me, Kathryn," he said, stroking his hands along her thighs, behind her knees, along her calves. He was kneeling between her legs, lifting her legs to rest on his shoulders.

"Tell..." He kissed her foot, turned his head and kissed the other. "me..." He nibbled her ankle. "what..." As his hands cupped her buttocks, his mouth etched a moist trail up to her knees. "you..." He bent forward as he lifted her. "want." His mouth was hot as he kissed her intimately, his tongue flicking her pulsing femininity.

He seemed to pull her outside of herself, until she was caught in a force so vast, so irresistible that she could only let herself be swept along to wherever he led.

Her spasms almost sent Erik over the edge. He fought his body's reaction as he gently brought her back to herself. What a wonderfully responsive woman she was.

As he lay beside her, stroking her relaxed body and willing himself to patience, he accepted that his memories had not played him false, after all. Over the years, whenever he'd remembered the single night with Kathryn, he'd told himself that nothing could be that good. But something could. Someone could. Even without coming to climax himself, he was more satisfied than he could have imagined.

A tentative touch brought him to full attention. A light caress along the still-hard length of him played hell with his patience. "Careful," he said. "I'm a little touchy."

Kathryn's laughter was warm, cocky. "I know," she said.

When her hand circled him, squeezed, Erik felt it clear to his toes.

"Tell me what *you* want," she said, her fingers exploring.

When she found even more sensitive flesh, she clasped it within her hand. Breath exploded from him, but he was able to contain the implacable force. Barely.

He drew a deep gasp of relief when she took her hands away. And disappointment. When her lips touched his navel, he inhaled again, spasmodically. His chest hurt, his heart pounded. He reached for her.

"Ah-ah!" she said, pulling back. "Mustn't touch. It's my turn, now." She swung herself astride him, holding herself just clear of his belly. Leaning forward so her breasts scarcely skimmed his chest, she kissed him, pulling his tongue into her mouth, simulating the joining he so desperately wanted.

He arched upward, his body demanding completion, but she was too quick.

"Oops," she said, "This wasn't such a good idea." Rolling aside, she stationed herself alongside him, still on her knees, twisted so her breasts again pressed lightly against his chest. Her lips closed his eyes, one at a time. Teased the tip of his nose. Lightly grazed his mouth. Her teeth nipped gently at his chin, her tongue wetted his Adam's apple.

Then her breath was warm on his chest as she dropped kisses at random, working her way down again to his navel. She tickled, she sucked, she bit, she tasted. Millimeter by millimeter, she crept lower and lower, challenging his restraint. Whenever he bucked in reaction to a particularly stimulating touch, she pulled away and let him calm himself.

When her breath warmed the hair at the base of his shaft, he shuddered in anticipation. *Touch me!* his mind screamed. "Ahhhh!" was all his mouth could manage. He released his grip on the sheets, no longer willing—nor able—to obey her stricture against touching. His hands found her head, tangled in the curls. "Now!" he commanded.

"Now," she agreed. The single word held anticipation, passion, and triumph. She touched him with her tongue. Took him into her mouth.

She toyed with him, drawing him deep, then releasing him and sitting back on her heels when he bucked against her hold. When he was still again, she traced from the base of his shaft to the tip, her fingers both curious and knowing. Once more she kissed him, looking along his body in question.

He took her hands in his, clasping them tightly around him. When she moved to lower her head again, he gasped, "No. Look at me, Kathryn. I want to see your face."

But he didn't see her face. Once he released the tremendous control he was exerting, it took but a tightening of her hand about him for him to explode, his consciousness shattering as he gave himself up to the release he'd been denying himself ever since he'd found Kathryn again.

Kathryn woke to a kiss and the smell of coffee. She stretched, aware of having slept better than she had in a long time. "Mmmm?" she said, without opening her eyes.

"Is that a way of being safe?" Erik's voice was amused. "In some book or other, the hero always made a noise like that when he didn't remember the name of the woman in his bed."

"Kathryn Elaine Pierson," she said, wondering why she didn't feel even a smidge of regret. She opened her eyes and scooted up to lean against the brass headboard.

"Huh?" He set a cup on the bedside stand and, carefully balancing another, slipped into bed beside her. His jeans were half unbuttoned and his feet and chest were bare. He looked as if he belonged.

"The name of the woman in your bed." She sipped her coffee, grateful. Although she'd fallen quickly into deep sleep almost as soon as Erik had wrapped his arm around her and pulled her close, she knew she'd need all the help she could get today. Even with a good night's sleep, it was going to be a long day. With fewer than six hours, she would be a zombie by eight tonight. "How can you look so cheerful on so little sleep?"

He slipped his free arm behind her. "I'm a morning person, I guess. I always wake up raring to go."

"Today that's probably for the best. I keep wondering what I've forgotten." Another sip. Surely there was something she needed to be doing, but she couldn't think of a single one. Having a half-naked Erik beside her in the bed was an instant and effective mind wipe. She drank more coffee, thinking that she really needed to get started. The Committee was meeting for breakfast at eight-thirty, and she had to get together with Amelia before that.

Erik lifted the cup from her hand. "You've had a half cup. That's enough." He pulled her close and kissed her, a hot, wet kiss full of promise and longing.

For a moment, Kathryn responded, wanting him just as much this morning as she had last night. Then reality intruded, in the sound of jake brakes on the highway. Today was the Fourth and she was in charge of the Social. She could let nothing interfere with her responsibility to her town. "Stop, please," she said, once she could pull her mouth free from his. An almost impossible task, because she hadn't really wanted to. "We can't. Not this morning."

Erik looked over her shoulder at the clock. "You're right, damn it. It's almost seven."

"Oh, no!" She rolled out of the bed, hardly noticing she was stark naked. Grabbing her robe, she headed for the bathroom. If she hurried, she could get her shower and still have enough time to go over everything with Amelia before breakfast.

By the time the Social officially opened at noon, Kathryn was already convinced that their estimates of attendance were going to be exceeded. People had been coming into town steadily since about ten, and already the fairgrounds parking lots were full.

The parade went well. She imagined people from Boise weren't too impressed, but as far as she was concerned, it was the biggest and best ever. The visiting high school bands played loudly and with enthusiasm, if not always strictly in tune. Each riding club was followed by rowdy clowns, wielding their scoops with smelly flamboyance. There might not be many floats, but the wagons full of costumed children and the clowns made up for the lack. Every Halloween costume in Sunset County must have been put to use. And how had the coach convinced the entire football team to paint their faces? Not that most of the boys didn't do a lot of clowning around anyway, even without makeup. Phil Cohoon was the cutest, with his bulbous red nose and Emaline's old purple satin dress straining at his broad shoulders.

So far—knock wood—everything was going smoothly. All the first shift volunteers had shown up, the equipment donated by local merchants was all working, and the truck from the beer distributor had just arrived. They wouldn't open the beer garden until four, but she was relieved to know that they would be ready to do so.

Even the hurriedly built tables and benches looked good. Erik had called made a call to Portland and convinced the company president that Hells Gate Timber should contribute to the Social, a first for the town. Ever since the original owners had sold it, about thirty years ago, the sawmill had used Sunset County trees and labor, but had done nothing else to be part of the community. Today there was seating for several hundred picnickers, put together practically overnight with materials and labor supplied by Hells Gate.

Kathryn checked her watch. Almost one and everything was still going smoothly. Now, where were Janine and the kids?

"Katie!" Kathryn craned her neck, trying to see who had called her name. "Katie! Over here!"

A hand was waving over the crowd, from the direction of the Baptist Church booth. She wove her way through the crowd. "What's the problem?" she asked the aproned woman behind the counter who was holding the end of an extension cord.

"We can't keep it plugged in. Every time someone walks between the booths," she pointed next door, where tempura and teriyaki chicken on skewers were selling like hotcakes, "they trip on our cord and unplug the coffee maker."

Kathryn measured the distance between the booths with her eye. "Why don't you pull one of your cars into the space a little way, then run the cord under it? Then you could stretch some flagging tape across whatever gap is left. I'll see if I can find Erik and send him over with the tape."

"That ought to work. Thanks, Katie." The woman dropped the cord and spun around to call to a co-worker, "No, not those onions. Use the ones in the blue container first."

Kathryn was heading for the high school, to check supplies in the rest rooms, when she heard her children calling her. Turning around, she saw Kyle and Ginger racing across the picnic area, dodging adults and tables. Janine and her children were following at a more leisurely walk. She knelt and waited, marveling again that these two wonderful children were hers. When they reached her, they bowled her over with their enthusiastic greeting.

"Mama, did you know Phil's wearing a *dress*!" Kyle demanded, as soon as he'd given her a big hug. "And one of the guys has his hair dyed purple and tattoos all over his tummy."

"And...and...and we saw a bee-u-tiful black car with its top down and a license plate that said 'ZOOM,'" Ginger added, showing where her interest always centered. Jon swore she'd drive the Indy 500 some day.

"I want a hamburger," Kyle said, still hanging on her, even though she'd stood. "And lots and lots of ice cream and a hot dog and some cotton candy, and—"

"And maybe I should leave them with you tonight," her cousin's wife said, giving Kathryn a quick hug, "if he's going to eat like that."

"Oh, Jan, if only you could, but I've got to—"

"I was kidding," Jan said. "You'll be on the go until all hours, if this is anything like it's always been." Janine had done her share at the Social in years past and she knew whereof she spoke.

Kathryn was guiltily conscious of relief. If the children were to stay with her tonight, Erik wouldn't. And she so desperately wanted him to.

After the confusion of the Social was over, she wouldn't dare let him stay in her house, unless the children were there. And she wouldn't ever, ever let him make love to her if there was a chance in a million that her children might discover them together. Tonight would be all they had.

Perhaps ever.

"I see some of the guys from school," Jace said. "Can I go to the carnival with them, Ma?"

Janine dug in her purse and handed him some money. "Go ahead honey. Just be sure you meet me at Aunt Katie's at five o'clock."

He was gone almost before he could agree.

"I'm really, really hungry, Ma," Abby said, tugging on Janine's free arm.

"Me, too." Ginger rubbed her tummy.

"Well, me, three," Kathryn agreed. "So. Where do we eat?" Usually there were only two food booths to choose between, besides the ice cream stand. This year featured the Baptist booth, where hamburgers and hot dogs sizzled, the Obon Festival booth with its Japanese food, a barbecued ribs and baked beans feed put on by the Larch Mountain Grange, plus an Idaho Spud booth, where one could get potatoes fixed every way but raw. That was not to mention the cotton candy stand, two soft drink stands, and the beer garden, which would feature pizza by the slice along with its domestic and imported beers.

"Ice cream!" Denny said.

"Hangoobers," Kyle demanded, using a pronunciation from his terrible threes.

"I want some of that stuff on sticks," Ginger said. "And french-fries."

"Can I have a hot dog, Ma?"

Kathryn laughed. "Let's make a list. Then you kids can go save us a place at a table and Aunt Janine and I can get all the food, okay?"

They all agreed and repeated their requests for Janine to write down. With happy shouts, they ran toward the picnic area. "I'm not sure we are going to be able to carry all this," Jan said. "Or that they'll be able to eat it all."

"Probably not," Kathryn agreed. "I never could, but Gran and Gramps always let me have whatever I wanted, just this one day."

"That's what Jon said, too. Oh, well." She chuckled. "if we have an epidemic of belly aches tonight, he can get up with 'em." They parted to get the varied foods for their children.

* * *

Erik caught Kathryn between the First Aid tent and the not-yet-open beer garden somewhere around three. As she was passing the beer truck, an arm snaked out and pulled her into the narrow gap between it and the tent.

"C'mere, you gorgeous morsel." His voice imitated a movie gangster's.

"Ooooh," she sighed, fluttering her eyelashes, "please don't hurt me!"

"Baby, what I want to do to you won't hurt a bit," he growled, before taking her mouth in a deep, hungry kiss.

She melted. The temperature was still in the low seventies, but she felt herself sizzle as his kiss deepened. Caught between his body and the truck behind her, she didn't quite trickle down into a puddle at his feet, but she felt as if she should.

"There," he said against her lips a long time later, "that should hold me for a little while."

She kissed his bearded chin. "An hour or so," she agreed. "Not one second longer." He felt so good. All she wanted to do was stand here in the circle of his arms and let him turn her blood to fire and her body to fluid compliance.

"But what I *have* to do is get on back to the stage. There's some problem with the sound system." He released her, leaving her standing shakily on legs that had somehow lost their starch.

"And I've got to deliver this sunscreen to the First Aid tent." She shook her head. "I can't understand why people don't come prepared. Our most common medical emergency is sunburn."

"Be glad it's nothing worse," Erik said, reluctantly releasing her. "Gotta go." With one hand he caught her nape and kissed the tip of her nose. "Catch you later."

His leer promised an unspeakably delicious later. Kathryn knew she was grinning like a clown as she went on her way.

* * *

Erik had to admit that today was at once the most exhausting and the most interesting day he'd spent in years. Despite the constant need to cope with minor emergencies, he was having the time of his life. Getting to know these people was the best part of it. He'd lived in the Washington, D.C. area for eleven years now, on and off, and he knew fewer people than he did in Garnet Falls—and not nearly so well, either. He couldn't think of a place he'd ever been where he felt so at home.

Kathryn was a big part of his feeling like he belonged, he was sure.

Glancing at his watch, he stopped to purchase a cola and headed across Jefferson Street. His feet were tired and he could use the excuse of making sure the kids' games were going smoothly to sit on the bleachers for a while.

Most of the foot traffic between the park and the playing field was children running pell mell in all directions. Several times Erik had to step out of the way or be run down. The third time it happened, the boy—ten or so, he estimated—begged his pardon before running off. Three smaller children were pursuing him, yelling.

My god! That little girl had to be one of Kathryn's twins. Her black, curly hair and stubborn little chin were duplicates of Kathryn's, and her mouth had that same sweet little curve to it that made her look as if she were about to smile.

But it was the younger boy who held his attention. Who was he? Erik *knew* he'd seen the child before, seen him many times, but where?

He followed the children, or tried to. Since the playing field was the only possible destination in this direction, he kept on going that way. When he arrived, he climbed higher in the bleachers than he needed to, just so he could look over the crowd.

Where have I seen that child before?

He scanned the crowd. If he could only get another look at the boy, he would know.

The miniature Kathryn was at the side of the field, jumping up and down. The third child, another girl, was beside her, carroty hair a beacon in the bright sunlight.

Where was the boy? Ah, there, pulling a gunnysack over his legs, along with a dozen or so other boys, all much bigger than he.

Erik watched, straining to make out the child's features. Even his motions seemed familiar. He half kept his eye on the boy as he made his way down to ground level, almost afraid he'd disappear before he was identified.

The sack race began before he could get near enough to see the boy's face well, so he stood as close to the two little girls as he could, assuming the boy would return to them, since he'd seemed to be their companion.

The short course was littered with fallen children before the race was decided. The boy whom Erik was watching fell about a third of the way through the race, and lay on the ground, laughing uproariously while the other boys hopped and staggered their way along. The winner was a tall, skinny kid with a gap between his front teeth, and the boy who'd collided with Erik was second.

After awards were presented to first, second, and third places, with lesser prizes to all the contestants, the two boys returned to the little girls. Erik watched as the smaller one approached. He watched and wondered if he were seeing a ghost.

Gail and Erik were not twins, but might as well have been. Less than two years apart, they were inseparable. If Gail had been a little bossy, Erik had been a good follower. His big sister never left him behind when she went places with her friends. She had never called Erik a baby, or told him he was dumb, or even beat on him, as some of her friends did on their little brothers and sisters. Erik and Gail were a unified front before their mother's gloom and despair. It had been to Gail that Erik owed what laughter and happiness his childhood had held.

He still missed her, and it had been twenty-six years since...damn! He still felt as if he'd failed his sister!

The child came closer. Erik met his eyes and lost touch with here and now. Gail's eyes had been an unusual color, lighter than Erik's own dark brown, the rich yellow-brown of Baltic amber. Her nose, even at ten, had been long and straight, with a faint indication of a cleft at the tip. A matching cleft, deep enough to be called a dimple, marked her chin. Erik was blond, but Gail's hair had been lighter, almost silvery, and dead straight, lacking even the slightest wave.

Erik looked into his sister's eyes. "Gail?" He heard his voice tremble as his hand reached out to the tow-headed child.

"Uh-uh. I'm Kyle."

"Let's go," the larger boy said. "I want to show Ma my prize."

"We're gonna do the three legged race," the red-haired girl said. "You're just gonna have to wait, Denny."

"Aw," he said.

"You promised, Denny," Kathryn's image said. "You promised, and you gotta stay. So there!" Her little chin was set, just as he'd often seen Kathryn's.

Erik licked suddenly dry lips. "Kyle?" He touched the younger boy on the shoulder. "Do you live here?"

"Who are you, mister?" Denny's voice challenged him. He moved to stand between Erik and the girls, and was trying to push Kyle behind him as well.

"I'm Erik Solomon," he said. "Who are you?"

"I'm Virginia Elaine Pierson," the dark-haired girl said, "and that's my cousin Denny and my cousin Abby and my brother Kyle." She smiled with heartstopping pride. "We're twins."

"Ginger, you're not supposed to talk to strang—"

"He's not a stranger, Denny. He's Mama's assistant. I saw 'em talkin' earlier." Her smile was as lovely as her mother's.

But Erik couldn't appreciate her smile, for he was, as always, tongue-tied and unable to think what to say to this charming little girl. He was also still mesmerized by the uncanny resemblance between the boy—Kyle Pierson—and Gail.

Could he be...? No, it was impossible! His mouth went dry, his heart throbbed heavily in his chest. He had to ask.

"How old are you, Kyle, seven?"

The boy looked to his sister, reminding Eric of how he'd always let Gail take the lead. "Not for a while yet."

"Our birthday's the third of August," Ginger said.

"Mine's next week," Abby said, obviously not liking the twins to hog the spotlight of his attention. "I'm older."

"Pooh," Kyle scoffed. "Only three weeks."

But the children's squabbling only registered peripherally. Erik mentally counted on his fingers.

CHAPTER NINE

"Mama!" Ginger's high, sweet voice sounded over the constant mutter of the crowd. "Mama, look what we won!" She and Abby were slipping through the crowd like little eels. Kathryn held her breath as her niece nearly knocked the plate of barbecued ribs out of an older man's hands.

"Look, Aunt Katie!" Abby held up a shiny disk on a plastic cord. "It's a medal!"

"I got one too," Ginger said. Hers was bright blue to Abby's green. Both were inexpensive but pretty, the way they split the sunlight into a thousand shards on their rainbow surfaces. "We came in fifth."

"I didn't even finish the sack race," Kyle said, coming up and leaning against her. He looked tired, but happy. "But they gave me a prize anyhow." He dug into his shorts pocket and pulled out a tiny plastic figure. "See. It's a dinosaur, but I don't know what kind."

"It's a stegalopolis," Denny said, with the dogmatic confidence of his ten years. "I saw one in a book at school."

"Of course it is," Kathryn agreed, trying hard not to crack a smile. "Did you get a prize too?"

"Yeah, but it isn't much," Denny said. One grimy hand opened to show her a tin whistle, about an inch long, attached to a red lanyard. "Its only got one note." Demonstrating, he nearly broke her eardrums. The one note was loud and shrill. "And a ribbon." He puffed his chest out, calling her attention to the red rosette with a big gold "2" in its center.

"Oh, my goodness," Kathryn said, "I'll bet you're proud of that."

Denny allowed that he was, but his attention had wandered. "Come on, you guys. It's time to meet Ma."

Without another word, they all abandoned her, at a dead run as usual. Kathryn sighed, feeling unnecessary, but grateful. Denny was so good with the younger children, so responsible.

She stood, aware that her feet were tired. Perhaps she should have worn her old sneakers today, instead of these new ones with their bright pink trim. But they matched her blouse, and she'd wanted to be beautiful in Erik's eyes. He'd said pink was her best color, but he'd been speaking of blushes, not blouses.

Her skin grew hot just thinking about the conditions under which Erik had admired her blush. It hadn't been restricted to her face.

Speaking of Erik, her radar was telling her he was nearby. She wished she were a little taller, so she could see over the heads of the crowd. She'd never seen so many people in Garnet Falls in her life. Surely they were approaching the projected attendance.

Golden hair shone in the sunlight and she raised on tiptoe. Kathryn knew she was smiling all over her face. While there was no place they could go where fifty people wouldn't be watching, she just wanted to be close to him, to touch him, for a moment. Then she would be revitalized and ready to tackle a few more crises.

He looked at her, but didn't stop walking toward the food booths. He looked at her and didn't seem to know her.

No, that was wrong. He knew her. She could see that, even at the twenty-five or so feet that separated them. Erik's stare bore into her like a long, sharp icicle, freezing as it penetrated, draining all the warmth from her.

A clot of people moved between them. Kathryn stood, dazed, staring at where she'd last seen him.

The clot thinned, dissipated, but he was no longer there. She craned her neck, looking frantically in the direction he'd been moving, but he had vanished.

"Katie?"

A deep voice penetrated the fog in which her mind groped. She turned. The sheriff was standing behind her, looking impatient. "I asked you if you were ready to go to the bank with me?"

Oh, lord, she'd almost forgotten. A deep breath gave her back her voice, but not her equanimity.

Why had Erik snubbed her like that?

"Yes, Wally, I guess we'd better," she said, checking her watch. "I hadn't realized the time." They'd made arrangements for him to escort her to the bank with the money from all the food booths, so none of them would have too much cash on hand during the supper rush. She had been supposed to meet him fifteen minutes ago.

They stopped at the Baptist Church booth. "Hi, ladies. Have you got lots of money to go to the bank?" She forced herself to smile. Surely Erik had been distracted and hadn't even seen her.

If she was going to get through the rest of the day with her sanity intact, she had to put him out of her mind.

"Things are goin' pretty smooth," Wally commented as they walked back to the park after making the deposits. Driving was out of the question, with two lines of cars nose to tail along every street in town. Wally had closed most of the side streets to traffic anyway, except for service and emergency vehicles.

"Don't say that," she told him. "It's like a flat tire—don't mention it and maybe it won't happen." She showed her crossed fingers to him. "I've been concentrating on positive thoughts for the past week."

Maybe that was why she couldn't really believe Erik had deliberately snubbed her. Surely he'd been focusing on something else and hadn't even seen her.

"Well, keep it up for a few more hours," Wally said, "until after the concert." He touched two fingers to the bill of his hat as he left her at the ice cream booth.

There were no more emergencies, so her crossed fingers must have been effective. They didn't, however, prevent minor hitches, so it was well after the concert began before she was able to take a break. And she didn't see Erik again, though she watched for him all evening.

Thanks to an excellent sound system, she at least got to hear Trace Pickett sing.

Kathryn didn't know where he was, where he'd slept. Erik hadn't come to her house last night, as he had said he would. The Picketts had still been in his room over the Wooden Nickel, so he'd had nowhere to go.

"Katie, are you listening?"

She jumped and almost knocked over her coffee mug. "I'm sorry, Amelia. I was wool gathering."

"Well, pay attention. Wally needs an answer as soon as possible."

An answer? She hadn't even heard the question. "I'm sorry," she apologized again. "I can't seem to wake up. What is it Wally needs to know?"

"Those motor homes. Some of the people want to stay at the fairgrounds until tomorrow. He says it's our responsibility. Something about insurance."

Kathryn shook her head, trying to clear it. "Insurance? Oh, sure. Our special liability policy covers us until Monday morning.

I don't see any reason why they can't stay, as long as they don't make a mess."

"That's what I told him."

Well, why did you ask me? Kathryn's head ached already. She knew Amelia wasn't usually this indecisive, for she'd sat through numerous County Commission meetings where her friend had kept the men to the topic at hand until a resolution was reached. "When is Erik coming in?" she said, hating herself for needing to know. If he hadn't cared enough to let her know he wouldn't be home—listen to her!—wouldn't return to her house for a second night, she should care if she ever saw him again.

"Probably not until tomorrow," Amelia said. "He decided to go with the Picketts when they left, early this morning." Amelia's voice held a gentle question, one Kathryn hoped she wouldn't put into words.

"Oh." She tried to make herself sound nonchalant. "He didn't tell me, but I guess there's no reason why he should. Who's going to take care of the money, then?"

"Everything's copacetic, Katie." Lester reached across her plate to top off her hardly-touched coffee. "Something wrong with your eggs?"

She looked down. The liquid yolks were stirred into her hash browns and the whole congealed mass sat in her plate. She poked her fork into it and realized that nothing could convince her it was edible. "I guess I'm just not hungry," she said apologetically. With an effort, she took a bite of her toast. It was cold and she almost gagged as she forced herself to swallow.

"Erik and me, we counted all that money last night and made out a deposit. I'll take it to the bank first thing tomorrow." He pulled a chair from a nearby table and straddled it at the end of their booth, leaning his massive arms on its back. "He and Trace hadn't had much time to catch up on old times, and I told him to scat. I didn't do much gettin' ready for the Social, so's the least I can do it help clean up afterward."

Lester had been generous with contributions of food and other supplies for the Social in the past, but he'd always said he was too busy to give his time. Kathryn wondered how Erik had managed to convince him otherwise. Or had it been Amelia?

She pressed her lips together to keep from asking Lester if Erik had seemed angry with her. "Look, I've got to go. It's not that I don't trust everyone to clean up their messes, but—"

"Go along with you," Amelia said. "I'm just going to have just one more cup, and I'll be off myself." She smiled at Lester and held out her cup. His answering smile made Kathryn ache with loneliness. Erik had smiled at her just that way a little over twenty-four hours ago. And now he was gone without a word.

"I figure she got herself knocked up on one of them business trips." Alf Wallace's words echoed in his memory as Erik tried to push his foot through the firewall of Charlie's car.

No! Kathryn would never be so dishonest as to use him to father her child...children, and never tell him he was a father. Kyle's uncanny resemblance to Gail was simply one of those bizarre coincidences.

That's all.

Coincidence.

He had been careful. In his entire adult life Erik had never assumed the women he was intimate with were on the pill or otherwise protected against pregnancy. He wasn't a stud, but he was human. If the opportunity presented itself and he liked and respected the woman, he'd never walked away from a sexual encounter. It was a matter of pride with him, however, that almost all of them had been long-term, rather than one night stands.

All but one of them.

A one night stand. Wasn't that what one of the fellows in the tavern accused Kathryn of? Or had the words been his? He didn't know. It didn't matter.

Damn Charlie Bittenbusch anyhow. Late last night he'd pounded on Erik's door. "I've got a deal you can't afford to pass up," he said, hinting that it would complete the funding package for Wounded Bear Meadow.

Erik had agreed to come with him this morning because it was still too soon to confront Kathryn.

"Here we are," Charlie said, pulling into the parking lot of McCall's biggest and poshest hotel. He led Erik into the restaurant, where three men, about Charlie's age and having much the same air of wheeler-dealers, were waiting at a table.

Charlie introduced them, but their names went in one of Erik's ears and out the other. They were easy to tell apart, however. One had artfully coifed hair that was both too black and too thick for a man his age. Another looked like a Prussian field marshal, And the third was so nondescript, so colorless and expressionless, that he faded into the background.

Charlie pulled out a chair between the Prussian and the hairdo, leaving Erik to sit more or less facing them all. Feeling like he was about to undergo interrogation. Or brainwashing.

The three were the major investors in a consortium—High Country Homes—that had its collective eyes on the Zenger Ranch. Erik was assaulted with the most concentrated, most overpowering sales pitch he'd ever experienced.

"Whenever you have time, we'll fly you over to Sunriver so's you can see how they've managed their environmental protection," the Prussian promised. "We've planned for about the same housing density, or maybe even a little less."

Hairdo broke in. "We've already talked to some people up at Billings who're putting together a homeowners' agreement for us. It'll set up restrictions for access to the meadow. Any trees that have to be cut down will be replaced. We figure on movin' a good number of them, as long as they aren't too big."

The third man's voice was as colorless as the rest of him.

"The hotel and golf courses will be where the main ranch buildings are now, so we won't have to construct new access roads. And we'll hire the best engineering firm to plan the interior roads to do the least environmental damage."

And on and on and on. At three Erik looked at his watch for the fourth or fifth impatient time. Would they never run down?

"And that about wraps it up, Erik," Hairdo said, sitting back and beaming. "What d'you think?"

"I think you've put a lot of thought and time into your planning," he said, admiring in spite of himself, their apparent determination to construct what amounted to a small city with minimal environmental damage. "But I don't see what this all has to do with me. I couldn't invest if I wanted to. It would be a conflict of interest, since I'm representing NWT."

"We need Wound—"

The Prussian held up a hand, stopping Charlie's explanation. "Let me explain." He waved the waitress over for their umpteenth refill, waiting until she had poured before continuing. "You're the wetlands expert. We need you to help us plan so we don't do anything to mess up Wounded Bear Meadow."

Erik stared for a long moment. "Wait a minute! What makes you think you'll be allowed to build anywhere near the meadow?"

"That's what I was gonna tell you," Charlie began. "We—"

"Charlie, please." Again the Prussian waved him to silence. "Mr. Solomon, we've met with Jethro Zenger and convinced him that selling us the entire ranch would be in his best interests. I'm surprised he didn't tell you."

"The hell you say!" He hadn't spoken to Jethro for more than a week, what with spending all his time on the Social.

"As a condition of the sale, we've promised Mr. Zenger that we would retain you, or someone with similar qualifications, to oversee our planning for the preservation of Wounded Bear Meadow. We would of course, pay you your usual consulting fee."

The figure Hairdo named showed he knew what a good consultant was worth these days.

"I don't know what to say." All he could think of was that everything he'd done for the past month was wasted. He'd been so sure he could get the funding together, so sure Jethro would be patient until he could. Why hadn't he insisted on a contract, instead of a handshake?

"Just say you'll consider our offer," The Prussian said. "We'd like to send you some preliminary plans in a few days, have you look 'em over for potential problems."

Erik was in a daze as they left the restaurant. He'd take the consulting job, not for the money but to make sure they really didn't mess up the meadow. But he'd never be able to face his associates at NWT, not after losing one of the best wetlands the Trust had ever had a chance to obtain.

They got back to Garnet Falls about six. The first thing Erik did, after he got rid of Charlie, was call Kathryn.

No answer.

Then he called Jethro Zenger. One of the hands answered, told him Jethro was up in Montana.

"He figured to be back around the tenth, unless the fishin's extra good."

"Is there any way I can get hold of him?"

"I don't reckon so. He's likely to call, come Wednesday or Thursday. You want me to give him a message?"

Mrs. Zenger was also away, visiting her son in San Francisco.

"Thanks," Erik said, holding on to the last shreds of patience. "I'll call again after the tenth." He slammed the phone into its cradle.

There was no help for it. He'd just have to wait until Jethro returned to learn what was going on.

Now, which road did he take to the Double J?

* * *

He spoke as soon as she appeared, not even waiting for her to open the back screen door. "How long did you think you could keep them a secret?"

Kathryn stared up at Erik's grim face, slightly blurred through the wire mesh, her heart heavy in her chest. He was angry, and she hadn't the faintest idea why.

She pushed on the screen door, but had to wait while he moved aside before she could join him on the porch. "Whatever I did, we can talk about it better where Janine won't worry about what we're saying." She led him to the cluster of lawn furniture under the big weeping willow.

Kathryn sat, knotting her hands together under the table's edge. Ever since her grandfather had insisted she stand at attention for his occasional scoldings, she hated to do battle on her feet. Sitting down kept her relatively composed.

Erik gripped the back of a chair, his knuckles white and his fingers digging into the floral-patterned cushion. "I want an answer," he said. The cords in his neck stood out in harsh relief. "Now!"

"If I knew what the question was, maybe I could give you one."

"Damn it, Kathryn, I'm talking about the children!" His face contorted into an angry mask as the words exploded from his mouth. "How long did you expect to keep them a secret from me?"

Honestly puzzled, Kathryn frowned. "I *know* I told you about them, when you first came to town."

"Yeah. And you told me their father was dead." With one step he was before her, hands clenched on her upper arms, pulling her up to face him. "You lied, Kathryn. Didn't you?" The expression in his face frightened her.

"Yes." Writhing, she tried to break free of his grip. "Yes, I lied. What did you want me to say? That their father was an unknown?"

"Unknown? Bull! You know who fathered those kids." His hands tightened on her arms until she wanted to cry out with the pain.

"No!" She couldn't restrain the sob in her voice. "I never knew. I never wanted to know." The old agony came once more, with all the force and sharpness of long ago. As long as she didn't know the identity of the anonymous donor—a condition of the insemination—she could fantasize that Jesse had fathered her children. The fantasy had never replaced reality, but at first she had hoped it would.

"Think back, lady. Remember the first time we met?"

She couldn't meet his eyes. "How can I forget?" she whispered. "It was a mistake."

The crack of his laughter was like a knife at her chest. "I'll say. The worst mistake you'll ever make." Releasing her, he strode to the thick trunk of the willow, leaned against it, deceptively casual. But his spine showed tension, as did a twitching muscle in his jaw. Finally he said, "Did you really expect me to miss the resemblance?"

She drew a deep, steadying breath. "Erik, you aren't making sense. Now please, sit down and tell me what you're so angry about."

He dragged a chair right up to hers, threw himself into it. He glared directly into her face, close enough that she felt his breath hot on her cheeks. "Talk!" he commanded. "Tell me about their so-called father."

"My children were conceived by artificial insemination," she said, wondering where she had put the records. Not wanting the twins to find them until they were old enough to understand, she had kept her medical records separate from their birth certificates and other important papers.

"And reindeer fly," he sneered. "Come on, Kathryn, stop lying to me."

All at once she'd had enough. "Damn you, Erik Solomon! What gives you the right to come out here and call me a liar?" She forced herself to speak slowly, calmly. "It's none of your business, but I can prove what I say. Kyle and Virginia are the result of my being impregnated at a clinic in Portland. Do you want time and date?"

"By all means. Add some verisimilitude to your fiction."

She told him. The details were engraved in her memory. She had begun to care whether she lived or died at that instant.

"That was the day we met," he said. His voice was more subdued than it had been since his arrival.

"I went directly from the clinic to the airport. And I arrived at the conference in Seattle just a little before two." She remembered how emotionally exhausted she'd been that day. How she'd rather have done anything but sit in a conference and listen to a bunch of experts talk about saving a few marshes and bogs.

"And that night you seduced me."

Her voice caught somewhere in her throat, on a gasp of surprise and outrage. "*I* seduced *you*?" she managed to croak. For long seconds her mind whirled with confusion and fury. Through narrowed eyes she glared at Erik, trying to remember the exact details of that night. But all she recalled was finding momentary forgetfulness, a brief relief from deadening sorrow, in his arms.

"I *didn't* seduce you. I don't even remember how we...why we..." Taking a deep breath, she looked him in the eye. "Erik, I don't even know how you got into my room."

He searched her face, seeing sincerity. A pleading to be believed. And he stiffened his resolve. "I suppose you don't remember asking me to make love to you, either."

"I didn't do that!"

"Lady, you begged for it."

She stared at him, tears drowning her eyes. Erik suddenly

knew what it felt like to be a lizard hiding under a rock. Low. Lower than low.

"Oh, hell! Listen. I don't want to fight with you about this. All I want is the truth." He did his best to make his voice calm, non-belligerent.

"I've told you the truth!"

"You've told me the lies you've lived for so long you believe them," he said, and stopped. Now that the words hovered on the tip of his tongue, he was finding them hard to say. As if, by saying them, they changed from a theoretical possibility to reality.

He forced himself to relax, let the fat cushions enfold him. A bee was buzzing just outside the willow canopy, exploring the roses along the white board fence. Sunlight filtered through the branches and lay in long golden lines across the yard, highlighting Kathryn's face, heightening the green of her eyes and glinting off the tracks of tears on her cheeks. Erik was more aware of his surrounding than he had ever been, more aware of the mutter of a tractor somewhere, of far away children's voices, of the scents of July-hot grass and fresh-cut hay.

Reaching out to gather her hands into his, he pulled them from their rigid clasp in her lap. With one thumb, he stroked along her wrist, wondering if there was any right way to say what must be said. Deciding there wasn't.

"Kathryn, I'm the father of your children."

She giggled, a nervous, uncertain giggle. "No you're not!"

He held her hands, even though she was struggling weakly to pull free. "I am. There's no question in my mind that Kyle is my son." None. He'd wrestled with all the possibilities for two days now and there was just no escaping it. Coincidence could not account for such a perfect resemblance.

This time she was able to jerk her hands free. She jumped to her feet and strode to the tree, where she turned her back to him and leaned against its black bark. Silhouetted thus against the gold and green of the willow branches, she looked fragile. Fragile and vulnerable.

"Why are you doing this to me?" The pain in her almost-whisper cut him to the quick.

"Why did you do it to me?" he countered. Almost he'd convinced himself that she was as innocent as he, but not quite. Not quite.

"I didn't." Her shoulders hunched and her head bowed, she stood unmoving at the edge of the sink. "You're making a horrible mistake, Erik. There's just no way." Suddenly she stopped. Her hands gripped the edge of the sink. "Unless you—" She turned slowly, her eyes wide and full of accusation. "You said you'd protect me!"

"I did." He *had*. The condom resided in his wallet for a long time, just in case.

"Then how? How can you believe they're yours?" Her question resembled a wail.

"Kyle could be my sister, Gail—or her twin," he said. "The resemblance is uncanny."

"Coincidence." Her protest was almost a question.

"Sure. How many people have you seen with eyes that color?" He never had, anywhere in his travels. He would have noticed. "And the widow's peak? The almost-white hair? Did he get those from your family?"

"No, but—"

"His voice is like I remember Gail's. His mouth is shaped the same way. He's even got hitchhiker's thumb." Erik held up his hand, effortlessly bending his thumb back until it almost touched his wrist. "It runs in the family." Hating himself for the agony he saw on her face, he said, "Any one or two of those characteristics I could buy as coincidence, Kathryn. But not all of them.

"He is my son."

He went to her and slipped an arm around her shoulders,

pulled her with him back to the cluster of chairs. After an initial resistance, she allowed him to guide her. Bonelessly she collapsed, sitting slumped and defeated.

"I still can't believe you." Her eyes overflowed and she seemed unaware of the tears coursing down her cheeks.

"I tried to convince myself it couldn't be," he said. The last of his anger dissolved with her renewed tears. "I told myself you were pregnant when...that night in Seattle. But then I counted." Over and over he'd counted. "Condoms aren't a hundred percent foolproof." He shrugged, still unwilling to believe. "I guess we're the fools."

Ginger's birthday, and therefore Kyle's, was August third. Exactly eight months, three weeks, and six days after the night in Seattle. He'd used his modem, gone back into his work diary which, fortunately, he'd put on disk last winter when he'd been forced into temporary inactivity with a sprained ankle.

"Erik, You've got to be mistaken." She sat straighter, her tears gone now. "If you used a...protected me, and I was inseminated the day before, it's just impossible. Besides, I requested a donor with light hair and brown eyes." Biting her lip, she paused, then said, as if admitting something faintly offensive, "I wanted their father to look as much like Jesse as possible."

"That's sick!"

"You walk in here and claim to have fathered my children and you talk about sick?" Her hoarse cry should have strained her throat.

Somehow Erik felt as if he had been put on the defensive. "Never mind who's sick. I want to know if you're going to keep denying that you used me!" He'd fought the suspicion that he'd been nothing but a convenient stud to her, and thought he'd conquered it. Now, with her insistent denial, he was beginning to wonder if it might not be the only possible explanation. "What'd you do? Decide it would be more fun to do it the natural way? Go to Seattle, lure the first blond man you saw into your bed, and bingo! Natural insemination."

He stood with such force that his heavy wrought iron chair tipped. Pacing, avoiding the sight of her face, he snarled, "Well, think about this, lady. That boy is mine and I have every intention of his knowing his father. You can either cooperate or fight me. Either way, I'll win." He bent over her and waited for her to look him in the eye. When she stubbornly kept her face turned away, he lifted her chin with an inexorable pressure.

"If I have to go to a geneticist for proof, I will," he vowed. "I haven't any doubt Kyle is my son, and I intend to be his father. You've got a week to get yourself used to the idea. Then I'll take whatever steps I must to be part of his life."

CHAPTER TEN

"I don't believe you."

"Whether you believe me or not, Kathryn, I know Kyle is my son." Two steps took him to stand behind her, not touching, for the rage within made him afraid to lay a hand on her. "I want him."

"No!" Her gasp was as ghostly as a bat's wings in the night. "You wouldn't take him away from me?"

"Wouldn't I?" Her face was twisted with pain, but he couldn't let it affect his decision. "He's my son, and nobody's going to keep me from being a father to him." Even as he spoke the words, he was amazed yet again at his primitive need to know his son.

"I still don't believe you." Desperation and denial.

"I can prove it."

"How?" Incredulity and more denial.

"Ever heard of genetic testing? It's a simple process to take a small sample, look at the DNA, and tell that I'm one of Kyle's parents. Beyond doubt." He couldn't prevent a smug tone from creeping into his voice. Geneticists were doing incredible things. Proving paternity was only a small part of the miracles they passed before breakfast.

"Sample? Of Kyle's blood?"

"More likely of tissue. I'm not sure."

"You'd need my permission. What if I won't give it?" Now her voice and her stance were stubborn, but the denial was still there.

"I'll get a court order." He gave himself a mental reminder to call Wils tomorrow. Even if she stopped fighting him on this, he needed legal advice.

Her shoulders slumped. She refused to look him in the eye, hunching one shoulder and staring at the ground. For a moment she gnawed her lip. "Will you give me time?" she said. "I need to think about this."

He wanted to say no, because he wanted his son to know him. "Yes. I've got to go to Minnesota tomorrow. I'll be back late in the week." He hoped. The project in Minnesota sounded like one of those that dragged on three times as long as expected. "You have until then." He went to his car, had his hand on the door handle when she spoke, finally.

"Erik?"

"Yes?"

"What about Ginger? If Kyle is your son, she's your daughter."

Erik stared at her. Bitterly he heard again his mother's words, words he'd tried so hard to forget.

"I'll never forgive you, Erik. Never. You should have taken care of her. It was your responsibility."

Even now, so many years later, he cried out, in his mind, "I tried, Ma. I tried. But she was too big, and the water was so swift."

But his mother hadn't heard. In her grief and her anger, she'd raved on. "There's not a man in the world can be trusted to take care of a woman. You're just like *him*, just like your father. With no thought for the females you're responsible for. Oh, God! Why didn't he take you with him? Why didn't you go?"

Knowing his own limitations, and hating them, Erik could not turn to look back at Kathryn. "I just want my son," he repeated.

What would he do with a girl? He could no more be a father to her than he could fly.

Erik kept his voice low as he hunched over the pay phone in the concourse at O'Hare. Despite the sound made by hundreds of travelers, he wanted to be certain he wasn't overheard. At least four other members of the EA team were in the Chicago airport, waiting for the flight to Duluth. The way his luck had been running lately, they were in the adjacent phone booths. "Wils? Where have you been, man?"

"In court. We're finally going after Lithops Petrochemical." Wilson Bates's deep voice held a strong note of satisfaction.

"All right! Nail 'em to the wall." Erik knew how long and how hard Wils's law firm worked to put together a case against a major contributor to a toxic dump. "How'd you finally get them into court?"

"A little, tiny loophole. One of their legal staff missed it and it gave us an opening." Wils sighed. "The bad news is that this case is likely to drag on for months."

"Think of all that lovely money," Erik said, grinning. For years Wils had worked for peanuts trying to save the world. With the birth of his fifth child, he'd decided to be practical. Now he was a junior partner in a prestigious firm specializing in environmental law. "You ought to make enough from this to guarantee college for all of your rug rats."

"Fat chance. Have you any idea of the cost of braces these days?" His voice faded briefly and Erik heard him say something to someone at his end. "Look, buddy, I've got about ten minutes before I have to be back in court. What can I do for you?"

"I may have to prove a boy is my son. Can I get a court order for genetic testing?"

"What the hell?"

"Wils, don't ask questions. Just tell me: is a court likely to go along with what I want?"

"I'm an environmental lawyer. How should I know?" Again his voice faded. This time Erik heard a woman's voice in the background, sounding urgent. "Okay, I'll be right there. Look, pal, I can't give you an answer right now. Can I get back to you?"

Quickly Erik gave him the name and number of the hotel where he would be staying for the next few days. "All I need is a name, Wils. I don't have a clue who to call for this, but I know I need legal advice."

"I'll have some names for you by tomorrow. And buddy?"

"Yeah?"

"I want all the details. You hear me? *All* of them."

A quick glance at his watch told him he'd better get a move on. They were probably boarding his flight right now. "You'll get 'em. That's a promise." He hung up, but stayed in the enclosure for a few seconds, leaning his head against the cool plastic of the pay phone.

God! It was all so damn complicated.

"This is a new one on me, Katie, but I'll say right now that you'll have to let him have the children tested." Her lawyer looked genuinely distressed. "Unless there's no possible reason he could be their father?"

"No," she said wearily, "it's possible." She closed her eyes, not wanting to see the expression on his face. Another childhood friend of Jesse's, he had to be disappointed in her. Had to believe she'd cared so little about Jesse to have slept with another man so soon.

"Were there witnesses? Or is it his word against yours?"

"Witnesses? What on earth are you suggesting?"

He raised his hands, palms out. "I'm not suggesting anything, Katie, except that you may not have been a willing participant."

For just one reckless moment she actually considered it.

"No." The word came out a defeated sigh. "No, I knew what I was doing." Shaking her head, wondering yet again at her foolish and desperate attempt to escape a pain that had still been as fresh as the day Jesse died. "Or at least, I thought I did."

"Well, then, Katie, I'm afraid you have no choice. As long as you're willing to admit having been intimate with him, he'll win."

"Thanks, then. I guess the only thing left is for me to tell the children."

"Don't do that!" He came around his desk and knelt before her. "Not until you know he's their father." Dabbing at her tears with his handkerchief, the lawyer said, "It *could* be the donor, you know."

"But—"

"Katie, promise me you won't say anything. Not yet. It could jeopardize any case you might have."

"Case?"

"Once he's proved he's their father, he could challenge you for custody."

"No!" She grabbed his hands. "It wouldn't do him any good, would it?"

"I'd like to say it wouldn't," he said, "but yes. It could."

"I can't believe it. Erik would never—"

"Katie, we don't know what Erik will do. He seemed like a nice enough fellow, but we're talking here about some pretty primitive emotions. People do the damndest things when their kids are concerned."

Kathryn remembered the implacable expression on Erik's face when he accused her of concealing the twins from him. She believed him to be a decent, honorable man, but she'd seen he was also a man of stronger, more complex passions than she'd suspected.

Would he believe she'd never intentionally kept his children from him? Or would he take revenge on her for doing so?

"What's this?" Erik looked at the envelope the messenger had just handed him.

"Don't know, sir. Sign here, please." He thrust a clipboard under Erik's nose.

Impatiently Erik scribbled his initials. He was already running late. He'd just have to pay the premium on an empty gas tank, because there wasn't time to fill the tank before he turned the rental car in at the airport. Ripping the envelope open, he pulled its contents free and unfolded the thick stack of papers.

A summons! Quickly he skimmed down the top sheet. "Ferrous County vs. The National Wetlands Trust." The date was day after tomorrow. What the hell?

He tossed his jacket and briefcase onto the borrowed desk. Somebody had better have some answers, and fast. He had a plane to catch.

Fifteen minutes later a secretary was canceling his flight and Erik was closeted with the rest of the project team and a lawyer. "The county is *fighting* us? You've got to be kidding?"

"Not exactly," the project manager said. A lawyer with a background in land use planning, she was one of the best Erik had ever worked with.

"According to their counsel, they foresee a legal challenge and want to shortcut it up front. By having a judge rule on the validity of the county's claim, they'll have it on record that there is a conflict between recreational development on the old Blackstone Mine property and preserving the swamp. They aren't asking for a judgment on whether the development will affect the swamp, just on the existence of a use conflict."

"Do you really need me?" There was one more flight he could catch and still get to Boise tonight.

"You're our prime witness, Erik. We need to show that there's evidence of a subsurface flow between the pit and the swamp."

"I don't know that for sure."

"But you have some evidence that points that way, don't you?"

He'd just spent three days going over old well records and other historical documents. "Yeah, there's evidence. I couldn't swear to it, though."

"You won't need to. Just tell the judge what could happen to the swamp if the pit were flooded and a connection *did* exist."

"That I can do." He could paint a graphic picture of what happens to a swamp when the water level rises and it becomes a lake. He'd seen enough silvery skeletons of trees standing in deep and stagnant water where once highly productive ecosystems had existed.

Damn! He'd wanted to get back to Garnet Falls tonight. He wanted to see his son.

Difficult as it was for him to admit, he wanted to see Kathryn.

"Why don't you marry him?"

Kathryn stared at her cousin. Jon was usually a very serious person, little given to joking. "Excuse me?"

Jon pushed his platter aside, having left nothing of the sixteen-ounce rib steak dinner he'd ordered but the bone and a parsley sprig. Kathryn was still toying with her "lady's sirloin," a delicious steak but one that seemed to swell in her mouth as she chewed it.

"Ordinarily I'd be the last person to come off sounding moralistic, Katie, but this time I feel like quoting the old saw about lying in the bed you made." He waved to Sandy, who was making the rounds with a pot of coffee.

"You've got a lot a nerve," Kathryn snapped, just before Sandy filled their cups. She smiled her thanks and waited until her friend was back behind the lunch counter. "With your past, I figured you'd be sympathetic."

"Sympathetic, yes. God knows there's nobody better'n me to know how easy it is to give in to self-destructive appetites."

Jon's eyes grew shadowed, and Kathryn knew he was remembering the years after his return from the Army. He'd nearly destroyed himself seeking forgetfulness of the atrocities he'd witnessed in one of the incessant Central American revolutions.

"Our situations aren't exactly the same," he said, looking at her from under his dark brows. "I was trying to forget. You were trying to replace."

"That's not true! I was...I was..." She could not finish the sentence for the tears that threatened to choke her. Wordlessly she looked at Jon, wanting him to read her explanation in her face. Her eyes burned, just before her vision blurred.

"Let's get outta here," Jon said, pulling her to her feet. He tossed a couple of bills on the table and dragged her after him, ignoring greetings from several people sitting at tables between their booth and the door.

Once on the sidewalk, Jon put his arm around her shoulders and pulled her hard against his side. "Katie, what else were you doing if you weren't trying to find Jesse? Or someone who could take Jesse's place?"

Biting her lips, she tried to give his accusation careful consideration. "Put that way, you make me sound really sick," she said, not liking what she saw of herself.

"I didn't mean to," he said. "I don't think that's particularly bad, or even all that uncommon. When your whole world falls apart, it's natural for you to want to find something that will help you put it back together."

"Erik accused me of using him."

"We all use each other, sometimes."

"But if I did, it was, well, selfish. Dishonest. It was—"

"It was human, Katie. You were hurting and he helped you feel better. Sometimes that's excuse enough."

"Not this time." She wondered if there was any reason good enough to excuse her to herself. She *had* used Erik, even though she had not consciously chosen to do so.

"Hey, that's enough beating yourself for what's already done. When I said that about accepting the consequences, all I meant was that you should make the best of a bad situation."

They turned onto Adams and the lights of town faded behind them. Although the moon appeared gibbous, its light filtered through the tall pines and maples that lined the residential street. Jon's light tenor voice seemed almost disembodied, as long as she kept her face tilted down and her gaze on the sidewalk.

"You said I should marry him. How does that qualify for sleeping in the bed I've made for myself?"

"Looks to me as if you've got two problems," he said. "One is that, come hell or high water, Erik Solomon is gonna lay his claim to your kids."

"To Kyle," she corrected, again feeling pain for Ginger, who wasn't wanted by her own father.

"Your kids," Jon reiterated, and Kathryn knew that Erik would claim both of the children, or neither. Jon would see to that.

"Since your lawyer said you'd have to let 'em be tested to make sure Erik's their pa, let's just assume he is. That means you can either voluntarily give Erik custody for part of the time, or fight him to keep 'em all to yourself. Do you want to drag those tykes through the courts like that?"

"Oh, God, no!" She hadn't really given much thought to what a legal battle for their custody would do to the twins. She hadn't gotten that far. It had taken her this long to really assimilate the fact that Erik could very well be their father, and not some anonymous donor whose name was locked in the clinic's records.

"Then it looks to me like your best bet is to let him be a father to 'em. The likeliest way to do that is to marry him."

It wasn't the first time she'd considered the possibility, just the first time she'd done so seriously. Marry Erik Solomon? Share her life with him and not be alone any longer? Go to bed at night knowing he'd be there when she woke every morning to his sleepy kisses?

"I'll think about it," she said, knowing she was already sold, though still doubtful it would ever be more than a dream. He didn't even want both his children, let alone her in the bargain.

"You do that little thing."

They walked on, alone in the night, accompanied by soft voices from front porches and open living rooms, by swooping bats hunting among the trees and slinking cats bent on their own adventures. Kathryn knew every crack in the sidewalk, every shadowy lilac bush or drooping willow that made the sidewalk seem a mysterious, dangerous place. She'd walked this way so may times, day and night, summer and winter, that its sights and sounds and impressions were a part of her.

They took the shortcut across the grade school lawn to Idaho Street. It was darker here, with the grade school on one side and the park on the other. Wally Blanchett had been agitating them for streetlights, but so far the city council had turned him down. There'd never been any kind of incident here, in this darkest corner of Garnet Falls, and the single light at the park restrooms shone among the trees, keeping the night from being pitch-black.

Marry Erik Solomon? She'd buried the impossible prospect for weeks, but now she could bring it out and examine it. Except for his irrational—and she had to believe temporary—rejection of Ginger, she found him everything she could want in a husband. She liked his sense of humor, his sensitivity. Erik was the only man she'd ever worked with who could help her cross a fallen log without making her feel like a helpless child. He'd given her a hand with the same matter-of-fact attitude he had demonstrated when helping Harry Lindholm up the courthouse steps or hoisting lumber out of the back of a pickup.

She liked his looks. Blond was too mundane a word for the molten gold of his hair in sunlight, and if his eyes were merely brown, she was the Queen of England. There might be a couple of models on Em's beefcake calendar who were better built than Erik, but they lacked his masculine sensuality, his aura of competence.

"Jon," she said, as they stopped at her front gate, "I just thought of something awful."

"What's that," he said, pushing the gate open and shuddering when it gave its usual rusty squeal. "Remind me to oil this damn thing, will you?"

"I can do it."

"You've been sayin' that for months. I'll take care of it."

Kathryn had her key in the front door when Jon said, "What awful thing did you think of?"

"What if Erik doesn't want to marry me?"

"He will, Katie." He patted her shoulder and, with a gentle push, moved her inside. Just as he pulled the front door shut, she thought she heard him say, "I'll see to that."

"Jon, wait!"

But his high-heeled boots were thudding across her porch. She leaned against the front door. Surely Jon wouldn't...no, he wouldn't. He didn't even own a shotgun.

Again she fought with her pillow, but this time only memories kept her from sleep.

One evening, after they'd exhausted themselves trying to anticipate every possible complication of the Trace Pickett concert, she and Erik had sat at her kitchen table, sipping herbal tea and trying to unwind. She'd asked him about his family.

"My sister, Gail, drowned when I was eight," Erik had said, sounding as if the words hurt his throat. "Afterward, my mother burned all photographs of her, cleared the house of every trace of her."

"Oh, Erik, I'm sorry," Kathryn said, laying one hand on his arm. If she hadn't had so many photos of Jesse, those first months after losing him, she didn't think she would have survived. And how Erik must still hurt, if this was his most vivid memory of his youth.

"My mother was...emotional." He stopped for a moment, as if wondering how to explain his childhood. "My dad divorced her when I was just a baby and moved to the West Coast. I don't know if she changed after that, or if she'd always been, well, incapable of relating to people." He wiped a hand across his mouth and Kathryn wept inside for a lonely little boy in a house devoid of love.

"She didn't like boys." The words seemed to burst from his mouth by accident, yet she could see the pain they caused. "I can remember." He paused until his voice sounded more normal. "I can remember how, whenever I'd misbehave, she'd say—" He stopped as his voice broke again. Then he swallowed, twice, and she saw him pull himself together.

"She'd ask why I couldn't have been a girl." With a swift chop of his hand, he cut off her expression of pity. "Then she'd say that if our father was here he'd know how to handle me. How could anyone expect, she'd say, a gentle, civilized woman to be able to understand a savage little boy like me."

"Oh, Erik, no!" She had reached out to touch his hand, but he had pulled it out of her reach.

"Oh, yes! But don't feel sorry for me. My mother made me what I am. She showed me how undisciplined I was, how irresponsible. Her inability to do anything with me forced me to take charge of my own life." He plainly rejected the warmth and tenderness she wanted to share with him. "I'd never have gotten to where I am today without her influence."

Kathryn couldn't help but wonder if he believed her incapable of dealing with Kyle—and himself incapable of being a good father to a girl-child. Surely he was intelligent enough to realize that his mother had been more than simply "emotional." She had been seriously deranged.

Could she overcome the poison his mother had poured into his young mind, or was he beyond redemption? Kathryn wanted to believe she could, because she no longer could imagine life without him.

Jace Pierson was bored. His best friend had a broken leg, and two of the other guys on the soccer team were gone to Scout camp. His pa was mowing hay. All the hired men were either haying or busy with other chores.

If he was fourteen, Pa would let him drive tractor. He thought he was old enough now—some of his classmates drove tractors on their places, and even trucks, sometimes.

To make matters worse, the littles kept following him around, bugging him to play with them.

What he really wanted to do was go camping with Pa. But he'd asked, and had been put off with a promise to go when the hay was in and the new pond up on Elderberry Creek was finished.

"You know what I heard in town?" Denny said.

Even his just-younger brother was better company than nobody at all. As long as Abby and the twins didn't find them, they could lay here on the hill back of the barn all morning in peace. Given time, he'd figure out something fun for them to do. He always could. Ma said what he couldn't think of hadn't been thought yet. "What?"

"Old Man Zenger is gonna sell Wounded Bear Meadow to some people who are gonna plow it up and build houses on it."

"Huh?" Jace sat up. "I don't believe you. Aunt Katie said that fella from Washington is gonna buy it and make it a place where nobody can hunt."

"You know that old Charlie Bittenbusch?" Denny turned over on his stomach and faced Jace.

Jace nodded.

"Well, he was talking to those old guys who always sit on the courthouse steps—you know who I mean?"

Again Jace nodded.

"Charlie said those people who want to build those condoms on the Zenger place said they wanted it all or they wasn't going to buy any of it. So Old Man Zenger is gonna sell 'em the meadow 'cause his wife won't spend another winter up here freezin' to death."

"Yeah. Old people don't like to be cold." Jace remembered their grandmother Caswell, who'd lived with them until she died when he was nine. She'd worn long johns all winter and two sweaters, most days.

"Anyhow, Charlie Bittenbusch said the conshum...consorm...those guys who want to buy the Z-Bar-Z are gonna give Old Man Zenger until the end of the month to decide. And he laughed at how they'd show that environmental fella that there's better things to do with land than give it to the bats and bunnies."

"Pa says we gotta start saving places like the meadow or there's not gonna be any wildlife when we're grown up." Jace had believed what his father had told him, because Pa had sounded so serious, not like his usual teasing way. He couldn't imagine not having deer around the haystacks in the winter, or pheasants and chukkar waking him with their calls on summer mornings. But Pa said all that would be gone, if people like Charlie Bittenbusch had their way.

"Yeah, well, that ain't what Ol' Charlie says." Denny sounded real disgusted. "He says we gotta get some of that tourist money that goes on up to McCall and keep it here. He says we need to have amities to offer the people who buy those condoms so they'll spend lots of money in Sunset County."

"I sure would like to see Wounded Bear Meadow," Jace said, "while it's still there. Aunt Katie says it's the prettiest place this side of heaven."

"Yeah, me too." Denny rolled over onto his back and shaded his eyes.

"How long do you figure it'd take us to ride up there?" Jace wondered aloud. An idea was forming in his mind. "We could go over Skunk Ridge, up behind the line shack. Wounded Bear Creek's the next one over. If we followed it upstream, we'd get to the meadow, sooner or later." He had a general idea where the meadow was, and didn't doubt his ability to get there.

"That'd take us all day." Denny didn't sound like he was arguing. "Then we'd have to come back."

"Yeah." All day to get there. Another day to get back. "Yeah!" It would work! "Look, Denny, you remember when Pa said I was almost old enough to go up to the line shack alone?"

"Last winter," his brother agreed.

"Well, I'm older now. So I'm old enough."

"I don't know," Denny said, sounding really doubtful.

"I do. Besides, what could happen? We've been up there a zillion times, and the worst thing that's happened was when the mice got into our food." It was beginning to sound like a grand adventure, and he was more determined than ever to go.

"Yeah, but Pa was with us."

Jace jumped to his feet. "He's busy haying." Starting down the hill, he looked back over his shoulder. "Are you comin' or what?"

"I'm comin'," Denny said, still sounding unsure.

They ran down the hill and across the wide driveway between the barn and the house. From the barn, Abby's and the twins' high voices told Jace they were at their never-ending game of saving the world. At breakfast they'd decided it was Ginger's day to be Catwoman. Just as they reached the house, Ma came out the back door.

"Hi, guys," she said. "I'm glad you're here." She set a covered dish on the passenger seat of the station wagon. "Ellen Greyhawk broke her arm this morning and I'm going over to take care of the babies while she goes to the clinic."

Jace drew a deep breath. "Ma, can we...?"

"Jace, you're in charge until your pa comes in. Keep the littles out of mischief. There's roast beef and ham in the 'fridge for lunch. I'll be home by five." She climbed into the car and pulled the door shut.

"Ma!" Jace could just see all his plans falling apart. "Wait a minute!"

She rolled down the window, looking impatient. "Denny, you help your brother, now. I've got to go. They're waiting for me." The engine caught.

"Can we go for a ride, Ma?" At least he wanted permission to take the horses out, a rule Pa was immovable about.

"As long as you take the littles," she said as she drove out the driveway.

Well, hell! Jace kicked at a big piece of gravel. They might as well stay home. Who wanted an adventure with three little kids tagging along?

"Well, can you get a message to him?" Kathryn drummed her fingers on her desk. She hated to make personal calls from the office, but this was an emergency.

Even more, she hated to be calling Erik. The less contact with him she had, the better she'd like it.

Liar! She would give her right arm—and maybe more than that of herself—to have him here right now.

She needed someone to reassure her that her entire life wasn't falling to pieces. Twice today someone had asked her how come Jethro had changed his mind. The first time it happened, she simply denied it. The second, she'd been just as quick with her denial, but she'd wondered. Was there something she didn't know.

Calling the Z-Bar-Z hadn't helped. The ranch-hand who answered the phone didn't know when Jethro would be back from his fishing trip. He'd decided to stay an extra week. He might call home sometime this week, but if he didn't, no one would worry too much. They were gettin' the hay in, and everything else was goin' just fine.

Ordinarily she wouldn't have worried. Jethro's summer fishing trips to the Three Forks area of Montana were as much of a local institution as the Social. It was the only vacation he ever took. But did his extended absence this summer mean he was avoiding questions? Had he really decided the money Charlie and his sleazy buddies were offering was more important than his word?

She couldn't believe it, unless his wife talked him into it. That woman could convince a bat to fly at high noon, when she wanted something bad enough.

"Tell him Jethro Zenger may have changed his mind. Tell him..."

She worried the tip of her nose. "Just tell Erik to call me, as soon as possible." Reciting her home and office numbers, she listened as the voice on the other end made it clear she didn't have the faintest idea of what she was doing. With a sigh, Kathryn hung up, certain Erik would get a garbled message, if he got one at all.

Should she leave a message on his answering machine at his apartment? No. That wouldn't do any good. By the time he got back to Garnet Falls, it would be too late.

The rest of the afternoon dragged by. Erik didn't call, nor did he that evening. If only she had some idea of where he was, but she wasn't even sure whether it was Minnesota or Wisconsin. Never having been east of the Rocky Mountains, she found all those states in the middle of the country confusingly alike.

Thunder grumbled across the sky as she prepared for bed.

Another summer storm. They'd been lucky to get through the Fourth without one, considering how they seemed to blow up more often than not when the weather got this hot. She lay awake, listening, and wondering if what she planned to do was right.

She really believed it would be best for the twins, but would it be best for her? For Erik?

Once free of the courtroom, Erik tried to call his Washington office. Getting a busy signal, he then dialed Kathryn's home number. No answer. Nor was there one at the Zenger Ranch. Jethro must still be fishing. Frustrated he dialed Wils Bates's number.

An answering machine thanked him for calling and invited him to leave a message. He did. It was short, succinct, and profane.

One more try. He waited through several rings before Walt Thomlinson answered. After giving a quick rundown on the progress of the hearing, Erik asked about messages.

"Let me see." Walt always took the message log home at night, since so many NWT staff people were in the field all day. "Erik? There doesn't seem to be anything here."

"Nothing?" He couldn't believe that he'd had no calls. That hadn't happened in his memory.

"Not a thing." Erik could almost hear him grimace. "I even had to show the temp who came in today how to use the phone."

"Damn it, Walt, you'd think we could get competent help!" Erik said, irritated out of all proportion and aware he was being unreasonable. "Well, if anything was really important, they'll call back, I guess."

"How'd the hearing go today?" Walt said. "Will you be done this week?"

"I doubt it, considering tomorrow's Friday." He realized he was snarling. "Hey, look, Walt. Don't mind me. I've got some things going on in my life right now that aren't a hell of a lot of fun."

"Well, let me know if I can help," Walt said.

"Thanks, but I'm going to have to straighten this out by myself," Erik told him, appreciating his associate's concern. "Look, I'll check my answering machine. Maybe she...they called there." Impatiently he cut the connection and dialed his apartment in Garnet Falls.

The only message on the tape was from Charlie Bittenbusch. The last person in the world he wanted to speak to.

Ginger lay in her sleeping bag, wishing she were home in her own bed instead of high in the mountains. The thunder stalked closer, only a slow count of eight between the last flash and its sound. That meant it was just a little over a mile away—close enough to be dangerous.

She pulled the bag over her head, knowing it wouldn't shut out the sound, but feeling a little more secure when she couldn't see the bright flashes, even through her closed eyelids.

It wouldn't be so bad if they were in the line shack. It sat in a sheltering stand of pine, all taller than it was. Lightning wouldn't strike it, if what her Uncle Jon had told her. It only struck the highest point around.

She hoped the tree under which they slept wasn't the tallest one in this particular piece of forest.

This was one of Jace's ideas she wished she hadn't been so ready to go along with. She couldn't believe she'd even helped him convince Denny that they should sleep out under the stars, instead of staying in the line shack and going on in the morning.

It had sounded like such a great idea, to go see Wounded Bear Meadow before they built a parking lot on it. That was what Uncle Jon said developers did—after they built a fancy hotel people had to drive their cars to. She didn't think that was so bad. When she grew up she was going to have lots of cars. She'd need a parking lot all her own. And a race track, for her Indy racer.

If there was a road up to Wounded Bear Meadow, she wouldn't be laying here waiting to be struck by lightning.

Tomorrow morning, she'd tell Jace she wanted to go home. Abby already did—she'd cried a little before she went to sleep—and Kyle kept worrying about what Uncle Jon would do to them. He hated to be scolded, especially the way Uncle Jon did, with eyes that looked right into you and a voice that made you want to shiver.

The thunder was closer. She just knew it was.

Wounded Bear Meadow might be the neatest place in the whole world, but she'd trade in a minute for her own bed back in town.

CHAPTER ELEVEN

Kathryn was in bed, wondering if tonight she would finally get some sleep, when the phone rang. "The kids went up to the old line shack this morning," Jon said. "It looks like they decided to stay all night." He sounded as if the children did something like this every week.

"Oh, Jon, did they go alone?"

"Well, yes, but I wouldn't worry if I was you. Jace may still be a kid, but he's a sensible, responsible kid. And you know Denny—he's real protective of the littles."

Kathryn couldn't believe Jon was being so calm about the situation. "What if...?"

Jon said, "I figure it'll do 'em good to stay up there. Maybe they'll get cold and hungry enough that they won't pull a fool stunt like this again."

"But," she sputtered, "but—!"

"Hey, Katie, it's okay. They'll be safe up there, and in the morning, when I go up an get 'em, they'll wish they'd spent the night in their own little beds."

She was partially soothed by the amusement in his voice. "So you're going to teach them about suffering the consequences of their actions the hard way?" She didn't approve of her babies having quite this strong of a lesson, but if Jon wasn't worried, she'd try not to be.

But what if...? Her vision wavered and her knees gave way. She was only dimly aware of the cool oak floor as she collapsed onto it. *NO! Not my children! Jesse is gone. Isn't that enough?*

"Katie, listen to me!" Jon's voice came from the receiver, now lying on the floor beside her. "The kids are all right. Do you hear me?"

She picked up the phone, put it back to her ear with a trembling hand. "I'll be there as soon as I can," she said, struggling to make her still-rubbery legs obey.

"You're not goin' anywhere but to bed, you hear?" His voice stopped her struggles. "Come first light, I'll be riding up there to bring 'em down. And it'll be a long time before any of 'em wants to go on an adventure again."

"Jon, what if...?" She didn't know what horrible situation she feared, but she knew her children were in danger. Terrible, life-threatening danger.

"Katie, you just listen to me for a minute, okay? I'll admit right now Jace wasn't too bright, taking the littles off like this, but I guarantee he's takin' good care of them. Do you believe he'd ever deliberately put them into danger? Any of them?"

Kathryn had to deny the possibility. Both Jace and Denny were good boys, mature and responsible for their ages. She allowed herself to be convinced that the only danger facing her children was a mild discomfort. "And if I know the boys," Jon said, "they'll have taken plenty of food. They might get a little cold, though, because we brought the blankets down to be washed and haven't taken them back up to the line shack again."

"But they're so little," she protested, her fright reduced to apprehension. "What if they get scared, all alone up there?"

"Then they'll not be so ready to go along with Jace next time,"

Jon said. "You know those three littles will do anything he suggests."

Yes, she knew. More than once she'd felt another hundred hairs go white when Ginger or Kyle related one of their adventures, all of them courtesy of Jace's fertile imagination. "I don't like it," she said, not yet willing to share Jon's confidence that a night alone in the mountains would be good for her babies.

"Katie, if I thought for a minute that those kids were in any danger at all, I'd ride up there tonight, but I don't. I'll be on the trail at first light, and they'll be home in time for lunch."

She drew a shaky breath. "Promise?"

"I promise. And they'll all be eatin' standing up," he said.

Kathryn didn't feel like laughing, but she couldn't help a smile. "Be my guest," she said. Jon had never laid a hand on any of the children, although he'd often threatened to. And she had a hunch that there had been times Denny, at least, would have far rather had a spanking than some of the more novel punishments Jon assigned. It had taken him much of last summer to reduce a fallen cottonwood to firewood.

With a few more words of reassurance, Jon said good night. "I'll call you when I get 'em back down," he told her. "Probably along about noon."

He hung up, and Kathryn was alone with her fears. No amount of telling herself the children were perfectly safe worked. She lay awake until exhaustion overtook her, her fertile imagination paining pictures of disaster.

How could she sleep when her children were alone in the mountains? Every coyote's call, every rustle of a night creature would bring them to full and terrified wakefulness.

Sometime in the night thunder rumbled, far off in the mountains. It pulled Kathryn out of a restless, nightmare-filled doze. Ginger, absolutely fearless about everything else, was terrified of thunder and lightning.

Toward morning it began to rain. Curiously, Kathryn was

soothed by the gentle patter on her roof and she finally slept soundly. That was why, when the phone rang at six twenty-seven, she practically jumped out of her skin. She hit the alarm clock with her usual groping slap, but the ringing continued until she came alive enough to realize it was the phone.

"Did I wake you?" Erik's baritone pulled her the rest of the way from sleep.

"Um, yeah." She rubbed her eyes, blurry and tender from too many hours of staring into the dark. Yawning, she pulled herself upright and sat on the edge of the bed. "Sorry. I didn't sleep much last night."

"I'm the one who should apologize. But it was call you now or not until tonight."

"'S'all right. The clock would have gone off in a few minutes." She hoped he was calling in response to her message about Wounded Bear Meadow and not because his lawyer had told him to take her to court over the twins.

The twins! Had Jon found them? Looking at the long shadows across a corner of the bedroom, she realized he couldn't have been on the trail for much over an hour, and it was a good two-hour ride up to the line shack. It was too early to be hoping for word.

"I need to know exactly what's going on with the meadow," he said, pulling her thoughts from her children. "Your message was garbled, because the person who took it didn't write it down. By the time we asked her about it, all she could remember was that you said something about the meadow being sold."

She told him what she knew, including her hope that Jethro would keep his word. "But I don't think he'll wait a day beyond the end of September, because his wife has her heart set on being in Arizona before the first snow," she warned.

"I don't think there's a problem. We made enough from Trace's concert that Walt thinks we can qualify for some matching funds from a foundation. He's looking into it and will get back to me as soon as he has any news."

"So I can tell Jethro that you'll have the money by September?" *If he ever comes home,* she added, to herself.

"No, not yet. Give me a few more days. I'm stuck in this trial now, but by the middle of—"

"Trial? What trial?" Was he taking her to court?

"It's a damned nuisance. I'm their expert witness, but they want me to listen...just a minute." His voice faded, as if he'd put his hand over the mouthpiece. She could hear the deep resonance of his voice, but not his words.

Finally, "Look, Kathryn, I've got to go. I'll call you this weekend, okay?"

"Okay." She heard him hang up but she sat, holding the receiver, until the angry blatt of an open line reminded her of where she was. What was wrong with her? She should be relieved that Erik hadn't brought up the subject of child custody, and instead she was disappointed that he hadn't even mentioned the twins.

The twins. How long until she could expect to hear from Jon?

Her jump at Erik's call was nothing to the state of her nerves by eleven. Every time her office phone rang, she snatched up the receiver while it was still ringing. Each time her heart leapt up into her throat and her stomach tightened.

None of the calls were from Jon.

Finally, at eleven-fifteen, she called Janine.

"No, I haven't seen him," her cousin's wife said. "But don't worry, Katie. The littles were on their ponies, and you know how slow they are, compared to a horse."

"But it's been hours," she wailed.

"And if one of the horses threw a shoe, it could be another hour or two." Janine sounded matter-of-fact, and her calm drained the panic from Kathryn. If Janine wasn't worried, why should she be? After all, Abby was only a few weeks older than the twins.

"I'll have him call you the minute he gets in, I promise."

"Thanks. I know I'm being silly, but I just can't help it."

"I'd worry too, if I were in town and not able to do anything."

After a few commonplace exchanges, Kathryn hung up. She was worrying unnecessarily. The twins were just fine. Jace and Denny had taken good care of them, and by now they were in Jon's capable hands.

But she didn't go out to lunch, because she might have missed Jon's call.

She was growing frantic all over again by the time Jon called at a little after three. "Are they all right?" she cried, as soon as she heard his voice.

"Now calm down, Katie. You're not doing those kids a bit of good to carry on like that."

"Something happened! It did, didn't it Jon? Something happened to one of them!"

"I don't think so."

"*You don't think so?* Jon, how could you not know?" Terror burst within her. "Where are my children?" She heard her own voice rise in a shriek on the last word.

"I don't know."

She could not produce a sound, could hardly breathe.

"They weren't at the line shack. I couldn't even find their tracks after they crossed the big meadow up on Skunk Ridge."

"I'm coming out there." She was shoving papers and folders into her desk willy-nilly as she spoke.

"I think you'd better," Jon said. "I've already sent a tracker out. He'll find their trail in no time, but you'll feel better for being here."

Kathryn knew he was just trying to reassure her. Tossing the phone in the general direction of its cradle, she grabbed her purse. If only she had brought the car to work today. Even if she ran most of the way, it would take ten minutes to get home. Another thirty minutes to the Double J.

Oh, God! She needed her riding clothes. Her boots. Thoughts scrambled through her mind while she ran, as fast as her dainty sandals allowed, toward home.

She had to find her children.

It took only moments to tear off her skirt and blouse and replace them with jeans and a long-sleeved shirt. Her boots and slicker in her hand, Kathryn was running out the back door when a thought struck her. Erik!

For a moment she hesitated, then went back inside. He deserved to be told. No matter what came of his claim to be the twins' father, he believed he was.

Why hadn't she gotten his number? Frantically she pawed through the slips of paper stuck into her address book.

Aha! A yellow sticky note emerged, bearing the NWT headquarters number. She dialed, pounded her fist lightly on the telephone table while it rang and rang. Finally an answering machine clicked on.

Impatiently she listened to the message. When it ended at last, she said, "This is Kathryn Pierson in Garnet Falls, Idaho. Please have Erik Solomon call me. It's an emergency."

She had almost hung up when she remembered that he probably didn't have Jon's phone number. Hurriedly she recited it.

Jace was worried. Everything looked so different, with the clouds hanging low over the mountains and the rain making it hard to see more than a half-mile or so.

He'd done the best he could. When the rains began, along toward morning, he'd gotten the others up and had them help him roll up the sleeping bags. He was really glad he'd insisted they all bring their slickers along, 'cause at least they were staying dry, even if they were kinda cold.

"I want to go home," Abby said, her tone very close to a whine.

"Oh, be quiet, Abby," Ginger said. "It's gonna stop raining pretty soon and then we'll be able to explore." She put an arm around her cousin. "Look. It's letting up already."

And it was. Jace was relieved to see that the clouds seemed farther away and not as dark, that the rain was not the heavy curtain it had been.

"I'll bet I could make a fire," Denny said. He showed Jace a handful of dry duff he'd scraped up from under the fallen log that offered them narrow shelter from the storm.

"Not yet," Jace said. First we gotta see if we can find some dry wood to burn.

At his direction, the children scattered, searching under large shrubs and near the trunks of the tall yellow pines. Jace studied the big log. The hollow under it wasn't big enough to hold them all, if it started raining again, but he'd bet he could stretch the tarp across here.

By the time the others came back with their pitiful collection of firewood, Jace had a snug little shelter waiting for them. They might not stay warm, but he'd keep them dry.

"Why haven't you called Wally?" Kathryn demanded.

"Because if Bob Wolfe can't find them, I doubt Blanchett could," he snapped. "Look, Katie, Bob's only been out a couple of hours. He's the best tracker around and he shouldn't have any trouble picking up their trail." He rubbed his hand across his face and Kathryn could see his worry and exhaustion. Had he slept at all last night? "And I've got all the other hands out looking, too."

She regretted her outburst, particularly when Jon put his arm around her and led her toward the house. "I wouldn't even be worried, if it weren't for the rain. It's been falling all night, up there." He gestured toward the high peaks to the west. "The creeks will be rising."

Creeks her children would have to cross on small, inexperienced ponies.

"The hell of it is," he said, holding the back door open for her, "is that I can't figure where they could he headed. Jace doesn't know that country, up back of Skunk Ridge. I've always taken him east, over along Pigeon Creek, when we've gone camping together."

"Are any of your maps missing?" She knew Jon had enlarged topographic maps of his ranch, annotated with his observations.

"I hadn't even thought of that. Let's go see." He led the way to his office. Kathryn wondered, as she followed him, where Janine was.

No maps were missing. But they were out of order. "I wonder," Jon said, when they saw which one was on top. "No, he couldn't have."

Kathryn saw a familiar map, one that matched the still larger map hanging on her office wall. "Wait a minute," she said. She pointed at the upper right corner, beyond the thick red line marking the Double J north property line. "Wounded Bear Meadow. You know, Jace has been really curious about what Erik's been doing."

"And I lost their tracks in the meadow up on Skunk Ridge," Jon said, pointing. "It's possible."

"How far is it?"

"I don't know. Eight to ten miles," Jon answered. His finger traced a path from the circle around his ranch house to the meadow. Between them, the topo lines were crowded and convoluted, signifying steep, mountainous country.

Were her children lost somewhere in those crags and canyons?

Jace didn't see how things could get much worse.

Actually, a lot of their troubles now were Ginger's fault. She'd been the one who talked the hardest to get him to stay and explore instead of starting home like he thought they should.

"We've come all this way," she said, this morning after they'd eaten gorp and oranges for breakfast. "It's not raining any more and I want to see what all the fuss is about. C'mon, Jace, don't be a dope. We can start home this afternoon."

So he'd given in, without much argument. It was what he wanted to do, anyway. Abby had been the only one who'd really objected, and they all knew his little sister was a girlie-girl, not very tough.

They went all the way across the meadow, clear to the bottom of the cliffs on the north side. Denny wanted to go back the long way, but Jace overruled him. "We've got to get started home," he said. "It's gonna be almost dark when we get to the line shack anyhow." And he wasn't sure he could find his way home from there in the dark.

Returning along their own trail, Jace found that creeks could rise a lot in a couple of hours. They had to wade several and once they had to go a long way to find a place shallow enough that it was safe to cross. It was a good thing the sun was shining, because they all got really wet.

"I'm cold," Abby whined, as they were squishing across a grassy field that had been dry when they crossed it before.

"Me, too," Kyle said, "and I'm hungry, too."

Jace didn't notice that the sunshine was fading until a bright flash was followed immediately by a deafening crack of thunder. Abby shrieked, Kyle yelped, and Ginger turned as white as snow and bit her lower lip. Within seconds it became almost as dark as night. Great big raindrops pelted them. Then came the biggest hailstones Jace had ever seen. "Sit down!" he yelled at the others. "Put your arms over your heads." He pushed and shoved until they were huddled close together, then he sat with them and tried to hug them all.

The hailstorm lasted a long time. When it finally quit, it didn't matter that they'd been sitting in puddles, because they were all soaked to the skin. A gentle rain was still falling when Jace ordered the others to join hands and follow him. He had to get them back to the horses and headed toward home.

A door slammed at the back of the house. "Jon?" It was Janine.

"In here," he answered. "Call Wally," he told Kathryn. "Tell him we may need the posse. We'll get back to him as soon as we can, but in the meantime, he should alert them."

"Have you heard anything?" Janine said as she came into the office. "Oh, Katie, I'm so sorry. I shouldn't have left Jace in charge."

Kathryn made the call while Jon told his wife of their newest suspicions, then she spent the next few minutes assuring Janine she didn't blame her for the children's absence. "If I know my daughter," she said, trying to sound calm instead of scared stiff, "this was all her idea." Somehow, her fear was more manageable when she had someone else to be strong for.

"I'm going to see if I can raise anyone on the radios," Jon said, striding out of the office. Kathryn and Janine followed, to end up in the kitchen.

"I'll make some coffee," Kathryn said, needing something to do with her hands. If only she could find something to keep her mind busy, too.

For the next two hours, she and Janine worked together in the kitchen. Their conversation was light, inconsequential. Deliberately so. Kathryn knew, if she were to speak of her fears, to bring them into the light of day, that she might lose what little control she had over her emotions.

At eight Jon came in to report that several of the hands had returned with the news that the creeks were indeed rising. They had seen no sign of the children to the south and west of the ranch. It was too dark to go on searching. They'd begin again at first light.

The tracker couldn't be contacted, but that wasn't surprising. The two-way radios worked only on line of sight, and if he were following a trail along a canyon, he would be completely out of touch.

The rains resumed at midnight. Heavy drenching rains accompanied by rolling thunder and long, jagged lightning bolts. Kathryn overheard Wally tell Jon that he was as concerned with falling rocks loosened by the rain as he was with the steadily rising streams. She contained her fear, barely. She refused to go to bed until Jon, rain dripping from the brim of his hat and his temper short, roared at her about midnight.

"Damn it, Katie! You're not doin' them any good stayin' up all night. Get yourself some rest." He waved his arm toward the ranch yard where volunteers of the Mounted Posse were setting up a communications center. "Everybody else's quitting for the night. It's blacker than Hades out there."

"Don't you tell me what I should or shouldn't do, Jon Pierson! I'm not going to bed until I know they're safe."

"Then stay up, dammit! Tomorrow you won't be worth the rope it'd take to hang you, but don't blame me." He stomped toward the back door.

"Jon," Kathryn called, immediately contrite. "You're right. I'll go to bed. Just wake me if you hear anything. Please?"

He nodded before continuing outdoors.

She did sleep, although the muttering thunder and the steady drum of rain on the roof entered into every dream she had. They were dark, terrifying dreams, filled with threat and danger. In many, she saw her children, but they were always just out of her reach. And always in danger.

* * *

A secretary handed Erik a message slip as he came into the conference room. Call Kathryn? An emergency?

He went to an adjacent office to use the phone.

A woman answered and he asked for Kathryn, identifying himself.

"Oh, Erik, thank heavens you called. Katie's frantic."

He had no idea who he was talking to. Then Kathryn spoke. "Erik? They're lost!" Her anxiety came over the wires as clearly as her voice. "Jon lost their trail in the dark and everything's flooded. You've got to come home!"

"Lost? Who's lost?" For a moment there was no answer.

"Solomon, Jon Pierson here."

Ah, Kathryn's cousin. The rancher. He listened as Pierson told him that the children—*his son*—was missing, could be in deadly danger. Could be already...no, he wouldn't allow that thought.

"I'll be there as soon as I can," he said, interrupting Pierson's account of what was being done to find the children. He ignored the protest and hung up. One call to the airport and he had a plane chartered, another to the car rental company to pick up his car, and a third to discover that a pilot in New Meadows was already on alert to fly search—as soon as the ceiling raised enough to let him.

He didn't ask if it was all right for him to leave, even though he hadn't yet given his expert testimony. He told, and he didn't care if he was slapped with a contempt charge.

His children needed him.

"Dammit, Katie! You don't have the experience!"

"I don't care! Those are my children out there, Jon Pierson, as well as yours. I'm going to help look for them, and you're not big enough to stop me!"

"You just try it, and I'll lock you in your room," Jon said, looking worse than fierce with two days' growth of whiskers caked with mud and his eyes bloodshot.

She wondered if he'd had any sleep at all last night.

"Now, Katie, we need you here," Wally Blanchett said, his voice mild and non-argumentative. "Janine can't keep up with sandwiches and coffee for this crew, and it'll be a few hours before the Posse Auxiliary gets here with the chuck wagon."

"You're joking!" Kathryn couldn't remember feeling so...so insulted. "You want me to stay here and make sandwiches while my children are out there," she waved a hand toward the north, "in danger?"

"Damn straight," Jon growled, slamming his coffee cup onto the drainboard.

"I want everybody to do what he or she's suited to do best," Wally said.

"But I—"

"But you've never spent the hours in the saddle that these folks have," he said, jerking his chin to indicate the members of the Mounted Posse who were unloading horses in the ranch yard. "And you don't know these hills like they do." He paused. "Do you?"

She had to admit he was right. "I just want to help," she said, feeling so helpless, so useless.

"Believe me, Katie, you'll be doing your share, keeping this crew fed," Wally said. "Let's go, Jon. I think I hear the radio."

The two men left the kitchen. Kathryn looked at the empty plates, the pile of coffee cups on the counter. Jon was right, although she hated to admit it. She didn't have the experience or the stamina to help with the search.

Damn!

"Good morning, Katie."

She almost dropped the pile of plates she was taking to the dishwasher. "Amelia!"

"I must be gettin' old," Amelia said, slipping out of a bright blue slicker. "I just don't feel up to spending the day in a wet saddle, so I figured I'd help you and Janine with the food and let the men folk do the dirty work." She put her arms around Kathryn. "They'll be all right, hon. Believe me."

"I keep telling myself that," Kathryn whispered, knowing her voice would tremble if she spoke aloud, "but I don't really believe it."

"You've got to. Otherwise you'll fall apart." She patted Kathryn's back several times, then released her. "Now, since I'm in here to help, not to fool around, what can I do?"

Swallowing hard, Kathryn found that Amelia's briskness gave her strength that Janine's shared apprehension hadn't. "You can load the dishwasher, for a start. I swear, those men took a clean cup every time they came in, all night long."

"Wouldn't surprise me," Amelia agreed, tying an apron around her middle.

"They found Bob Wolfe," Janine said, coming in with a basket full of freshly-gathered eggs.

"Found him? I though he was following the children's trail?" Kathryn's fear, contained for a while, burst forth with renewed force.

Janine set the basket on the counter and began sorting the eggs. "I guess you were asleep when his horse came in, about four," she said. "He had a couple of long scratches on one shoulder, looked like he'd hit a sharp rock pretty hard."

"How is Bob?" Amelia said.

"Broken leg," Jon said from the door, "and exposure. He lay out in the rain for about fifteen hours. Katie, can you set up the big coffeepot out by the radio van? We'll stretch a tarp and set up a table." He was gone again before she could even answer.

"He found the children's tracks before his horse fell with him," Janine said. "They seemed to be headed for Wounded Bear Meadow, all right."

"Then the men will go up there right away?" Surely if they knew where the children were, it was only a matter of hours.

"Some of 'em will, but they're not writing off the other trails up that direction."

Janine brought the fifty-cup percolator out of the basement, and Kathryn set about filling it. Perhaps time would go faster if she kept busy.

CHAPTER TWELVE

Erik felt as if he should get out and push. The small jet he'd chartered seemed interminably slow. It gave him too much time to think.

Was this how his mother had felt when they told her Gail had drowned? Had her chest felt empty, as if the heart had been torn right out of it?

From what he remembered of her, he had trouble believing she had ever felt so intense an emotion other than resentment.

He'd never known he was capable, either.

For the past few days he'd deliberately not thought of his newly discovered fatherhood. It confused him, because he wasn't sure how he really felt about having a child.

Children. No matter how scared he was of the awesome responsibility, he couldn't deny he had two children.

He just wasn't sure he had the ability to love both of them equally. His mother hadn't. He didn't believe, to this day, that she'd had the ability to love even one child. But if she had, it was her daughter, not her son.

She had said, so many time, "I didn't want boys, never should have had a son. God knows, I don't know what to do with you. Wild and noisy and rowdy. Not like your sister, so sweet and quiet."

Gail had been quiet, all right, but never sweet. She'd been as big a hellion as he, only with the sense not to misbehave when their mother could catch her at it. He'd heard someone say, once, that So-and-So had been "born civilized." That was Gail. She learned from others' mistakes, knew when to be quiet and ladylike, and slipped through life as slick as soap under a wet foot.

She'd fooled his mother, that was certain. After her death, he'd heard, over and over, "She was such a good child, like all little girls. Why can't you be sweet and gentle like she was?"

There were other kinds of child abuse than physical.

Intellectually he now knew his mother had been mentally ill. Emotionally he was still fighting her lingering influence on his reaction to little girls. He could admire them from afar—they were one of nature's miracles—but he simply could not interact with them. His body's reaction was peculiarly similar to an animal's fight or flee dilemma in a dangerous situation.

Look how uncomfortable he'd been when he'd met his own daughter for the first time. He'd been virtually tongue-tied, until he deliberately ignored her and spoke only to Kyle.

That's why he would be doing the right thing by leaving Ginger to her mother's care, assuming he obtained shared custody of Kyle. No little girl deserved the kind of unfit parent he might be. He would explain. Surely he could make her understand it wasn't that her father didn't love her, but that he didn't believe he could be a good parent.

He looked at his watch again. Surely the plane could go faster than this!

The helicopter was fueled and ready at McCall. Erik held little hope that they'd be able to fly in to Garnet Falls, let alone get up into the mountains where the search was going on. The cloud layer was the thickest Erik could remember seeing.

"We wait," the middle-aged pilot said, confirming Erik's suspicion. "I checked with the weather service while you were landing. They said it'd start clearing sometime this afternoon."

At least the rain had stopped, although the full roadside ditches and flooded fields told of hours of heavy precipitation. Erik checked his watch. Noon, and the clouds looked awfully permanent. "Maybe I should rent a car," he said, thinking out loud.

"Already checked that too. There aren't any available." His cigar, which Erik had never seen lit, shifted from one side of his mouth to the other. "If it keeps lifting like it has been, we should be able to get to Garnet Falls by following along the highway in an hour or so. My fuel truck's already on the way over. You had lunch?"

Erik couldn't even remember having breakfast. "I could use some coffee," he admitted, feeling spent. He probably should eat a sandwich, too. Falling on his face was no way to help search for the children.

To his surprise, the clouds did thin while they were eating. The pilot decided to try to make it to Garnet Falls and immediately went into his preflight. Erik stood watching, wishing he could help, just for something to do. Idle, all he could do was imagine the worst.

As a hydrologist, he was intimately aware of what a heavy rain could mean in the mountains. Every stream would be in flood, rocks would be rolling down steep hillsides, and mudslides might even be blocking trails. And there were five children out there, God only knew where.

They managed to get to Garnet Falls, although Erik suspected his pilot was relying on memory more than landmarks when he took them over the divide between Payette Lake and Goose Creek. Instead of setting down on the landing strip east of town, they swooped over the low ridge and headed out along Skunk Creek Road. Not too much later the Double J ranch buildings came into view. Erik could see a number of pickups, some of them attached to horse trailers, parked in the space between house and barn.

Several people waved as they circled and one man pointed toward a corral behind the barn. Another ran in that direction. Soon they were sitting in the corral, the helicopter's blades still turning as Wally Blanchett bent low to approach the cockpit.

"Good thing you made it," he shouted. "The creek's got the canyon blocked and the trail over the ridge isn't passable."

"Which ridge?" the pilot yelled back.

"That one Wounded Bear Creek cuts through. We're pretty sure the kids are up there somewhere. I've got some men trying to get in from Jethro's, but you know how rough that country is."

Just then another uniformed man came up with a bundle of blankets.

"Out you go, Solomon," Blanchett said, gesturing.

"I'm paying for this helicopter and I intend to be on it when we find them." Erik took the blankets and stowed them behind his seat. "Let's not waste any more time."

The pilot shrugged, obviously not caring who his passenger would be. The sheriff glared at Erik, his eyes narrowed as if he were measuring Erik's competence and stubbornness. Finally he too shrugged. "We'll keep trying to get a team in there over the ridge. Don't take any stupid chances."

"I'll do what I have to do," was all Erik would promise. The important thing was getting the children out.

"I'll send Steve out, then. He's got some EMT training."

Surprised at the sheriff's capitulation, Erik went aft to check out the hoist. He wanted to be ready when they got to Wounded Bear Meadow. There wasn't any doubt in his mind that the children were there.

* * *

Kathryn reached the gate to the corral as Steve Lindholm walked out to the helicopter. "I'm going with them," she said.

"Now, Katie," Wally said, "don't start that again. You don't have any training. You'd only get in the way."

"And you're not their mother, Wally Blanchett," she snarled. "It's not open to debate. I'm going." Jerking her arm free of his hold, she ran across the corral. There was plenty of room for her. And she *had* taken the advanced Red Cross First Aid course. The small duffel in her hand was filled with everything she could think of that might be needed once they found the children.

She grabbed the door just as Steve was pulling it closed. Quickly she climbed in, pushing past him to take a seat.

"What do you think you're doing?"

The familiar voice came from behind her. "Erik?" Kathryn dropped the seat harness and turned around. "Erik? What are you doing here?"

"That's what I asked you. Hold it," he yelled as the aircraft lifted.

"Don't you start. Those are *my* children out there and I'm as qualified as you to be here."

"They're mine, too,"

His face held a grim resolve that Kathryn had never seen before. She ignored it. "Are we going to sit here and bicker," she asked, knowing she could never win if she argued with him so she was willing to resort to emotional blackmail, "or are we going to rescue the children?"

Erik stared at her a moment, then gestured to the pilot. She felt the helicopter lift and breathed a secret sigh of relief.

The radio crackled several times as they skimmed close to treetops and ridges. Kathryn couldn't understand one word in three, but Erik evidently did. "The trail up to the meadow's blocked from the Z-Bar-Z too. It'll probably be tomorrow before they can get in on horseback," he said. He turned his back and continued whatever he was doing just behind the wide door.

Kathryn was left alone with her thoughts. *Oh, God, let my babies be all right!*

Abby was crying again. Kyle still managed to keep his own tears hidden from her, but it was getting harder all the time.

If only the horses hadn't run away. They could have gone across the creek, no matter how high it was, on Smoke and Taffy. But when they came back from their exploration of the meadow, the only two left were the ponies, Cooter and Sneaky. Jace said that Dumbo and the horses probably spooked when the lightning and thunder struck so close.

At least the creek hadn't come much higher. For a while there, after the logs had come thundering down and stuck in the bend, Kyle had been afraid he and Abby would have to climb a tree to stay out of the water.

"I want to go home," Abby said, for about the millionth time.

"Me too," he admitted. "Do you s'pose they're gonna find a way across the creek?" he said. He wished he knew where they'd gone after Jace had gestured that he and Ginger and Denny were going to try to find another way across the creek that had suddenly turned into a raging river.

That had been yesterday, close to dark. Kyle and Abby had waited for a long time, until it got too dark to see. Then they'd crawled under the tarp and huddled together, slowly growing warmer as their clothes began to dry. But sometime in the night he'd gone to sleep and their feeble fire had gone out. He hadn't been able to build a new one, because they'd used all the dry wood.

Sometime after it got light, he and Abby had opened and eaten a can of beef stew. It still sat in his tummy like a cold lump of ice. "I want my mother," he whispered, not wanting Abby to hear.

"Listen!" Abby's chin came up. "What's that noise?"

Kyle listened. It sounded like an airplane. He crawled out from under the tarp and looked all around the sky. Clouds still sat on the hills surrounding the meadow and everywhere he looked, he could see nothing but water.

The sound grew louder. Not an airplane. A helicopter!

Erik didn't know what to say to Kathryn. He wanted to reassure her that they would find the children safe and sound, but he couldn't. He knew how fragile life was, and how easy it was for a child to make the wrong choice and pay for it with his life. Hell, he'd seen a couple of adults who'd paid for mistakes with life or limb.

They topped the last ridge and Wounded Bear Meadow opened before them. It was a lake! Only the copse of trees where he and Kathryn had eaten their lunches was visible above the swirling, churning muddy waters. As they headed that way, his eyes swept over the entire valley. A few patches of willow also seemed to be above water, but he saw nothing that might indicate there were children here.

Had they been erroneously pinning their hopes on a few indistinct tracks and an injured man's almost incoherent account of a trail seen before he was thrown?

He saw Steve gesture. As the helicopter rotated, he lost sight of the copse, but was able to see that several other small, isolated islands still rose above the flood.

"There!" Kathryn's joyous cry brought him to her side. She was pointing. "I see two of them."

The pilot nodded his comprehension. Steve called the ranch while Erik went aft to rig the hoist. They'd already agreed he would be the one to go down if they couldn't land.

Where in hell were the other three?

Hell? Erik stared out over the valley. This was the wettest hell he'd ever seen. The water seemed to be backing up from the outlet through the ridge, probably dammed by debris where the creek had cut a steep gorge through the narrow limestone outcrop. It would be days before it drained enough that a helicopter could set down.

It was a good thing he'd done this before, he thought as he checked the line he would descend on. Rappelling down a swaying cable wasn't something that came naturally. He'd spent a long afternoon learning just what he could and couldn't do, before his instructor had let him down into that canyon in Montana to collect the stream gaging instruments. At the time, he'd sworn he'd never again play spider monkey.

As he hesitated at the door, Kathryn caught at his arm. He looked at her, seeing fear. And something else.

She said something to him, but her words were drowned out by the roar of the helicopter's engine through the open door. He shook his head.

She pulled at him, and he bent. Her lips touched his briefly, and her words penetrated the roar. "Bring them back, please, Erik. Bring our children back safely."

He nodded. He'd do his damndest.

Before he could think about it again, he let himself slide from the door and dangle on the cable.

The helicopter inched closer to the trees, setting Erik spinning slowly. He watched, knowing it would be a near thing whether he was able to find solid footing or would have to swing across the water and drop, like Tarzan from a vine.

As he drew nearer the island, he saw the children clearly. One of them was his son! Kyle was safe. But the other was not his daughter. For the first time he realized the icy knot of fear beneath his breastbone was for all the children, not just Kyle. And in that moment, he knew he could love Ginger as she should be loved.

The cable began to swing and he let himself slip lower. Soon he was passing over the edge of the wooded island every few seconds. He dropped lower yet, until he had to pull his feet up to keep them dry. One more swing, and he let himself fall, tumbling onto the narrow strip of wet grass between the creek and the trees.

Quickly he removed the blankets he'd wrapped around his upper body. The girl first. She clung to him, making it more difficult to enclose her in the warm wool. He handed Kyle a second blanket, telling him to wrap it around himself.

"We've got sort of a tent back in the trees," Kyle said, his voice trembling.

"Good. Can you show me?" He held the girl in one arm and grabbed the rest of the blankets with the other hand. Two steps and his feet were soaked. For a moment he regretted not taking time to change. Surely someone at the ranch would have had something more suitable for swamp stomping than his tasseled loafers.

At least one of the kids had some woods savvy he realized when he saw the sturdy canvas lean-to. A patch of ashes at one side showed that they'd had a fire, for a little while at least. He set the little girl down and slipped out of his knapsack. Quickly he inventoried its contents. "Where are the others?" he said as he began carving thin splinters from the underside of the fallen log.

"I don't know," Kyle said, sounding close to tears.

He told Erik how the older boys had held hands across the flooding creek, letting him and Abby cling to them as they half-floated, half-climbed across the human bridge. Then Kyle had seen the logs coming and Jace had barely gotten back to the other side before they tumbled by and stuck in the bend, just below the island. After that the water had risen swiftly and Jace had gestured that they were going upstream to see if they could find another crossing. Kyle had walked clear up to the end of the island on his side, and had watched them pass out of sight, still seeking a way across.

All the while Erik was cutting slivers for a fire. When he had a sufficient number, he pulled the sawdust and wax fire starter from the knapsack. Soon tiny flames were licking at the damp sticks he carefully fed them. When Kyle's account ended, Erik cupped a hand across his mouth. That had been eighteen hours ago. The trees sheltering Abby and Kyle were the only dense stand in the valley, other than willow thickets along some branches of the creek. That meant the other three children had been out in the rain all night without shelter, without fire, without food.

And the water had been rising all that time.

Kathryn chewed her knuckle. Erik had disappeared into the woods with the children. The helicopter was slowly flying in a circle, accomplishing nothing. She knew hysteria wouldn't help, but she wanted to indulge anyway. God knew she couldn't do anything constructive, and a short bout of hysteria might make her feel better.

The radio crackled. Not one word was intelligible, but from the alertness of the two men in front, she knew they must be hearing something important. Steve unstrapped his harness and came to kneel beside her seat. "It's two of the little kids down there. They're okay—just cold and hungry. But the others..." He shook his head. "We'll keep lookin'"

She grabbed his arm. "Which ones are...are safe?" She knew it shouldn't matter, but it did. Oh God, it did.

"Dunno. Erik didn't say." He went back to the door and began preparing to follow Erik to the ground. Kathryn was left to wonder if both her children were safe, or only one. And which one?

Again they hovered as Steve descended.

With her face pushed against the window, Kathryn stared across the almost unrecognizable meadow. They were pulling away from the copse, the downwash of their rotor making even the roiling, rushing water flatten and appear calm. As they drew farther away and climbed higher, she saw Erik emerge from the woods to meet Steve.

He waved, pointed upstream. Steve gestured, shook his head.

"Damn fool!" She heard the pilot clearly. The helicopter tipped in a sharp turn.

"What are you doing?"

He handed her the headset. As soon as she had it on, he said, "We're goin' to circle around and see if we can find the other youngsters," he said. "Erik says they went up that way." He pointed toward where the water was a turbulent sheet over what had been a wide meadow the last time she'd seen it. Only a few brushy clumps marred the new lake's surface. "Last night."

"But what about—?" Wordlessly she gestured at the trees, which concealed the two children and the deputy.

"They'll be okay with Steve while we take a look around. After we refuel, Wally and me'll pick 'em up. Erik's gonna see if he can find trace of the other three."

She hadn't thought she could be more frightened.

A long, thin log was caught in a tangle of brush and debris at the edge of the island. Erik measured the distance between him and the shallows beyond the flood channel. The log just might span it. He went to work.

The water was almost too swift. More than once it tried to tear the log from his grasp. But he shoved, and guided, and grunted, until finally he had the log wedged into the muddy streambank on his side. He hoped it was as securely seated on the other end. He could move it no farther, but that didn't mean it was fixed.

He stared at the log. It was almost completely submerged, the water spilling over it in a silvery sheet. Turning around, he looked back toward the shelter where Kyle and Abby were safe. Steve would care for them until the helicopter returned.

Erik had a space blanket and one wool blanket in his knapsack, several high energy bars, and a liter of water. A first-aid kit. His Buck knife was attached to his belt. Strips torn off one blanket were wrapped around his feet, better traction than leather-soled loafers.

One last deep breath and he straddled the log, feeling the icy water soak up along his legs. It gave when the current caught him, but it didn't break free. Inch by inch, he crossed, until his legs found a bottom. Then he scrambled onto not-so-solid ground under a foot of calmer water, no longer in danger of being swept away.

From hummock to hummock, from shrub to thicket, he made his slow way across the valley. Every few feet he stopped to call, until his throat hurt and his voice was a scratchy croak. He grew colder, then he no longer noticed. Sometimes he had to go far out of his way to find a route across wide channels, and once he was swept a quarter-mile downstream before he could grab a dangling willow and inch his way onto solid footing.

A flash of yellow caught his eye. He eased himself into yet another channel, this one only about five feet wide and as deep. The current was less strong than in most, so he was only swept a few feet as he half-waded, half-swam across. In an elderberry bush, caught on a branch that would be waist level to him under ordinary circumstances, a yellow, billed cap dangled, its Big Bird emblem one he'd seen before. On Ginger's head, the Fourth of July.

For a moment he held it close to his heart, wondering what he would do if he never found the other children. Never found his daughter.

No! He went on, determined not to think of the worst possibility.

One of the horses had not escaped the flood. He saw its carcass bobbing among a mass of debris behind an overflowing but still-intact beaver dam. He refused to allow himself to look for the children's bodies as well. They were alive. They had to be.

Working his way upstream, he managed to cross that channel about a quarter mile above the backed-up stream. The helicopter's drone drew nearer, and he knew it was still circling, still seeking. When it circled overhead, he looked up. The sky seemed lighter, as if the clouds were thinning.

An arm waved from the cockpit. It pointed, circled. Erik shook his head. God, but he was stupid! What was the pilot trying to tell him?

Another gesture. Ah! Time to refuel. He waved, surprised at how heavy his arm seemed.

Although he knew it would be less than an hour before it returned, he felt abandoned when the helicopter swept over the ridge and out of sight. He looked around him. Where was he?

The steep ridge at the lower end of the meadow was farther away than the last time he'd checked his location. He was making progress, although it sometimes seemed he lost five feet for every six he advanced, so twisted and meandering was the route he'd been forced to follow.

He called again, knowing his hoarse croak couldn't be heard over the rush of the waters for any distance. "Jace! Dennis! Ginger!" *Oh, God!* "Ginger!" He slogged on, the strips of blanket long since lost from his feet. It didn't matter. The cold water had robbed him of any feeling below the knees anyway.

More channels. Twice more he fought to snatch at overhanging branches, to save himself from being swept away. Once he found himself praying, although it had been many years since he had done so. "Let me find them. Please. Let me find them."

"No! I'm going back with them!" Kathryn shook Jon's hand from her arm. "My children need me!"

"Mine are out there, too," her cousin said.

His calm words stopped her as excitement would not have. She saw the exhaustion in his face, the fear. All night long, he'd been searching, in the dark and the rain. All day he'd been here, waiting. How did he stay so calm?

"Katie, let the men do their job," he said, putting his arm around her. "There's no room for you in that chopper, not this trip." He gestured. "Alf and Wally are trained. You're not. They'll go down and search, along with Erik and find the kids."

He didn't have to say the rest. She read the fading hope in his face. She knew that, with each hour, the chances of finding the other three children safe were shrinking.

"You come on in here, now, and warm up. 'Twon't do a bit of good for you to wear yourself to a frazzle." Jethro's arm went around her. She hadn't even known he was here. With a sigh, she let herself be led into the ranch house.

Amelia was talking quietly with Janine at the table. Janine looked as desperately frightened as she felt, but Kathryn could find no words to reassure her. She nodded to Amelia, and followed Jethro into the front room.

"Those youngsters are gonna be just fine," he said, wrapping an afghan around her and pushing her gently into Jon's big leather recliner, seating himself on the arm. "If that Solomon fella hasn't found 'em by the time the chopper gets back, then Wally and Alf and Steve will help him out. They ain't gonna give up until they find 'em."

She saw the mantel clock over his shoulder. Four. It would be dark in another four hours. Her babies couldn't survive another night in the open. "Oh, Jethro!" she wailed. The tears she'd stanched all day flooded forth.

He picked her up and slid into her chair. His still-strong arms gathered her against his chest, comforting her as if she were still a child. "Now you just have yourself a good cry, Katie, and stop that frettin'. They're gonna be all right."

Somehow she believed him more than she had any one else. She wiped her eyes. "I want to believe you." she faltered.

"You do it, hear? The good Lord ain't gonna take them youngsters away from you." His callused hand stroked her hair. She leaned against his flannel shirt, its faint scent of sunlight and tobacco-in-a-can reminding her of Jesse. He'd smelled this same way.

"I was just thinkin'. That Solomon fella might be the best one to find the youngsters," he said, after a few moments' contemplation. "Him bein' a wetland expert and all."

She wished he hadn't mentioned Erik again. Her terror for the children was no greater than her anxiety for him. "But what if something happens?" She could not complete the question.

"You fallin' in love with him, girl?" Jethro's gruff question forced her to pull free of his comforting embrace.

"I...I think I fell in love with him a long time ago," she said. She could no longer deny, even to herself, that the feelings she'd had for him almost at first sight had never entirely died.

"Don't you think it's about time you told me all about it?"

Another kind of fear caught in her throat. "All about what?"

"You think I ain't got eyes, girl? If that Solomon fella ain't the twins' pa, he's a damn close relation."

Kathryn stared. Of all the people in the world who should have been angry at her betrayal of Jesse's memory, Jethro had the best reason.

"I worried about you," he said, "back then after Jesse was taken." One wide hand gripped his nape, rubbed. "You took it too danged hard. Didn't seem to be gettin' over it like you should have. You wantin' to be inseminated worried me some, but not as much as the way you dragged around, half dead yourself."

"Oh, Jethro, I didn't mean to trouble you." He had lost his cherished son. She hadn't been the only one grieving.

"Shoot fire, girl! You didn't trouble me. I hurt for you as much as for me." Again the rubbing of his nape. "Katie, you're as much a daughter to me as my own's ever been. And I'm no fonder of my blood grandchildren than I am of Kyle and Ginger."

She leaned against him. Her biggest fear—after the possibility that she might lose custody of her children—was that Jethro might never forgive her for betraying Jesse's memory. "I don't think there's much doubt he's their father." There! It hadn't hurt to say it. Probably because, sometime in the past terror-filled day and night, she'd accepted the reality of Kyle's appearance, of Erik's claim. "Will you ever forgive me?"

"Forgive you? For what? You didn't do nothin' to hurt me, and Jesse was gone. You couldn't lay yourself in his grave, alongside him."

A tiny glimmer of peace woke inside her. For the first time she really believed that the children could be safe.

Erik would find them. He had to.

CHAPTER THIRTEEN

Erik fell,his foot sinking into deep mud. For a moment it seemed almost too much to ask of his exhausted body to rise. But there was a stick poking him in the gut and so he rolled, struggled, and finally came up onto one knee. That's when the sound finally penetrated his misery and hopelessness.

He looked around, seeking the source. The island he was on was small, one side bordered by the overflowing beaver pond, the other higher, still several feet above the flood. He made it to his feet, climbed the low rise.

The water had cut through a larger island, leaving a steep-sided channel, was still cutting, for even as he watched, a clump of soil fell from the edge of the next island. All that seemed to be holding it from total destruction were several fair sized pines, surrounded by a narrow but dense willow thicket.

He looked again. Beyond the willows, nearly hidden by tangled stems and gray-green leaves, he saw a spot of color. He shouted, "Ginger! Jace! Dennis!"

"Help!" This time he heard clearly. The color moved, resolved itself into a child's arms and body, burrowing through the dense branches. "Help! Help!"

Ginger emerged, her face scratched and pale, her coat torn. Erik had never seen a better sight in his life.

She came to the edge of the island, jumped back when another clod broke off and fell into the raging creek.

"Stay there!" he yelled. "Are the others all right?"

She called something, but the sound of the water drowned her words. But her nod was enough. They were all safe!

Erik set three flares while he walked the length of his island, seeking a way across to the children. He wondered how they had come this far in relative safety. In that same time, both islands grew appreciably smaller, though his seemed to be shrinking at a faster rate than the one holding the children. Probably because there were no willows where he stood.

Finally the 'copter found them. It circled, while the sheriff peered out the door. There was no place for it to land because of the tall pines. Erik watched while Wally attached something to the hoist that extended out over the door. Soon a cable began to descend, a pointed, silvery device dangling from it—a forest penetrator, he remembered it being called.

When the penetrator touched ground, Erik saw how three flanges could fold out, revealing webbing straps. He waved his understanding, then called out to Ginger, pointing at the device. While she watched, he straddled a flange. The webbing went around his waist and he wrapped his arms around the round body of the penetrator. "Ginger!" he called. She nodded her understanding.

Oh, God! She was only seven years old. Would she be able to tell the boys what to do? Would they listen?

Dismounting, he folded the flanges back up and released his hold on the cable. Slowly the penetrator rose and swung across the stream. After twice being deflected by the dense willows, it finally slipped between two pines and disappeared from his sight.

Erik waited, watching while both islands grew steadily smaller. The water seemed higher, and swifter. Finally Wally waved from the open door of the 'copter. The penetrator rose slowly from the treetops, three children clinging to it, their arms and legs tangled together.

He could do nothing more. Except pray.

Now that his task was complete, now that his children were safe, Erik realized just how cold, how tired he was. A bone deep exhaustion swept over him and he sank to his knees.

The world seemed to tilt. That was when he realized that more than exhaustion was affecting him.

Upstream a logjam broke free. He saw the mad tumble of dirty foam and black-wet logs just as it struck the pitiful remnant of his island. He saw the penetrator, starting to descend for him.

He saw the thick branch, just before it struck him.

"We'll find him." Kathryn heard Wally's promise, but she didn't believe it. Couldn't believe it.

"You left him," she said, again. "You left him up there to die!"

"Dammit, Katie, Steve's still looking. And the chopper's on its way back. Those kids needed medical attention."

Guiltily she looked toward the ambulance, where the EMTs readied her daughter and nephews for the trip to the clinic in town. They'd chased her away, told her not to hover.

There hadn't been room in the helicopter for Abby and Kyle. They would be brought out on the next trip. Steve's last radio message had assured her they were both safe and comfortable, now that they'd been fed and wrapped in dry blankets.

"You coming, Kathryn?" The EMT was closing the doors of the ambulance.

She was torn. To go to the clinic with Ginger, to stay until Kyle was brought in? Until Erik was found.

"I am," Janine called, running from the house, her purse and a jacket in one hand.

"Then I'll wait for Kyle," Kathryn said. Wait for Kyle and word about Erik.

He *had* to be alive!

Warm. His back was warm.

He'd been cold for so long. And wet.

Slowly he became conscious of water pulling at his feet and legs, trying to drag him along in its rush.

Erik clawed himself higher, away from the water's clutch, feeling the cuts as his hands slipped along sharp edges of long, narrow leaves, the only things he could catch hold of.

God, but his head hurt!

His body screamed protest as he rolled to his back. A lowering sun shone bright in his eyes, the source of the warmth.

Why was he lying in the sedges? He was supposed to meet the attorneys for the county at two. It had to be later than that, but how much later? Turning his head, he tried to see his watch without raising an arm that weighed a ton. His wrist was bare, below the jagged end of a torn sleeve.

And why was the water so loud? Blackwater Swamp had no running water.

Where the hell was he?

He tried to sit up, but as soon as he lifted his head, the world spun and sharp pain radiated from his forehead. Dragging his hand along his body, he inspected the source of the pain. His fingers came away bloody.

The mere touch again caused the world to spin. Erik felt his hold on reality slipping.

Sometime later, when the warmth was all gone, he woke again. Someone was leaning over him, someone vaguely familiar.

"Can you move?" the man demanded.

Erik tried. He really did.

"Wake up, man! Can you move?" The man's voice was insistent.

With an effort, Erik raised himself on one elbow, but the pain in his head sapped his strength and he flopped back down.

"Move your legs!"

He did, although it cost him most of his strength.

"Arms!"

Again he complied.

"Turn your head!"

That didn't hurt as much as lifting it. Not quite.

The man did painful things to his body after that. At one point Erik felt as if he was being lifted into the air, but he refused to open his eyes. Hallucinations hurt almost as much as the reality that kept fading in and out. It was easier to keep the world shut out. That way the man didn't ask him to do things that hurt.

Once he thought he heard Kyle's voice. But never Ginger's.

Who were Kyle and Ginger?

Someday, a long time later, he felt a gentle hand on his cheek. "You're going to be all right, Erik," a hauntingly familiar voice said.

"I'm staying here," Kathryn said, glaring back at Dr. Franklin.

Slipping an arm around her shoulders, he led her to a chair in the brightly lit hall. "Then you're going to do what I say. This is my hospital." He pushed and she found herself unable to resist sitting.

"Only if you'll let me in to see him."

"As soon as he's in his room, you can do anything you want but climb into bed with him," Ed Franklin agreed.

Kathryn fought the urge to burst into laughter. Into tears.

She clutched at the doctor's sleeve. "He's really going to be all right, Ed?"

"He's going to hurt like hell for a few days, and be on crutches for a couple of weeks. Other than that, it's just a matter of letting time heal the cuts and bruises."

The doctor stood, shaking his head when Kathryn started to do the same. She relaxed back into the chair, grateful for its support. She was *so* tired!

"When can I take him home?" When she took Ginger and Kyle home, tomorrow morning, she wouldn't be able to stay at Erik's bedside. But if she had him on the sofa bed in her sewing room, she wouldn't be torn between her children and the man she loved.

"We'll see. I want to keep an eye on him until we're sure he doesn't develop pneumonia," Ed said. He looked down at her as if he were trying to decide something. "Look, Kathryn, I probably don't have any business saying this, but is there something between you two?"

Kathryn felt the hot blood rush to her face. "I love him," she said, not knowing what else to say.

"That's pretty obvious," the doctor said. "But there's more, isn't there? Something's coming between you."

Kathryn nodded. "We've got some problems to work out," she admitted. "But nothing major. We'll be fine."

He seemed doubtful, making Kathryn wonder what Erik had told him.

"I hope so. He was pretty wild for a while there, before we got him sedated. I don't think he was aware of what he was saying, but he kept yelling that something was his, and you weren't going to take them away from him."

"Did he..." Kathryn swallowed the enormous lump that had somehow formed in her throat. "Did he say what he thought I was trying to take away?"

"No. Just, 'They're mine. Don't take them away. They're mine,' over and over. Sometimes he'd plead with you to let him share 'them'." Ed was obviously trying not to let his curiosity get the best of him.

Kathryn chewed her lip. She'd already told her lawyer and Jon. Jethro had figured it out all on his own. How long before the whole town knew the identity of the twins' father?

Motion down the short hallway caught Kathryn's attention. The two EMTs emerged from Erik's room pushing an empty gurney. She half rose.

"Go ahead," Ed said. "Just don't disturb him tonight."

Kathryn almost ran to the still-closing door. Barely inside she stopped. Light from behind her shone on the bed, and the man it held.

He lay so still. Bandages covered his forehead, one arm, and the other shoulder. The sheet, pulled just above his waist, was tented over his legs, and she knew that the left one was encased in a cast. She tiptoed to the bed, stood next to him. An IV was inserted into the back of his left hand. His face was gaunt, with scratches marring his cheeks and chin.

The room was silent. Carefully she laid one hand on his chest, needing reassurance that he was indeed breathing. His skin was cool and his heart beat slow but strong under her palm.

Without thinking, she leaned over and kissed him, feeling his breath on her cheek, soft and faint. "I love you, Erik Solomon," she whispered, her lips almost touching his, "and I'm going to marry you."

She stood beside him for a while longer, before going back to the room that held her children.

How was she going to tell them they had a father?

Erik called, "Come!" in response to the light tap on his door. Dr. Franklin had told him arrangements were being made for his release this afternoon, but wouldn't give him details. Why did medical people act as if being injured diminished one's intelligence? He'd noticed the phenomenon before, and he hadn't liked it then, either.

The door opened and Jethro Zenger stepped into his room. "Mornin', young fella," he said. Without being told to, he pulled the straight chair the Sunset County Clinic deemed appropriate for visitors to the side of Erik's bed and sat. "You gonna live?"

Biting back a chuckle, Erik admitted he probably would. "I'm not sure I want to, though. Everything hurts."

"That was a brave thing you did," Jethro said.

Erik felt himself blush. The volunteer who'd brought his breakfast had been full of comments on his heroism and he hadn't known quite what to say in response. He had only dim memories of anything since the night before the Fourth. And they were tangled with all too familiar nightmares. A child spilling from a boat and being carried away. His throat growing raw from his screams as he called, "Gail, Gail! Ga-a-ail-l-l!" over and over until strong hands pried his fingers from the gunwales of the old rowboat and pulled his shivering body from the rushing water. A new vision, of a pixie-face peering through tangled willows, scratched and bruised, but wearing a smile bright enough to light up all outdoors. Then tumbling, churning debris, sweeping down on him, and after that, nothing. Nothing except pain and cold. He'd been cold, so cold.

Even now he felt as if he'd never be completely warm again.

He now knew he'd rescued the Pierson children from a flood, but the details eluded him. The praise for his bravery embarrassed him, since he remembered none of it. He almost felt as if he should deny doing anything out of the ordinary, since his cast wouldn't let him scuff his toe in the dust and mutter, "Shucks, 'twarn't nothin."

Jethro's next words brought him back to reality

"'Course, you'd 'a been a lot smarter to leave it to them as is trained to do that sort of thing."

This time he chuckled, and never mind how much it hurt. "Mr. Zenger, that's exactly what I've been telling myself ever since I woke up in this bed," he said.

They chatted of inconsequentials for several minutes. Jethro explained why the children had needed rescuing, and Erik found that he could remember snatches of a nightmare time when he'd been almost bereft of hope.

"Jon Pierson, he grounded the lot of 'em," Jethro said. "No Little League, no camping, and no floatin' down the Boise River for them this summer." Jethro leaned back and scowled. "Course, I woulda' tanned their little bottoms good, but then I'm not their folks."

Erik agreed that the kids would probably prefer to be spanked. Five more weeks of summer vacation and no place to go. How he would have hated that at their ages.

Once the subject of the children had been thoroughly covered, Jethro sat silent for a minute or so. He seemed to be thinking. Erik was also silent, relieved that Jethro didn't seem to require entertainment. He liked the old man, found him comfortable to be with.

Eventually Jethro reached into the inside pocket of his vest and pulled forth an envelope. Tapping it on his palm, he studied Erik, eyes narrowed.

"Doc Franklin tells me you can't remember what happened?"

Erik nodded. The only vivid memory he had was of Kathryn's voice, telling him he would be all right. Telling him the children were safe.

"Well, that's probably for the best. Both you and Katie said some things that oughta be forgot, and if you're smart, you will, even after your memory comes back." He cleared his throat. "Now, then, I got somethin' to say."

Erik waited.

"Those kids of Katie's, they're just like my own kin," Jethro said. "I reckon Jesse would have been proud to claim them."

Remembering the warmth that had drawn him, a lonely, friendless teen, into Jesse's orbit, Erik had to agree. "He was a good man."

Jethro nodded. "Right from the first I thought of them as my grandkids, even though they're none of my blood. I guess that makes you some kind of shirt-tail kin, too."

For a moment, his words failed to penetrate Erik's comprehension. When they did, they triggered a burst of memory, so that everything that had happened in the past two weeks was totally, painfully clear. Before he could say anything, before he could even think how to respond, Jethro handed him the envelope.

"You can think of that as a thank-you for savin' those youngsters, if you want, or you can call it their inheritance," he said, holding Erik's gaze. "I don't care. But you take good care of it, and don't never let it be changed."

He stood and put his hat on.

"I told the missus last night that we got more money than we'll ever be able to spend, if we live to be a hundred," he went on. "I figure a man has to do more than leave behind his kin when he goes, and I haven't done nothin'.

"I'd take it as a kindly gesture if you'd put up some kind of memorial to my boy, out there in your preserve."

He was out the door before Erik found his voice. With trembling hands, Erik tore the envelope open. It contained a deed—a deed to Wounded Bear Meadow, "for the sum of one dollar and services rendered."

Kathryn caught her breath when she saw him. Now that she acknowledged the relationship, she couldn't get over how much he and Kyle looked alike. Why hadn't she seen it before?

"What are you doing here?" Even in a wheelchair, covered with bandages and bruises, Erik radiated strength and charm. And impatience.

"I came to get you. Didn't Ed tell you?" She frowned at the doctor, who shrugged sheepishly. The coward! "You're staying at my house until you get your walking cast."

"No way!" Snatching his crutches, he struggled to stand up. "I'm going to my apartment."

"Not without help," Ed said, shoving him back into the chair with a hand on his shoulder. "You didn't read the fine print. I released you with stipulations." Kathryn heard the laughter in his voice.

Erik was still muttering rebelliously as he struggled into her car. She wondered if she was making a mistake.

No. She was doing the only thing she could. Giving them time together to settle their differences. At least that had been the theory, when she'd volunteered to care for him until he was free of the crutches.

"Supper's ready."

Erik looked up from the book he'd been halfheartedly reading. Agatha Christie was not his favorite mystery writer, but it had been lying on the coffee table, easier to lay his hand on than those in the book case across the room.

He reached for his crutches and found himself reminded that his upper arm had eleven stitches holding it together.

"Are you all right?" Kathryn's quick question told him she'd seen his wince of pain.

Ignoring another twinge from the stitches, he swung himself upright. Blood drained from his head and he had to concentrate on keeping his balance. "Fine," he grunted. "Just fine." In a few seconds the world stopped spinning and he was able to follow her to the kitchen.

He'd forgotten how long her downstairs hall was.

"I hope you don't mind soup," Kathryn said, as he painfully levered himself into a chair. The bowl she set before him was redolent with herbs and ham.

His stomach growled. "Delicious." Bean soup was just about his favorite supper dish, even on a warm summer night.

"Erik, we have to talk about...about the children."

While his bowl was almost empty, hers was still almost full. Crumbs and fragments lay scattered around her plate, telling him that she'd eaten very little of the delicious cornbread.

"What about them?" He still didn't know what he was going to do. He was glad they were out at the Double J. A day or two from now, when he felt a little stronger, would be soon enough to see them. Too soon, for it would be the last time.

"The only thing our fighting about custody of Ginger and Kyle will accomplish is to confuse and hurt them. I've acknowledged that you're their father, but I don't think that's enough. They want—they *need*—a father-in-residence. Someone to go to soccer games with Kyle, someone who can watch the races with Ginger. They need a father who'll be there on parents' night at school. And when they're older, Kyle will need a role model and Ginger an ideal."

"I'm not sure—"

"Please," she said, "let me finish. You really hurt me when you said you wanted just Kyle. I couldn't understand how you could reject your daughter, just like that." She snapped her fingers. "Then I remembered what you told me about your mother."

When he finally raised his head and met her eyes, he read understanding.

"You need Ginger and Kyle as badly as they need you, Erik. You need to be loved, so you can learn to love."

He wanted to tell her he had learned, but his throat ached with a lifetime's tears. All he could do was reach across the table and take her hand, clutching at it as he would at a life preserver.

"I want you to live here, to be a father to the twins," she said, her voice breaking on *father*.

"Here?" The word came out a croak.

"Here," she affirmed. Without another word, she was around the table and crouched before him. Her hands were soft on his cheeks, her breath warm on his mouth. "Erik Solomon, will you marry me?"

Before he could answer, she kissed him.

It was a mind-bending kiss, a memorable kiss, a kiss for all time. Erik's world narrowed to this instant, this place.

This woman.

Kathryn knew it was her last chance. She'd seen him do it before—pull himself into a hard shell of brittle charm, so powerful that no one could get past to the real person. There was a vulnerable, gentle part of him, but he kept it so well armored that few people saw it.

Well, this time she wasn't going to let him. With a last, lingering exploration of his warm, inviting mouth, she pulled far enough back to be able to look him in the eye. "You heard me. I want you to marry me."

She waited.

Almost sitting on his lap, looking into his eyes, she had no idea what he might be thinking. He seemed to be staring at something far away. His lips were parted slightly, his brows pulled into a slight frown.

And still she waited.

Finally his hands circled her upper arms, forcing her away. Without a word, without even a change of expression, he pushed her into a chair.

She watched as he awkwardly stalked back and forth across her kitchen, managing the crutches better with every pass. He seemed incapable of thinking unless he was pacing.

Words bubbled to her lips, but she held them back. All the reasons why she needed him, why they'd be good together. And all the reasons why it would be best for the children. She locked her lips over the words and let him think. For he had to come to her willingly, with no more persuasion on her part.

She'd stated her case. The decision was his.

Erik's greatest regret was that he'd spent so many years of his life with no one to love.

With no one to love him.

Expecting to die in the next moment, Erik had seen that he had never really lived, for he'd always been alone.

And now Kathryn was offering him another chance.

Even better, it was exactly what he'd come to realize he wanted, once his life had been given back to him.

He stopped before the sink, looking out to where vines shaded the window from the setting sun. Slowly he turned around and faced her.

She remained sitting where he'd moved her, her back straight, her eyes enormous and questioning.

Her expression hopeful.

"I can't."

He watched her crumple, like one of those Mylar balloons with a tiny puncture.

Quickly he swung back to the sink, using the window above it as a mirror because he could not look at her. "Kathryn. Katie, sweetheart, I want to. But I can't. I can't marry you, just because Kyle and Ginger need a father."

He bowed his head. "I was going to tell you tonight," he said, fighting the quaver in his voice. "I'm not going to claim paternity."

Kathryn waited until she heard him go into the sewing room, then she crept down the stairs. Carefully avoiding all the creaky boards, she tiptoed to his door, listened carefully. The thump of his crutches, followed by a faint clatter told her he had put them down. He muttered, and she was sure it was a curse.

She waited some more, until the line of light under the door went out. Then, with infinite patience, she eased the door open.

Entered.

Found the edge of the bed and pulled back the covers.

"What the hell?"

"Shut up, Erik. You'll wake the neighbors." Quickly, before he thought to resist, she snuggled up beside him where she believed she belonged. "Good night." Even though he couldn't see her in the dark room, she closed her eyes and feigned sleep.

He turned on the bedside lamp. The mattress leaned, telling her he was propped on an elbow, staring at her. Kathryn pretended for all she was worth.

"Get out."

She opened one eye, saw him looming over her, and wanted to close it again. "Won't." Opening the other eye, she challenged him to evict her.

He was naked. At least, what she could see of him was a gloriously bare as the day he was born. Kathryn resisted the powerful longing to stroke her hands across his chest, to kiss the black and purple bruises marring his masculine beauty. She kept her hands tucked under her head, while what they really wanted to do was rip the sheet back and lose themselves in erotic exploration.

"Kathryn." His tone held warning and threat.

"Erik." Hers spoke of promises and commitment. Did he hear?

No, because his hands were on her, pushing her away. Kathryn wrapped her arms around his waist and held on for dear life.

"No. You're not going to push me away again," she cried. "Listen to me Erik! You don't know what you're turning down."

"Yes I do." He grabbed for her wrists, but Kathryn managed to keep her fingers interlaced, and he didn't have the leverage to separate them. She felt an instant of shame, picking on him like this, with his bruises and bandages and all. Just an instant, though, because if he were in full fighting trim, she'd never get away with what she planned.

As it was, she had a real fight on her hands. It was time to get sneaky.

She went limp. Well, almost limp, for she kept her arms tight around him, and even managed to inch closer until their hips were plastered together with only the sheer batiste of her nightgown separating them.

He wasn't indifferent to her. She smiled secretly.

"What do you think you're doing?" he gasped.

Good! His injuries were telling. She had the upper hand.

"Trying to make you hold still and listen." She took advantage of his distraction to climb atop him, until she was sitting astride his waist but not letting him take her weight. She was aware of his incipient arousal against her buttocks, but she forced the knowledge to the back of her mind. Right now she had to arouse his intellect, not his sex.

She leaned forward and clasped his wrists, forcing them, against very little resistance, to cross on his chest. With one hand, she held them there, knowing that even token effort would pull them free of her clasp. "Will you?"

"Will I what?" He'd stopped resisting.

"Will you listen? Without interruption, without argument, until I'm finished?"

"If you'll let me say something first."

She didn't trust him, not for a minute. Still, she nodded. "Go ahead."

"When you asked..." He took a deep breath and began again. "You took me by surprise, earlier. I though you hated me."

"I was awfully angry with you for a while," she admitted. "I couldn't understand how any man could accept one of his children while rejecting the other."

"I wasn't rejecting her," Erik said, his voice growing stronger. "I was scared to death of her, scared I'd hurt her."

"Scared?"

"My father ran away from his responsibilities, leaving us with my mother."

She nodded when he paused and stared into the distance—

into the past? Erik had told her much of this before, but he seemed to need to explain. It was almost as if, by doing so, he would be able to come to a decision.

"And my mother, well, I don't think she was entirely sane. She idolized my sister, acted as if she couldn't stand the sight of me. And she was always going on about how boys were little barbarians."

Kathryn couldn't help but smile, because sometimes that thought had crossed her own mind. About both her children.

He cleared his throat, but his voice was still a little uneven. "After Gail...after my sister died, Mother got worse. She insisted that it was impossible for a woman to understand a son, or for a man to understand a daughter. I know she tried to get my father to take me, but he'd remarried by then and had a new family. He didn't want to be bothered with me, especially after she was through telling him what a monster I was."

"Oh, Erik—" How could any woman do that to a child? She ached for the pain in his voice, longed for the opportunity to soothe his ravaged heart.

"It's okay, Kathryn. I've worked through it, mostly, although I won't deny it took me a long time. She really was mentally ill, you know, so you can't blame her."

"*I* can," Kathryn said, wanting to do violence to the woman. "That nonsense about not understanding you because you were a boy—it was so much bull-pucky. She couldn't handle the responsibility any more than your father could, so she made it your fault." Leaning forward, she kissed him gently, trying to put all her love and all her understanding into it. "You're not your parents, Erik. You have a lot of love to share with your children."

"I always believed I was what they'd made of me, emotionally and genetically. But when I thought Ginger was...oh, God! When I though I'd lost my daughter before I even had a chance to know her, I...I just couldn't bear it! I love her, love them both more than my life!"

"Oh, Erik!" She understood. Forgave. Loved.

"I though the best thing I could do for them was go away, before I could mess up their lives the way mine was messed up. Then you asked me to be their father and I found there was one thing that could hurt me more than leaving them." Another deep breath, this one causing his whole body to shudder.

"At first I wondered if you wanted a husband so you could have more children." He smiled in the dark. "And found myself thinking what a good idea that sounded.

"Then I decided you wanted child-support, until I really looked around and saw how well you're providing for your—*our*—children without my help."

Again Erik remembered the timeless moment as he watched the mass of tangled logs rushing toward him. "I thought I was going to die. And what I regretted most was that we'd wasted eight years."

"Really?"

"Eventually, I accepted what I've been fighting for weeks. I love you, Kathryn. I really do. In a way I never thought I could love anyone." He buried his face in her hair, loving its every curly strand, drawing a deep breath of its lilac scent. "I need you, because the contemplation of a life without you is more than I can bear. But I won't marry you for the children's sake."

"I love you," she said then. "I think I have ever since..." She hesitated. "I never forgot you, but I didn't—couldn't trust my feelings. That night in Seattle, I was still hurting too much, still missing Jesse too much. Then, when you didn't answer the Christmas card I sent, well, I figured you'd written me off as just another one night stand."

"I've still got it," he said, thinking of the humorous little card he'd kept in a drawer under his handkerchiefs for so many years.

"If all I'd wanted was a man around the house," she said, a note of smugness in her voice, "I've had several candidates." He saw her grin as a flash of white in her shadowed face.

"I'll bet you have," he almost snarled, thinking of her kissing those faceless, worthless men.

"Then you came back, and I knew why none of them had been more than friends. They weren't you." Her shuddering breath told him more than the tremble in her voice.

Suddenly he moved. In an instant they were on their sides, her legs still clasping his waist. The stitches in his arm pulled, but he didn't care. Kathryn loved him!

He kissed her.

No, he consumed her.

With lips and tongue, he explored her mouth, her face, her neck. His mouth burned her, wherever it touched, all the way down her throat and across her chest. The thin fabric of her gown offered no protection from the questing, plundering exploration.

"Erik!" The word came out as a squeak, when his teeth found and gently held her beaded nipple. "What are you doing?"

When he raised his head, his breath cooled the wet fabric of her gown. "Making sure you don't change your mind." His smile was diabolic.

Lowering his head once more, he teased and coaxed and suckled, until she wondered if her entire soul was being drawn into his mouth.

"What do..." His free hand found the hem of her nightgown and lifted. "you—"

Now his fingers stroked the tender flesh of her inner thigh, almost distracting her from the explorations of his mouth.

She managed one final, gasped word, "—want?"

He touched her. Probed.

Kathryn arched into his hand, crying out in her need.

"I think that's perfectly obvious."

His words caused waves of fire to sweep from her toes to her belly.

"I want the whole package." His finger found exquisitely sensitive flesh.

Kathryn shattered.

He held her while she shuddered in the throes of completion, forcing his body into unwilling patience. When her spasms faded into gentle twinges, Erik could wait no longer. He moved her just so and slipped inside her. The hot, tight wetness of her almost made him explode. Grimly he forced his thoughts into other paths, recalling cold rain down his collar and ice crusting on his lashes.

Tiny aftershocks still tightened her around him, until he could hold back no longer. One thrust, and another. The third carried him after her, into completion and satiation.

She turned in his arms, snuggling against him, holding him close with her arms around his waist. "Eight years ago I wasn't ready," she said. Her voice was almost a whisper, her breath warm and moist against his shoulder. "Jesse...it was only a few months since Jesse—"

He touched her cheek, felt tears. "Do you still love him?" He couldn't, he wouldn't, compete with a ghost.

"Of course," she said. "Just as I still love my parents and grandparents." Her hand crept up to lie lightly across his mouth. "But I said goodbye to Jesse a long time ago, Erik. I can love you now, but I couldn't have, eight years ago."

Erik understood. He still regretted the lost years, but he understood he'd been no more able to love her then than he was able to give her up now.

He hoped he was able to love her now. "I'm not very good at relationships." He remembered more than one of the women he'd been involved with accusing him of being frozen inside, unable to release his emotions.

"We'll just have to keep working on it, then, won't we?" Her tongue touched his chest, just over his breastbone, and left a damp trail to the side, where it toyed with his nipple.

Erik felt a renewal of desire. "Then you'll teach me?" he managed to gasp as her hand found him, stroking and teasing.

She guided him to herself and, with a quick shift of position, took him within her. "Erik, was there ever any doubt?"

"Not any more," he said, knowing he'd finally made the right decision.

EPILOGUE

"Are you still mad at us?"

Kathryn looked into the rear view mirror, meeting her daughter's eyes. "I wasn't ever mad at you, honey. But I wanted you to have time to think about what you did and why it was wrong."

"I'm not ever, ever going anywhere with Jace again," Kyle said. He still, according to Janine, woke with bad dreams. Mostly they were of losing Ginger and not being able to find her.

"Well, I will, but I'll tell you first, Mama," Ginger said. No bad dreams for her. She had insisted on helping Jace and Denny with the added chores they'd been given, saying she'd been just as bad as they.

Kathryn smiled a secret smile. Kyle might have inherited his father's genes for appearance, but Ginger had received all his adventuresome ones. Kyle was more like her, content to live a quiet life, with only moderate excitement once in a while.

"When will we know our surprise?" Ginger wanted to know. "As soon as we get home?"

"It's not exactly a surprise," Kathryn told her. She and Erik had decided to bring the children back in from the Double J for a few days, giving them time to get to know him. She'd kept them away from him before, wanting him to be pain and pain-killer free for their first real encounter.

She hoped they would accept him. If they didn't...she refused to allow that thought completion.

They crossed Garnet Creek, the bridge timbers rumbling beneath the wheels of her minivan. Only a few more minutes.

Erik was sitting on her front steps. His bruises had faded to faint but colorful greens and lavenders and his walking cast wasn't nearly as dramatic as the plaster one had been. He held a bouquet of the fragrant pink roses that arched over her front gate.

Kyle was out of the front door almost before she stopped. Ginger was slower, unable to open the sliding side door. Kathryn waited for her daughter, while listening to her son.

"Hi."

Erik grinned. "Hi yourself."

"Did you get all those bruises rescuing us?"

Kathryn saw Erik's mouth twitch. "Nope. Only a few of them. The rest I got when I had a fight with a log."

"Logs can't fight," Ginger said. She was looking suspiciously at Erik. "What are you doin' on our front steps?"

He looked at Kathryn, his expression pleading. She smiled but refused to help him. He had to learn to deal with the twins all by himself.

"I was waiting for you two" he said, finally, laying the roses aside. "I wanted to ask you a particular favor."

"What's that?" Ginger demanded.

"Yeah, what?" her brother said.

"I wanted to ask if I can marry your mother."

Kyle's mouth widened in a delighted grin. Ginger frowned suspiciously. "Why?" she said.

"Because I love her."

The little girl didn't move. She just kept staring, her eyes moving over Erik's face as if to memorize each feature. Finally she turned to look at Kathryn. "Is he our father?"

"If you want him to be." Kathryn wondered what convoluted pathways her daughter's mind followed.

Ginger nodded. "I pretended he was, ever since the Social. Kyle looks like him, a little." She turned back to Erik. "Okay. You can be our father."

"Will you come to my soccer games?" Kyle wanted to know.

Erik said, "You couldn't keep me away." He held out a hand to each child. Kyle immediately went to him, snuggling close as Erik awkwardly hugged him. Ginger moved more slowly, as if she sensed his lingering uncertainty about relating to a girl child.

"I love you, too, Ginger," he said softly, "and I'll be the very best father I can be."

Ginger let herself be drawn into his embrace. Once there she relaxed. Her eyes closed and an expression of sublime happiness covered her face.

Kyle looked up at him with eyes full of hero worship.

Oh, lord, Kathryn thought, seeing the shape of the future. *Now I'll have to listen to years of "Erik says."*

~THE END~

About the Author

Judith B. Glad grew up reading pulp magazines, watching action hero serials, and collecting comics: Wonder Woman, Superman, Batman, Captain Marvel. So is it any wonder that she grew up wanting to create her own worlds in which the good guys—male and female—always won, where right always prevailed, and where love was the most important force in the universe?

Sidetracked by reality, she started a family, followed a couple of careers, and went back to school. Eventually she ended up slogging through wetlands, running sampling transects through sagebrush, counting rare plants, and writing technical reports. Now those reports may be important documents, but they aren't too satisfying to someone whose fantasy world always seemed more believable (and far more interesting) than the real world. So one winter when business was slow, she sat down and wrote a romance.

What fun! she thought. *Much more fun than technical reports.* A lot harder too, but eventually she figured out how to do it right. Now she alternates between writing sensual contemporary romances and exciting historical novels.

Judith lives with her husband in Oregon, where flowers bloom in her yard every month of the year. Three of her four children and two of her three grandchildren live not too far away.

Visit Judith's website at www.judithbglad.com, and while you're there, take a side trip to her other webpages where you'll meet her family and find links to some unusual and interesting places.